MACHINATIONS OF A MURDERER

A 1940s Philip Bryce story

Peter Zander-Howell

Copyright © 2023 Peter Zander-Howell

All rights reserved

Certain well-known historical persons are mentioned in this work. All other characters and events portrayed in this book are fictitious, and any similarity to real persons, alive or dead, is coincidental and not intended by the author. Real-world locations in this book may have been slightly altered.

No part of this book may be reproduced, or stored in a retrieval system, or transmitted in any form or by any means, electronic, mechanical, photocopying, recording, or otherwise, without express written permission of the publisher.

INTRODUCTION

There are at least two reasons why Robin Whitaker wants to eliminate his wife, Dulcie.

He is not allowed to drink any alcohol, nor to gamble. Dulcie controls his life to an extent that he finds intolerable. But she is also wealthy, so merely leaving her is not an acceptable option.

In most circumstances Dr Whitaker thinks and acts like the very intelligent and highly-educated man he is.

However, he has somehow convinced himself that the action of killing his wife is justified. He is also certain that his innate brainpower will give him a significant edge over any police detectives, and allow him to outwit them with ease.

What are his thoughts? How does he make his decisions? What does he do? Will he get away with murder?

FOREWORD

Philip Bryce is an unusual policeman. A Cambridge-educated barrister, and something of a polymath, he joined the Metropolitan Police in 1937 under Lord Trenchard's accelerated promotion scheme.

After distinguished army service in WW2, by 1949 he has become Scotland Yard's youngest Detective Chief Inspector.

Bryce has a number of interests – railways and cricket perhaps near the top of the list.

CHAPTER 1

Sometimes, momentous events arise out of comparatively insignificant actions. Perhaps the best-known example is that of the two pistol shots fired in a small city in Eastern Europe on 28th June, 1914. Tragic enough, because two people were killed. But as a result of that shooting, around twenty million more – as many as half of them civilians – were to die in the ensuing war.

At the other end of the scale, and thirty-five years after the Sarajevo incident, a routine action by the driver of a railway engine set in motion the murder of a woman by her husband.

It may be that some later event would have precipitated the same foul deed, just as some other pretext might have been found to start the Great War. But in both cases, what happened, happened.

****

Ray Little was at the controls of a big Princess Royal class locomotive, travelling towards Euston at sixty-five miles per hour and fast approaching the Castlethorpe water troughs. Five hundred yards long, the troughs' contents were critical to the engine's function. The optimal speed for taking on water at Castlethorpe was about forty-five miles per hour, although on the West Coast Main Line there was special dispensation to do so at up to seventy-five. That top speed, however, left very little margin for error for the fireman, whose job it was to lower and raise the scoop.

Even at this locomotive's rather slower speed, there would still only be about sixteen seconds to carry out the procedure from start to finish.

Little's train was already running seven minutes late, and knowing his fireman, Reg Baker, was very adept at handling the scoop, he maintained his sixty-five miles per hour. Baker carried out the exercise successfully enough, although collection at that speed inevitably meant a considerable volume of water was lost, sprayed either side of the train.

Robin Whitaker, oblivious of these technicalities, was slumped with his head against the window frame in a third-class compartment, asleep and dreaming. A tiny trickle of saliva ran over his slack lower jaw as he occasionally twitched and flinched through his snores. The dream was not a pleasant one, replicating as it did his real-life misery.

In the locomotive's cab, Little was

increasing speed again as the train cleared the troughs. The engine had barely gained a couple of miles an hour before he saw a signal ahead with its black-and yellow arm in the horizontal position. At the same moment, Baker bellowed out over the noise of the engine, "Wolverton distant is on, Ray!"

The purpose of the distant was to give a driver adequate slowing time. Although permitted to pass this semaphore, it was a clear warning that the next, home signal, was likely to be standing at danger, and Little knew his heavy train would need most of the interval between the two signals in which to make an orderly stop. He cursed, realising he'd be hard-pressed to make up any more lost time before reaching London. He closed his regulator, and made a controlled application of the train brakes.

By no means emergency braking, Little's action nevertheless caused Whitaker's head to bump lightly against the window frame, jerking him awake. In that brief moment between dream and reality, and with his brain not yet functioning fully consciously, Whitaker's decision was made. His wife must be removed from his life.

And the only way to accomplish this was to remove her from her own.

CHAPTER 2

Whitaker was a scientist. That is to say, he had a very good degree in science from Oxford, and a couple of years before the war had earned a DPhil to go with it. Despite his academic excellence, he was currently employed as assistant curator in a provincial museum, a job which required none of his scientific specialism.

The museum, run by the Draycaster City Council, was small, under-funded, and mostly ignored by the city's residents. Apart from routine trips by local teachers chivvying their bored classes around the uninspiring exhibits, most of the few visitors were people who dropped in to shelter from a rainstorm. There was not a single object in the museum of sufficient merit to attract anyone to the city just to see it.

Working at the museum was a tremendous backwards slide in Whitaker's career path. On receiving his doctorate, he was immediately appointed to a lectureship at Oxford. His prospects had been exceptionally good. During this period of academic ascendancy he courted, and very shortly afterwards married, the pretty young daughter of the Master of his college – a widower of considerable means, with Dulcie his only child.

By the time of his train journey to Euston, Whitaker should have been a Fellow, followed – such was his ability – a few years hence by a Chair at another acclaimed university. Even a Regius professorship at his own university had been forecast for him.

Something had gone badly wrong.

Two serious personal defects were Dr Whitaker's undoing. Both began to appear as incipient problems soon after his wedding, but the advent of war somehow suppressed them to manageable levels. By 1945, as he returned to Oxford, these flaws in his character became increasingly apparent.

First, he was an inveterate gambler. He frequented racecourses and dog tracks, where he placed large and usually unwise bets. When unable to get to a racecourse, he made use of bookmakers' 'runners'. Illegal though this was, many others did the same. Regrettably, Whitaker wasn't like the many others who enjoyed a 'flutter' occasionally. He was now addicted to gambling.

Initially, he was able to finance his habit thanks to Dulcie, who received a generous allowance from her father. Raising no objections, she would meekly turn most of it over to her husband each quarter. Initially, his wife's money and his own salary had been adequate. After a while, they ceased to be so.

As if the gambling wasn't enough, he was on the verge of becoming an alcoholic. Prior to his marriage, he had taken the odd pint of beer, or a glass or two of wine with a meal. Over time, this changed. After every visit to a race course or dog track he habitually downed several beers, matched pint-for-pint by whisky chasers. The drinking gradually escalated in step with his increasingly heavy gambling – and his increasingly heavy losses.

Of these two vices, it was the drinking, now excessive on a daily basis, which had the first major effect on his life. When he showed up at work drunk, and completely unable to deliver a lecture, his professor took him aside, and issued a sharp warning about his conduct. It should have needed no more than that to sober up an exceptionally intelligent man like Whitaker.

Yet within a fortnight, he arrived for an important college dinner, incorrectly dressed and very much the worse for wear. Two eminent guests, who were being cultivated with a view to extracting significant donations, were not impressed. Nor were Whitaker's senior academic colleagues, especially when the expected donations failed to materialise.

His status as son-in-law to the Master

couldn't save him. He was summarily dismissed.

Dulcie, embarrassed and deeply disappointed, nevertheless chose to stand by her husband. Some string-pulling, by his wife via her father, saw Whitaker take up a lectureship at the lesser University of Draycaster. Using capital inherited from a maiden aunt, Dulcie bought a charming house for them in a suburb of the small city, and looked forward to a fresh start in the autumn of 1948.

The couple had hardly finished hanging pictures and setting out ornaments in their new home when the Master died unexpectedly. In due course, Dulcie became sole beneficiary for a second time, this time inheriting a very substantial sum indeed, together with the freeholds of several rental properties in Oxford, and large holdings of equities.

Within six months, Whitaker, repeating his earlier pattern of squandering his wife's money and behaving unacceptably, found himself unemployed for the second time.

Fortunately, the university didn't make a public fuss about his dismissal, and he was able to secure the museum post in the spring of 1949. The board of governors, mostly local councillors with no business acumen and very few active brain cells, didn't ask any searching questions to ascertain why an academic, with positively glittering qualifications, should apply for such a mundane, dead-end, position.

Once again, his wife stood by him, but this time there was a significant difference. Dulcie made it very clear that in future none of her money – income from capital and the capital itself – would be available to him without her personal approval. She told him she would enforce this rule for even the most trivial expenditure.

If this wasn't (from his point of view) bad enough, Dulcie imposed severe restrictions upon him. Without her, he was forbidden to enter public houses or bars under any circumstances, and no alcohol would be kept in the house. He was barred from going to racecourses or dog tracks. Dulcie didn't know about bookies' runners, but with her drastic curtailment of funds he could make very little use of such a service now, anyway.

He was required to account for any appreciable length of time when he was away from the house or from work. He was even required to submit to having her smell his breath after he had been out.

Whitaker was given no choice regarding this regime. His wife's new dominance was backed up by a threat: if she discovered he'd gone to place bets, or if she detected the smell of alcohol on his breath – and above all, if he lost his job yet again – she would leave him immediately and change her will.

This threat was frightening to him, and

thus very effective. As a result, Whitaker adjusted his behaviour to appear alcohol and gambling-free. By the time he took his window seat in his third-class carriage, he was becoming desperate for release from what he perceived to be a living hell.

On the day of his journey, Whitaker was returning from a weekend visit to his parents' home near Manchester. Dulcie had suggested the trip and made all the arrangements herself. Opting not to accompany him on this occasion, she told him it would be a chance for him to prove that he had mended his ways.

Whitaker gave no thought to mending his ways. Instead, he used the time to establish whether his parents might somehow enable him to make an early escape from Dulcie.

His father was senior engineer at a large factory complex and was, Whitaker believed, well-remunerated. He knew both parents had come into money when relatives died, and wondered whether he might persuade them to release a decent lump-sum to him.

He was disabused of this prospect as soon as he surreptitiously inspected their accounts and private papers. It turned out the bequests received had been modest, and his father's salary rather less than he had assumed. Although they were financially 'comfortable', his parents weren't at all rich. Moreover, both were in their early sixties, and their health was such that at least one could reasonably be expected to live for a further twenty years.

Simple arithmetic showed Whitaker they would need the modest amount they had accumulated to support themselves through old age. Equally as bad was the realisation that, eventually, he would have to share with his siblings whatever his parents left. By the time he said goodbye to his mother and father, he knew there could be no advance on his inheritance.

Whitaker was nursing this disappointment to his hopes as he took the train home to yet more of Dulcie's suspicion and supervision. Not so long ago, he thought, when travelling on any main-line service with refreshment facilities, he would have made straight for the bar and stayed there. Now, he was conscious of the breath test to which he would be subjected on arrival home.

This was how he came to be passing the time dozing in his compartment, dreaming his increasingly febrile dream.

In his sober, wide-awake and rational moments, Whitaker fully understood that Dulcie standing by him a second time was a tremendously lucky break. His behaviour might have precipitated a change to his wife's will many months before he boarded the train. Knowing he could have brought this calamity upon himself was bad enough. But running through his subconscious as he drifted into sleep was something worse. Something he knew about – but over which he had no control – might yet trigger a cataclysmic change to his fortune, and sooner rather than later.

Dulcie was having an affair.

The liaison had started shortly before Whitaker lost his second university job. When his brain wasn't befuddled by alcohol, Whitaker remained an observant and highly intelligent man. From Dulcie's behaviour, he had deduced the existence of a paramour within weeks of the start of the affair. Eventually, by dint of some amateur but effective surveillance, he proved it to his own satisfaction. This proof, however, brought with it an acute awareness of the threat the affair posed to him.

The man in question was Brian McNamara. A local lawyer in private practice, the Whitakers had met him at a university function soon after they moved to Draycaster. In the friendly conversation of those newly introduced to one another, McNamara explained how the law faculty occasionally called upon him to lecture on legal ethics. Forty-five years old, powerfully broad-shouldered and very handsome, he was twelve years older than Dulcie and married with young children. Ironically, Whitaker had liked McNamara very much and, at the time, there was no hint of any mutual attraction between the solicitor and Dulcie.

The affair had been running for many

months. Careful though the lovers were, Whitaker, using his superior intellect combined with the cunning often found in alcoholics, gradually gleaned a number of facts. The most useful of these was that McNamara sometimes picked Dulcie up during the day when her husband was presumed to be at work. Dulcie never went to McNamara's house. Nor were they ever to be seen together in restaurants, theatres, or any other venues in Draycaster.

After three abortive attempts to follow the pair, perseverance and patience rewarded Whitaker. Sensing Dulcie was up to something one morning, he found an excellent reason to take the car for the day. As Dulcie disappeared into the bathroom to ready herself for her tryst, he drove their black Ford Anglia further down into the large turning circle of their cul-de-sac, and parked on the bend. That way, neither front nor rear number plate could be seen if McNamara or Dulcie should happen to glance in his direction. With his head turned away he pretended to study a road atlas, the brim of his hat adjusted to screen his face. Satisfied that he was just an anonymous man in a common black Ford, he waited. He knew if the couple came out they must, perforce, leave in the opposite direction.

And that was exactly what happened. McNamara arrived a little after nine o'clock in his green Ford V8 Pilot and turned into their drive. In less than two minutes he reversed out again, Dulcie beside him. Whitaker felt intense irritation as he imagined his wife gloating about how easily he could be deceived, and it took an effort of will to concentrate on driving in traffic, not losing sight of the Pilot. He hoped it would be easier to follow them without being noticed after they left the city environs.

And so it proved. McNamara drove at a sedate pace to a town thirty miles distant. There, the Pilot pulled into a hotel car park just off the main street. Whitaker didn't attempt to follow. Driving on, he parked out of sight around the next corner.

Not knowing the town well, he mooched around, aimlessly looking into the few shop windows displaying goods of any interest to him. He wondered if he was allowing sufficient time for the lovers to have a cup of coffee in the lounge – or do whatever it was the duplicitous pair did when they first arrived in a hotel at ten o'clock in the morning.

Thirty minutes later, he could contain himself no longer. He walked back to the hotel and pushed his way through the revolving door. A look around the spacious lounge showed him it was empty. Nobody was on the reception desk either, and it took him very few seconds to inspect the register, lying open and facing towards him. The only entry for the day showed a Mr & Mrs Angus Wilson. He was surprised to see the address recorded was in Draycaster. Whitaker thought it was probably false but nevertheless committed it to memory, quickly leaving before any hotel staff appeared.

Making his way back home, he called in at the local post office and asked for directions to the address given by the 'Wilsons'. As he surmised, no such road existed. He apologised to the clerk, explaining that he must have misheard the address when given it over the telephone.

His suspicions were confirmed.

That was all well and good as far as it went; except now he was forced to think about the danger presented by McNamara. Yes, the man was currently married. But divorces were possible, for both McNamara and Dulcie. Whitaker had read somewhere about an obscure functionary called the King's Proctor who would, in certain circumstances, interfere in divorce proceedings; prevent them even. But a solicitor would presumably know how to avoid the attentions of such an official. Once both parties were divorced, Dulcie would be free to marry her paramour.

He felt sick at his next thought. Solicitors also knew how to draft wills.

CHAPTER 3

Whitaker made no further attempt to follow the lovers, or to collect more evidence after the hotel incident. He reasoned it was imperative that Dulcie should remain ignorant about her secret being known to him, fearing premature disclosure could precipitate a decision to divorce him and trigger an immediate altering of her will.

Time dragged on, but Whitaker's circumstances remained the same. He became more and more determined to loosen his wife's grip on her money, and resume his former lifestyle.

Then came the Manchester visit to his parents. When Dulcie arranged the trip, Whitaker was sure she would be consorting with McNamara in his absence. He had no particular animus towards the lawyer for cuckolding him. No; his problem exclusively concerned the future use of Dulcie's money, and any action he took would be calculated to serve that outcome and no other. If the solicitor should prove to be an impediment, then, logically, he must be removed.

To achieve his objective, Whitaker consciously and subconsciously considered the possible elimination of McNamara. If he caught the two *in flagrante delicto*, surely he might justifiably kill the solicitor? He slowly realised that this solution was not wise.

He had a vague idea that the defence of *crime passionel* wasn't strictly available even in France, and would likely carry no weight in the English courts.

But even if he got away with it, Dulcie might simply console herself with another lover. He would be no further forward.

Also, she might divorce him anyway.

Dulcie had always been completely faithful before their move to Draycaster. She had never once even hinted at divorce for any reason other than if he fell off the wagon again. It might have been, had he kept sober and free of the betting mania, his wife would have tired of her older lover and turned her affections again to the man she once thought was wonderful.

Unfortunately, this possibility never occurred to Whitaker, and he would have discounted it anyway. Bending to Dulcie's will, and suppressing his drinking and gambling to the extent required, were twin forms of slow suffocation for him. He knew that long-term fidelity to his wife's cause of 'cleaning him up' was impossible.

And so Whitaker came to be fantasising more and more about life without Dulcie, but with all of her money. Shaken wide awake by his bump against the window and, with the die being (in his mind) irrevocably cast, he used the rest of his journey to start forming his scheme.

Planning to extinguish life in another human being was not an easy matter, he found, and various aspects of his decision demanded his full attention. But by the time he reached Euston, he was satisfied he had mentally organised the most essential action points in order of priority.

First: A rough timescale must be worked out; and from this moment on Dulcie must be given no hint that anything untoward was to happen.

Second: At least one, and preferably more, alternative suspects must be made available; each with a credible motive.

Third: A suitable method must be found, ideally appearing accidental or self-inflicted.

Fourth: He must have an unshakeable alibi himself.

****

On returning home, Whitaker tried to appear absolutely contented with life, and continued to conceal knowledge of his wife's doings. He was very successful in this regard. Indeed, his life improved marginally, although the financial reins were not loosened to any extent.

Whitaker decided to work through his little list in sequence. For the timescale, he provisionally set himself three months to complete all the tasks, but resolved not to constrain himself too rigidly. *Carpe diem* would be his policy.

His mind moved on to the second stage: finding some false suspects, or 'patsies', as they were called in the American pictures he enjoyed. He viewed this stage as precautionary, because he aimed to achieve a means of despatching Dulcie which would result in a verdict of misadventure, or accidental death, or even suicide. He realised from the outset, however, that there might be limitations to this aspiration. If the result of his chosen method (or some hitch in carrying out the action) failed to clear the 'accident' or 'suicide' hurdles, it would be too late then to try and set up his patsies.

He would therefore make no attempt to tackle the third and fourth stages until suitable candidates were found for stage two.

Without question, Brian McNamara presented as an excellent patsy and was, Whitaker realised, far more valuable to him alive. It might be reasonably thought by any investigating officer (he knew there would have to be one of those) that a cheating husband would do anything to prevent his own wife finding out about his deception and betrayal.

Whitaker could think of several ways of implying – or even baldly stating – that Dulcie was unhappy, and eager to extricate herself from the relationship. This was a scenario he felt he could work very nicely indeed. He would suggest that Dulcie had threatened to expose their liaison to the solicitor's wife.

Oh, yes; there was no question that McNamara could be used most effectively one way or another, and Whitaker knew he would derive tremendous satisfaction in creating plausible lies with which to ensnare him.

However, ideal as McNamara undoubtedly was, he alone was insufficient. At least one more credible suspect was needed. The possibility occurred to Whitaker that, depending on the method and location he eventually chose, an unknown number of innocent bystanders might conveniently come under suspicion.

No. He would trust nothing to happenstance. Not only did it go against his scientific training, it was also obvious that fortuitous help to his scheme couldn't be foreseen, much less relied upon. Someone more predictable must be found.

Nearly two weeks after his return from Manchester, an unexpected opportunity to fill this need arose, when, by complete accident, a welcome bit of scandal came to his attention.

The Whitakers' dentist, Keith Forrest, was ostensibly a pillar of the local community; a school governor, churchwarden, county councillor, and Rotarian. These activities occupied him so extensively that he now only practised dentistry part-time. But, like Brian McNamara, Forrest found time to spend with a mistress, and the day came when Whitaker happened to be in the right place, at the right moment, to discover this.

The museum was planning a large new exhibit, to be opened in October. The whole of September had been earmarked to organise this, but by the middle of the month it was clear that some overtime would be needed, and Whitaker was required to work late on several occasions.

After one of these extended days, and having just missed a bus home, he decided to take a shortcut and wait for the next bus a couple of stops along. On the point of emerging from an alleyway into a quiet street, Whitaker observed Forrest's distinctive sports car pass and pull up a few yards away. Something made him pause and wait out of sight in the alleyway.

Even under the limited illumination of a street lamp, Whitaker could see Forrest inside the car, kissing and embracing a woman for several minutes. His passenger eventually got out, straightened her clothing – which included a very deliberate flash of stocking-top for Forrest – buttoned up her coat, and entered a nearby house.

Patricia Forrest was one of Dulcie's bridge

partners. The two women regularly shared lifts to their weekly bridge club meetings, and he also knew Patricia from occasional social events. This was not her.

Whitaker waited until the sports car drove off before leaving the alley to check the number of the house.

His excellent brain worked rapidly as he continued walking to the bus stop. Money was what he wanted, and he wondered if a heaven-sent opportunity had been revealed to him along with the stocking top.

Whitaker could justify murder to himself with no qualms, but he rather perversely considered blackmail to be a filthy crime, employed by the worst dregs of humanity. The idea of 'squeezing' Forrest was entertained for only a few seconds before he rejected it.

Instead, he decided the police could be usefully guided towards Forrest, just as he could lay a trail to McNamara. Nobody would ever find out that Dulcie was unaware of the existence of Forrest's mistress. He would suggest, at the perfect moment of his own choosing, not only did she know, but that she had threatened the dentist she would inform her friend of Keith's misconduct.

Whitaker regretted that this was a very similar scenario to McNamara's; he would have preferred a patsy with an altogether different motive. However, this didn't deter him from seeking to implicate the dentist in the same way he planned to embroil the solicitor, if necessary. After all, it was hardly his fault that *two* men of his acquaintance were adulterers. Correspondingly, he reasoned, it was entirely their own fault if he used their salacious and reprehensible conduct against them. (Amongst the many twists in Whitaker's personality was a strong 'holier than thou' streak, but without any balancing sense of self-awareness. He genuinely condemned adulterous conduct, but felt no compunction about his own intended actions.)

By the time he reached home, the accidental discovery seemed more than a lucky coincidence, and he seriously wondered if some higher power was looking after him. Having found two possible candidates with almost no effort on his part, Whitaker, mindful of the exhortation that *'God helps those who help themselves'*, decided he must surely be able to find a third patsy himself, if he put some thought into the matter.

Such an opportunity arose not long after. The Whitakers – or more particularly Dulcie – had befriended a couple of about their own age. Paula Kent worked in the city library. Her husband, Geoffrey, until recently manager of a local brewery, was now redundant following its closure. The couples were in the habit of spending one evening a week together, generally alternating between their two houses.

On Saturday, while at the Kents, Paula suggested a trip to the local pub. Whitaker, under previous instructions from Dulcie, knew he was expected to behave like an overgrown schoolboy on such occasions, and drink ginger beer. This time, he decided on a different course. Pleading a sudden headache, he assured the genuinely concerned Kents that he would prefer to sit quietly in their lounge.

With the house to himself, Whitaker wandered listlessly around the living room, deploring the poor selection of reading material available to help him while away the evening. In one corner of the room was an open, roll-top desk, absolutely full of papers. He hadn't set out on his little stroll with the intention of snooping (unlike when at his parents' house); he was simply restless and stretching his legs. But as he passed the desk for the third time he caught sight of the corner of a document whose colour and texture he instantly recognised. Barely protruding from beneath a pile of other papers was a Post Office Savings Book.

He hesitated for a moment, the beginnings of an idea coming to him. Pulling out a clean handkerchief, he used it to protect his fingers as he drew out the book. The cover identified the account holder as Geoffrey Richard Kent. Avoiding touching the book with his bare fingers, Whitaker opened it and saw the current balance was only one shilling and tuppence.

With virtually nothing in the account, and Kent currently without any employment income to pay into it, Whitaker reasoned it was most unlikely that Kent would be making use of the book in the near future. He quickly converted his emerging idea into action, and slipped the book into his jacket pocket.

When the others returned he was reading a novel. To the solicitous enquiries of the Kents – and another from his wife which sounded solicitous but wasn't – he replied that his headache was practically gone. Soon afterwards, he and Dulcie made their farewells and walked the quarter mile back home.

****

The next day being Sunday, Dulcie went to the eleven o'clock service at the local church as usual.

As soon as the front door closed behind his wife, Whitaker positioned himself out of sight to one side of the lounge window, and watched until she disappeared out of the cul-de-sac.

Crossing the hallway, he went straight to the small room which Dulcie styled their 'snug', thinking it a more homely name than the more usual 'study'. In here, a large bookcase-cum-bureau held all of their domestic records.

Although Dulcie's paperwork was not quite as untidy as the Kents', she was not much more methodical in her own record-keeping.

Beyond grouping similar papers into bundles, she didn't do much filing, and was inclined to hoard every little thing.

Whitaker took a pair of thin leather driving gloves from his pocket and stretched their suppleness over his hands. Lowering the desk slope of the bureau, he first poked amongst the stuffed pigeonholes for Dulcie's current cheque book. Locating and then extracting the book, he was delighted to see it was practically new, with only the first two cheques used. Greatly relieved, he yet again felt he was being 'looked after'. He had already realised that if hardly any cheques remained he would have to abandon his plan, as the risk of Dulcie writing several cheques in quick succession – thereby noticing the missing one – would be far too great.

Pulling up a chair, he settled himself. Carefully, he tore out the last cheque in the book, and without filling in the counterfoil, replaced the chequebook in the bureau. Next, he rummaged in a drawer for an envelope containing a bundle of Dulcie's old cheques, which the bank had automatically returned after clearing. With two recent examples of his wife's writing in front of him, he picked up her fountain pen and made a few practice scrawls on a bit of scrap paper. The pen quickly ran dry. With exceptional concentration (knowing tell-tale spills could be his undoing), he re-filled it from a bottle of black Quink, and continued exercising his forgery technique.

Dulcie's writing was, naturally, very familiar to Whitaker. Apart from a slight slant to the right, it had no special style, and might have been termed 'undeveloped', being not dissimilar to that of a typical ten-year-old child.

Even better for him, was Dulcie's custom of writing cheques using print, rather than a cursive hand. He gazed steadily at the old cheques for a few minutes before slowly and deliberately printing *'Geoffrey Kent'* in the space for the payee on the new cheque, and *'Two Hundred and Fifty Pounds only'* in words and numerals in the correct places, imitating without difficulty his wife's examples in front of him. He post-dated the cheque for the following day.

Forging Dulcie's signature on the cheque presented only slightly more difficulty. Using another piece of paper, he made about twenty near facsimiles. He knew he needed to produce a version which wouldn't cause some bank employee to reject the cheque when presented for clearing, but which could, at some later date, be shown to be fraudulent. Eventually satisfied with his efforts, he signed the cheque using all Dulcie's initials, exactly as she would.

He returned the old cheques to their repository, simultaneously wondering why on earth Dulcie never destroyed them, along with all the other outdated and apparently useless paperwork. He folded the forged cheque into his wallet, and closed the bureau. Only then did he remove his gloves.

Taking his practice sheets to the kitchen, he opened the fire door of the Rayburn and consigned them to the little inferno within, the heat from which was gently cooking a small brisket pot roast and an apple charlotte.

When his wife returned, he was happily humming to himself whilst engaged in the domestic task set for him: preparing the potatoes and greens for their Sunday lunch.

CHAPTER 4

Whitaker's workplace was a little over a mile from his house. Some days, he walked to the museum. On others, especially in inclement weather, he took a convenient bus from the stop a few yards from their cul-de-sac. On Monday morning he walked, as he wanted to think about his next move, ensuring there were no flaws before he carried it out.

His mind was constantly occupied as he strode along. By the time he reached the museum he had not only finalised the smallest details of his afternoon's task, but also reinforced to himself that, whenever he was amongst people, he must always behave normally. No colleague, acquaintance, or even a chance-encountered stranger, should ever be able to say his behaviour was in any way odd, much less suspicious.

Arriving at the museum, he spoke, as always, to one of the two men employed in the role of general factotums – doormen, guides, movers of exhibits, and so forth. Entering his office, he greeted the two people who shared the room with him, one of whom was Whitaker's fellow assistant curator. Now approaching sixty, she had joined the museum as a bright young graduate some thirty-five years before, and become more disillusioned and cynical with every passing year. (This lady would never know it, but she was, in a way, somewhat instrumental in shaping Whitaker's destiny. He looked at her and saw himself in the future, dreading what he saw.) The other occupant held the grandiose title of 'Secretary to the Director'. As the director only appeared two days a week at most, it meant the bulk of her time was spent in typing and other clerical work for the curators.

He suffered the tediousness of his day's workload and joined in the grumbles of his colleagues in the usual way, restraining himself from constantly checking the time on his wrist, or from watching the hands on the office clock creep their way around its dial.

His luncheon break was an hour long and ample for his needs, with the added bonus of being flexible and taken to suit himself. Using a Kelly's directory to find post offices at which he might pay the forged cheque into Kent's account, Whitaker had settled on one in Flixton Street. This was a poor part of the city, and some distance from his house and the museum.

He opted for a late, two o'clock break, to be sure he didn't arrive during mid-day closing. Rather than stand in full view of the museum at the nearby bus stop, he walked a good distance in the opposite direction to which he was aiming. He boarded a bus; and presently alighted not far from his chosen post office.

It hadn't occurred to him before, but his own appearance was remarkably similar to Geoffrey Kent's. Whitaker now appreciated that if either one of them had been a vastly different weight or height; or wore a beard or moustache, he could not have taken the savings book on Saturday and pursued his current course only two days later. As it was, the two men were the same age and with the same hair, alike in both colouring and cut. Clean-shaven and within an inch of the same height, they even wore the same style of spectacles. He also knew Kent possessed an overcoat practically identical to the one he wore today. This final similarity was helpful to his plan, and as it was near the end of October, wearing the coat was unremarkable.

The chosen post office was positioned at one end of a dreary little shop. The woman behind the counter looked thoroughly harassed as she dealt with a line of customers, most of whom, Whitaker guessed, were collecting their weekly pension money.

He took his place in the queue behind an elderly lady. Another man swiftly arrived behind him, followed almost immediately by another elderly lady. This suited Whitaker, as it made it less likely that the postmistress would be able to spare any time querying his transaction.

Wearing his gloves – unremarkable again, given the weather – he drew the savings book from his pocket and opened it at the page showing the embarrassing one and tuppence balance. He positioned the cheque over this page, and when he reached the front of the queue simply passed the book and cheque under the grille, with a barely audible "'afternoon."

Scarcely glancing at him, the experienced postmistress didn't need to be told this was a paying-in. She wrote the amount in the book, banged a rubber stamp first onto an ink pad and then down onto the book and cheque, and handed the book back with an abrupt "There you go."

It was all over in moments. As soon as he was outside Whitaker breathed a sigh of relief. He hadn't really expected any trouble at this stage, but one never knew.

He would have to replace the book under the papers on the Kents' desk, of course, but he didn't foresee any difficulty there. He'd already decided he would make a performance of doing some overdue decorating in their living room first thing on Saturday morning and, under this pretext, arrange a consecutive visit to the Kents in the evening. He anticipated no problem with this, as the exact thing had happened in reverse a few months earlier, when Geoffrey Kent's decorating had overrun.

No, the next real risk would arise sooner

than next Saturday. In perhaps two or three days, the cheque would come up for clearing. Whitaker knew, from when they were on better terms, that Dulcie regularly converted her rental income into shares and bonds, writing cheques to her stockbrokers and others for sizeable amounts. Two hundred and fifty pounds was therefore not an especially unusual amount for his prosperous wife and shouldn't, of itself, raise any eyebrows. He wasn't too sure how the system worked, but, taking everything into consideration, he still felt confident his forgery would pass muster.

It turned out replacing the book was even easier, and completed far earlier, than he anticipated. As soon as he arrived home that evening, Dulcie told him he had narrowly missed Paula, who had dropped in on her way home from work. He learned that Geoffrey wanted a chat with him after dinner, about a possible job the Labour Exchange had suggested. A quick decision about the vacancy was needed, and Kent hoped Whitaker might have some sound advice to offer. The women had agreed the two men should have a man-to-man talk in the Kents' house, while Paula would come to the Whitaker's house to keep Dulcie company.

Inevitably, Kent left the room a couple of times during the hour and a half they were together and, on his first exit to make coffee, it took Whitaker less than thirty seconds to slip on the gloves he'd secreted in his pocket, and slide the Post Office book back out of sight under a large pile of papers.

Whitaker was quietly elated when Kent returned with the beverages, and the two men talked for some time. There was little in the way of advice he could give his host, but he made some sensible observations and suitably supportive comments, leaving Kent happier after their chat.

CHAPTER 5

Utilising his brain far more of late than was ever required at the museum, Whitaker frequently reviewed his plan, looking for weak points. On his walk home from the Kents he realised he had made a couple of assumptions which might not have been correct, and spent some time assessing them.

First, Mrs McNamara might already be fully cognisant of her husband's affair and, moreover, the solicitor might know she knew. If so, any theoretical motive for killing Dulcie more-or-less disappeared.

Second, as he had made no attempt to find out the identity of the woman in Keith Forrest's car, it was possible he had seen no more than a one-off fumbling, with no continuing relationship to use to advantage.

He decided he would have to live with these possibilities. If either of them should arise after the event, he would have to deal with it then. Instead, he turned his thoughts to more foreseeable, and rather more pressing, risks.

It was dawning on him that he must

despatch his wife before intervening, unhelpful events could scupper his scheme. Dulcie noticing the missing cheque, along with Geoffrey Kent somehow discovering his unexpected windfall, would become ever-present dangers as soon as the cheque was cleared. As more time passed, the chances of one or both of these catastrophes occurring increased – and so did his peril.

Aside from these possibilities was the fact that the bank always returned cleared cheques. When they did, Dulcie could hardly fail to notice the forgery.

Frustratingly, Whitaker had no idea what the interval might be between a cheque being presented and then returned to the drawer after clearing. He knew clearing took some days, and he calculated that the forged cheque couldn't possibly appear for at least seven days. If he was lucky, he might actually have a month or more, but he realised it would be unwise to risk that. The postman didn't make the morning delivery until after he had left for work; so intercepting any correspondence from the bank on a weekday was not a viable option.

By the time Whitaker slipped his key into the front door lock, he realised he must give urgent attention to Stage Three. Curiously, he hadn't given the method any thought at all following his train journey, anticipating he would have more time. But, having grabbed his opportunity with Kent's savings book, he was forced to confront what would be his most important decision. He spent the rest of the evening evaluating his options.

The first was to use his Webley Mk VI ·455 service revolver. His possession of the gun went back almost to the outbreak of war, when he obtained a commission in the Army. In many ways he'd been an ideal candidate: physically fit, highly intelligent and supremely well-educated. He had also spent several years as a cadet in his school contingent, at that time part of the Officer Training Corps. The Army recognised his eminent suitability, and duly issued Second Lieutenant Robin Whitaker with, *inter alia*, a revolver.

Almost six months later, Whitaker having never left the country, and having never heard a shot fired in anger, someone in the warrens of Whitehall belatedly realised that a better use could be found for a physicist with knowledge of electronics – rather than using him as cannon fodder. He was whisked away from his depot at a moment's notice, and sent to assist Watson-Watt in the development of radar.

Initially, this annoyed him. Far from being a coward, Whitaker had made no attempt to evade active service. But he rapidly became engrossed in the project, grasping the significance of the new technology and enjoying his part in its development. Dulcie moved to Suffolk with him and, in hindsight, these could fairly be described as the best years of their time together.

For some reason, probably owing to a bureaucratic blunder, Whitaker retained his commission. Although essentially a civilian, he was even promoted twice during his time at Bawdsey Manor. Crucially, when he was eventually demobbed in 1945, nobody took steps to recover his revolver.

It had lain at the bottom of a trunk ever since, safely housed in a cardboard box, alongside two smaller boxes each holding twelve cartridges. The Webley had never been taken out during either of the Whitakers' subsequent house moves. Dulcie was originally aware of the gun's existence, but hadn't mentioned it since they lived at Bawdsey. It was even possible she wasn't aware of its continuing presence in the house.

But her knowledge, or lack of it, didn't matter. It was far more important that, almost certainly, no other living soul knew. Obviously, the first method to be considered must be the revolver.

However, although there was merit in the idea of using the Webley, there were definitely disadvantages. To be shot with a heavy-calibre revolver meant either suicide or murder. Accident was so unlikely as to be impossible. It would be very difficult, he thought, to produce evidence to show Dulcie entertained thoughts of suicide. And as for murder, well, he had always hoped he might find a method which would avoid such a verdict.

Whitaker held the revolver option in abeyance, and considered other methods. Poisoning was, of course, a classic way to dispose of one's enemies. Again, though, accident was an unlikely verdict. Poisoning through eating some fungi which Dulcie might have gathered in woods or fields should lead to a verdict of misadventure. But his wife had never shown any interest in gathering mushrooms, and it would certainly be suspicious to suggest she might have started to do such a thing now.

He told himself that there must be hundreds of poisonings where the authorities never suspected murder. Or, if they had, where the lack of evidence meant the perpetrator was acquitted or – better still – never charged. He considered some of the infamous cases of the last eighty or so years, about which he had read. Armstrong eliminated his wife using arsenic. Seddon killed his lodger, again with arsenic. Crippen used hyoscine to kill his wife. Cotton poisoned her stepson, and very probably three husbands and other children, with arsenic. Pritchard used antimony to remove both wife and mother-in-law. Edmunds killed the wife of a man she fantasised over, using strychnine.

None of these provided Whitaker with a very satisfactory template. All six were convicted and the first five hanged – hardly the outcome he was aiming for. The only example he could think of where a probably guilty person had been acquitted was the case of Adelaide Bartlett, who allegedly employed liquid chloroform.

The one-in-six odds for successful commercial chemical poisonings were not looking attractive to him, but he wasn't quite ready to abandon this medium. He considered the matter of how to get his wife to ingest something laced with a toxin, which of course would have to be at such a time when he himself was elsewhere. This appeared to present insuperable difficulty. Unless, he thought, he used something slow-acting. Thallium sulphate was a substance he'd heard about. But what if the early symptoms were recognised by a doctor? And after such a failed attempt, even if by some miracle he wasn't identified as the potential culprit, he could never have a second attempt via any other method.

Anyway, apart from the uncertainty and poor odds, there was another problem. He imagined it would be quite difficult to obtain any of these well-known poisons, the authorities having rightly legislated to make it hard to do so. He turned instead to the extraction of poison from everyday substances, or from plants. He had read that rhubarb leaves contain potentially dangerous quantities of oxalic acid. Foxgloves, oleander, and nightshade were others known to have even more deadly content. But he was totally ignorant about the quantities required, and to ask at the library for a book on toxicology would be to invite disaster – not least because there was a chance Paula Kent would see him and mention it to Dulcie. In any case, he could hardly carry out experiments in their kitchen.

Without completely rejecting the idea of poison, Whitaker put it aside for the time being. He felt sure there must be something better.

What about a fall? This he dismissed almost immediately. A fall would mean a push. He would have to do the pushing, making a decent alibi impossible. Besides, there were no convenient cliffs or tube stations nearby.

What about a knife or axe? No, absolutely not. Whitaker wasn't notably squeamish, but did baulk at the idea of getting blood all over himself. He also felt bladed instruments were rather ungentlemanly. He gave no corresponding thought to the fact that each and every one of his savage intentions would put him a lot lower than 'ungentlemanly' in decent people's eyes. The parameters of conduct were always set where Whitaker put them; with his own actions fully justified and condemnation exclusively applied to others.

Strangulation was rejected – he vaguely remembered reading somewhere how the police could successfully link the marks on a victim's throat to the murderer.

Drowning whilst swimming, then? A better idea. Dulcie enjoyed this particular form of recreation and exercise in some of the local waterways. But then again, no. She'd hardly be swimming anywhere outdoors and alone at this time of year.

Perhaps 'falling' overboard in mid-Channel? He would have to persuade her to take such a trip within the next few days, and be there himself – so no possibility of an 'out of range' alibi. And he wouldn't put it past his vindictive wife to swim ten miles to land if necessary (she was an excellent swimmer), just to foil his scheme and spite him.

The bath? There was the one classic case in 1915, during which an eminent pathologist demonstrated how easily such a murder could be carried out. Unfortunately, the notoriety of the 'Brides in the Bath' realistically meant no one else could follow suit today, and have any hope of claiming it was an accident.

He toyed with various ways in which Dulcie could be electrocuted. This at least felt a more familiar method to him, so to speak, since it involved his scientific specialism of physics. However, nothing remotely feasible suggested itself, although he'd heard the women in the office discuss a recent case involving interference with an electric kettle.

Again and again, he came back to the fact that he wanted to be able to blame a third party, if possible. It was no use choosing a method which called for a patsy to be in their house for a lengthy time making preparations. Moreover, in the particular scenario of electrocution he would only be able to point to one patsy. He could hardly suggest that Forest, McNamara, and Kent not only had a compelling motive, but that *all* had been in the house with enough unsupervised time to adapt an electrical appliance.

Gas? Yes, a strong possibility. He knew that a high percentage of coal gas was highly toxic carbon monoxide. Most of the rest was highly flammable hydrogen and methane. He considered two options: direct gassing; or triggering an explosion after a sufficient build-up of gas.

Yet again, though, he couldn't see how to accomplish his desired outcome. Dulcie was a heavy sleeper, but might still wake up if he opened the tap on the bedroom gas fire and she heard the hissing. Coal gas being lighter than air, opening a tap downstairs instead would certainly overcome the audible hissing factor and, given enough time, the gas would of course rise and fill the house. However, it would be a longer and slower process for the gas to waft upstairs, and there could be no guarantee his wife wouldn't wake up and smell it, long before being overcome.

He thought about creating some sort of

timer to produce an electrical spark after the ground floor was saturated with gas. Although building such a device would be child's play to him, he felt sure it would be discovered, and the likelihood of one of his patsies having the know-how was slim. Whitaker rejected that idea too, realising that any method which involved physics would inevitably shine a light on him, and should therefore be discounted.

He went back over his options time after time, and considered a few more, which were really only variations on his original thoughts. He eventually decided it simply wasn't possible to devise anything which both guaranteed Dulcie's departure from this mortal coil, and which also looked like an accident. He was forced to reconsider his first, simple, direct option. The revolver.

He weighed up the benefits of the Webley. The gun was something he already possessed and, as far as he knew, nobody else in the world was aware that he did. Hundreds of these guns were in circulation, and it could be disposed of very easily afterwards.

It would be quick.

(Lest it be mistakenly thought by anyone that Whitaker was finally considering his wife in this last 'advantage', they should be corrected. As ever, he thought only of himself, and his getaway.)

So much for the positive side of the

reckoning. On the negative side, the gun had lain unused for ten years. It might not work. The bullets might be 'duds'. It was noisy.

Whitaker decided noise wasn't an insuperable problem – or even a problem at all. Their house was detached, with a decent enough gap between them and their neighbours on either side. Both of these properties were occupied by elderly widows, one of whom was stone deaf and the other routinely took sleeping powders. But anyway, there must be something with which to attenuate the sound to such an extent that it could hardly be heard outside the house. He would think about what to use.

There was a further risk, he realised, relating to the patsies. One, or conceivably more than one, might have a similar weapon himself. If so, a comparison of bullets would largely clear that particular suspect. Whitaker decided he must accept this possibility, but reasoned that the probability of all three being able to produce a ·455 handgun was effectively zero, so there would still be alternative suspects.

The revolver it would be.

CHAPTER 6

Feeling confident in his decisions about the earlier stages of his project, Whitaker felt able to move to stage four – working out his alibi.

Once again he considered various options, but in the end it really came down to his being – or appearing to be – a good distance away when his wife was shot.

Although not appreciating it at the time, fate had already lent him a helping hand in the matter of alibi. Several months earlier, the museum had been invited to send a representative to a symposium, to be held sixty miles away, in Bristol. The director couldn't attend, and the senior assistant curator didn't want to go. The invitation was duly passed to Whitaker, and he accepted it almost without thought, merely looking on it as a chance to get away from Dulcie for a night. Now, he realised, it was an opportunity for much more.

The symposium was to be held over one day, with delegates requiring overnight accommodation making their own arrangements – their sponsoring institutions no doubt reimbursing all reasonable costs. Whitaker, booking well in advance, was in time to reserve a room in the Arden hotel – a place he had stayed in before and which, handily, was also the venue for the symposium. He had arranged to stay overnight on the Monday, returning home after the final session finished at five o'clock the next day.

On his previous visit, a loquacious fellow guest in the bar had given him some information. Apparently, if a gentleman wished to bring a 'lady' to his room, this could be arranged in complete secrecy. He learned about a back door to the hotel, which opened conveniently onto a quiet side street. It seemed this door was left unlocked until four-thirty am. (Why four-thirty was not explained, and at the time the hour held no significance at all for Whitaker.)

Apparently, this facility was arranged by the night porter so that he wasn't embarrassed (nor indeed did he cause embarrassment) by refusing entry to a guest's unregistered lady friend. Whitaker's confidant told him there was a sort of 'honesty box' system in operation. Anyone making use of the arrangement was expected to tip the porter before he finished his shift at nine o'clock the next morning.

Whitaker had automatically made his reservation at this familiar hotel as soon as he accepted the invitation to attend the symposium. He booked without any thought of bringing a 'lady of the night' back to his room – he couldn't think of anything more degrading and beneath him than using such a woman. But the more he thought about his earlier visit and the chat at the bar, the more it seemed to provide an excellent means to set up a perfect alibi.

If he were to slip out of the hotel at, say, midnight, it would take him less than an hour and a half to drive back home. Traffic would be almost non-existent. He would allow thirty minutes to park well away from his house, enter, deal with his wife, and return to his car. Another hour and a half for the return journey would see him back at the hotel by three-thirty – a good hour before the locking-up time.

He realised he couldn't enquire directly – or even indirectly – whether the facility remained extant when he arrived at the hotel. That would be a fatal blunder if the police subsequently checked up. He was only staying for one night, and it would simply be a case of trying the door when the time came. If it was locked, he must postpone the scheme and think again.

Should the door be unlocked as he left, but locked on his return, all would not be lost; he could go away for a few hours and return well after the front door was re-opened, as though returning from an early walk. The chances of anyone noticing he was coming in, without apparently having gone out, were not very great, he thought.

Satisfied that his arrangements for points three and four of his scheme were perfect, he decided to go ahead on this basis.

****

The middle of the week passed uneventfully. On Friday, Whitaker put on a faultless performance of normal behaviour at work and at home. In the evening, after an early supper, Dulcie went to collect Patricia Forrest for their bridge club session. Loafing in a chair as she left, he instantly became active as the Anglia's headlamps cleared the driveway.

He retrieved the boxes containing the revolver and ammunition and took them to the garden shed. With a portable storm lantern providing necessary light, he inspected his weapon and ammunition. The gun, wrapped in oilcloth, looked as good as new, but he nevertheless set to work with the oil and cleaning brush which were also stored with the Webley.

Servicing of the weapon completed, he next ground off the gun's serial number from each of the places where it was stamped. It wasn't a very neat job, given his limited tools, but certainly adequate to prevent anyone tracing the revolver if it was ever found.

Ideally, he would also have liked to test the

state of the ammunition by firing a few shots, but finding a suitable venue would have been difficult at the best of times, and quite impossible in the remaining time Dulcie would be out. He abandoned the idea, and considered where to hide the gun until he left for Bristol. Inserting it into the car's spare wheel bay would have been his preference, but that was out of the question as Dulcie had taken the car. Instead, he hid it temporarily in a large crate containing old tins of paint, left by the previous owner of the house. Dulcie hated spiders and never went into the shed, so he had no fear of her discovering it.

The shed may not have been as handy as the spare wheel bay, but it was still a good place to keep the gun until Monday. Inevitably, he would need to shuttle back and forth down the side passageway between the drive and the shed, carrying out his usual inspections of oil, water, and general roadworthiness of the car, as he always did before a long journey. The gun would be transferred to the spare wheel space under cover of these routine jobs.

With his weapon prepared and hidden in the shed, he had one more crucial task, and very little time to accomplish it. He must somehow dispose of the remaining eighteen rounds of ammunition, oil can, and brush. Nothing could be left to suggest he ever had a gun.

Returning to the kitchen, he threw the boxes and cleaning rags onto the glowing coals of the Rayburn.

Then, pulling on his dark overcoat and hat, he walked briskly towards the nearest bridge spanning the River Dray. Alone and unobserved, he unscrewed the lid of the oil can and threw everything into the dark flowing water below.

By the time Dulcie returned, Whitaker was arranged in exactly the same relaxed pose he'd adopted when she and the Kents found him a few nights before: book in hand and looking as though he hadn't budged from his comfy armchair all evening.

****

The weekend also passed uneventfully, just like most of their weekends.

On Monday morning, Whitaker breakfasted with Dulcie as usual. No regular visitor to the household would have noticed anything remotely out of place in his manner. He checked his appearance in the hallstand mirror as he always did and, when ready to leave for work, bade Dulcie 'goodbye' as he always did (without any kiss – all such affectionate gestures had ceased when he lost his first job).

At the museum, he worked at his normal pace and with his normal level of efficiency. No one would be able to state that he was anything other than himself.

Surprisingly, Whitaker found the hours sped past. He skipped his lunch break and then left work early because, as he casually reminded his colleagues, he must drive sixty miles to Bristol.

To pleasant farewells and a cheery "Safe journey, Robin," from the Director's secretary, he made his way to the bus stop and home.

Whitaker's preparations of the car went like clockwork. He took leave of Dulcie for the second time that day in exactly the same manner as before.

As he engaged first gear in the Anglia he experienced a rush of pure elation. But instead of enjoying the thrill of what he believed was the start of his freedom, his scientific brain quickly prevailed, and he began reviewing and refining the last details of his scheme.

He was happy enough with the timescale for getting out of the hotel and back again, and knew his exit and return must be accomplished unobserved.

However, the very opposite was true for the rest of the time. It was essential that suitable people saw him – and remembered him – late into the evening, and also throughout the next day.

How should he achieve this?

Bristol boasted many hotels and guest houses, but as the Arden was the venue for the symposium, other delegates would inevitably be staying overnight. Although he probably wouldn't know any of them, he thought it should be easy enough to spot one or two by their clothing, or their demeanour, or whatever. If so, it would be worthwhile suggesting that two or three of them dine together.

Even if that wasn't possible, and he had to dine alone, he knew he absolutely must be noticed in the bar as late as possible. And it would probably be advantageous to appear the worse for wear as he finally tottered off to bed. Then the hotel staff would be obliged, if approached, to tell the police he couldn't possibly have embarked on a road trip of a hundred and twenty miles.

Assuming he could get back into the hotel secretly, he would also need to be in the dining room for breakfast as soon as service started. He guessed that would be at seven o'clock, but resolved to check the point on arrival.

At breakfast on the Tuesday morning, regardless of the fact that he would have enjoyed very little sleep, it was essential for the waiting staff and the other residents to see him behaving naturally. If it appeared nobody was taking sufficient notice of him, one or two targeted conversations might be initiated, in order to ensure that the correct impression was made on someone. He would rehearse a few *'Hail fellow, well met!'* openings, as he drove along. It couldn't hurt for him to be remembered as thoroughly pleasant, as well as thoroughly awake.

Whitaker's thoughts shifted back to the Webley. He knew he must dispose of the gun as soon as possible after using it. But he didn't intend to stop his car on the same bridge he had used on Friday night. The risk of his car being observed by a vigilant night watchman or a strolling insomniac was perhaps not very great; but he preferred to eliminate it altogether. He would need a different place.

He recalled what he knew about the location of the Arden. It had no car park of its own, but that didn't matter – he didn't want the car parked nearby anyway. Not far from the hotel were the Bristol docks. He was satisfied he could find a place to leave the car which, when he returned, would be only a short detour on foot to drop the gun into a dock before letting himself back into the hotel.

Surely all was now set?

Whitaker realised there was one aspect of his return home which he'd not yet considered. Exactly where should his wife be? Obviously, when he arrived at about one-thirty, she would be in bed. But if a patsy was to be blamed, might it not be more realistic if she had come downstairs in her night attire?

Yes, the idea had merit. On the other hand, Dulcie would be very much awake when he came to deal with her. It was all very difficult. After thinking the point through, he decided to wait, see how things developed, and improvise.

A final question came to mind. Depending on whether he left Dulcie in the bedroom or brought her to the lounge, he would need to utilise either two pillows or two cushions to muffle the sound. No difficulty in that, as both would be available. But should he remove these from the house after the deed was done, so there was no link to them? No, he thought that was pointless. He would leave them wherever they lay – just as he would leave Dulcie.

CHAPTER 7

Whitaker found an excellent parking place in Bristol. Leaving the gun safely stowed in its spare wheel hiding place, he took his small suitcase and walked the few hundred yards to the hotel and signed in.

His room was on the first floor, with a poor view overlooking the rear. He unpacked and went for an exploratory tour.

Within a few yards of his room, he found, as expected, a back staircase. He descended to the ground floor and immediately spotted the back door; working out it must be positioned almost directly beneath the window of his room. A quick inspection showed him there were only storage and caretaker cupboards near the door, with no guest rooms at all on this level. He was quite alone as he reconnoitred the area.

The back door was fastened by means of a heavy wooden bar. There was also a lock, but no key. By stooping and peering a little, he could see the lock was open; the bar being the sole means of keeping the entrance secure against anyone entering from the street.

Satisfied with his survey, Whitaker returned to his own floor, not having encountered a soul on his little sojourn. Continuing his orientation exercise, he discovered the three bathrooms on his landing were at the opposite end of the corridor. Even if a fellow-guest needed to pay a visit in the middle of the night, he or she wouldn't come along even as far as his own room.

The distance he would have to travel within the hotel from his room to the back stairs was so short, it might take him only five seconds to cover it. He was completely confident the chances of anyone seeing him in the middle of the night were infinitesimal. He could not have been allocated a more suitable room.

At six o'clock, Whitaker wandered down to the hotel lounge bar. He was experiencing a strong craving for alcohol, but was very conscious of the risk of taking even one alcoholic drink and not being able to stop. He ordered an Indian tonic water and sipped it as he leaned on the bar and looked around the room. There were ten or twelve people present, mostly males, and all apparently alone. He was considering which of these he might approach, and try to attach himself, when a man, standing a few feet further along the bar, nodded to him and enquired pleasantly:

"Are you by any chance here for the history symposium tomorrow?"

Whitaker was delighted that Fate was again assisting him. He responded with genuine pleasure to his new acquaintance, a man in his seventies and looking like an archetypal university don. "Yes," he said, accepting his companion's offered hand, "and very much looking forward to it. Robin Whitaker's the name. How do you do?"

"Splendid; splendid! Sebastian Hamilton, Cambridge professor emeritus. I'll be giving the first talk on -"

"The Importance of Fossils in the Silurian Shale!" Whitaker interrupted him with faux enthusiasm. "Your talk is the highlight of the programme as far as I'm concerned, sir."

The lie was delivered with what he thought was exactly the right amount of sincere-sounding gush. Whitaker had no intention of ruining anything he did, or said, by over-egging. His every move was to be considered, consistent, and above all, credible.

After ten minutes of amicable chat, during which both men confirmed they intended to dine in the hotel, three more guests arrived one by one at the bar. They didn't appear to be together. The genial professor took it upon himself to enquire whether they might also be attendees, and was pleased when the answer was affirmative for all three.

Further introductions established the newcomers were Anita French, Bernard Harris and Jonathan Armitage. The group moved to a table in the bar. Considering the disparity in ages, they got along very well. They did, of course, have something of a shared interest, but in fact the conversation was of a far more general nature.

Half an hour later, the little group swelled to six. Moira Lachlan had been one of Hamilton's students twenty years earlier, and she joined the group to talk to her old professor.

Almost by tacit agreement, the party decided to dine together, and at seven o'clock they were called to their table in the dining room. Whitaker had previously decided that his persona throughout this early part of the evening was to be one of calm; always showing he was genuinely interested in the current conversation and with nothing else on his mind. He therefore took great care to maintain the appropriate facial expressions, and continued this over dinner. He spoke quietly, mainly when spoken to, as perhaps befitted the youngest at the table.

He also remained completely alcohol free, and when one of his companions commented on this, he laughed the subject away. "Oh, I long ago developed a preference for not muddling the distinctive flavours of food and alcohol. I find I rather lose the pleasure of both, if I do. After dinner I shall definitely have a few snifters before bed, though. No better way of ensuring a good night's sleep in a strange bed!"

The meal was a convivial one, and Whitaker found himself particularly drawn to the elderly professor. For a moment, he allowed himself to think how, not many years before, he'd envisaged a similar career for himself. He even (quite ludicrously) told himself that one day he might return to the groves of academe. His brain didn't seem to encompass the fact that he was intending to eliminate the only person who might prevent his inevitable, self-destructive spiral of renewed drinking and gambling.

The group finished a leisurely meal a little after nine o'clock, Mrs Lachlan immediately excusing herself and retiring with a headache. The original group of five agreed on coffee in the lounge bar, and Whitaker decided this was the time to appear to drink so much as to incapacitate himself.

As everyone else took their seats in the lounge he remained standing, and asked who would be his guest and join him in "A tot of something good to go with our coffee."

Thanks, followed by requests for a small brandy, came from all four of his companions. Instead of calling for a waiter, Whitaker went to the bar himself. Ordering four brandies and a neat double whisky, he casually emphasised that the latter was for him. He also expressed his intention to enjoy more of the same later.

Craftily, he invited the bar tender to "take one for yourself," believing this would aid the man's memory in his favour, in the unlikely event of his being questioned.

Whitaker managed to convey the impression of drinking, with remarkable ease, even though not a single drop of alcohol actually passed his lips. His method was absurdly simple – he poured the contents of his own glass into a large tub containing a parlour palm – there was one conveniently sited on each side of his chair. This wasn't a coincidence; he had adroitly led the group into the lounge after dinner, having pre-selected both the table and his own seat.

Anticipating possible difficulty in distracting attention sufficiently in order to dispose of his drinks, Whitaker had prepared some ingenious ruses. However, as the evening wore on, he found deliberate deflections were unnecessary. Several opportunities arose quite naturally, the first as soon as he returned with the tray of drinks and set them down before his companions. Anita French spotted someone else she knew, and went to greet them, promising to return very shortly. The professor stood up at the same time and said he would take the opportunity to "see a man about a dog", prompting Armitage and Harris to do likewise.

A few minutes later, when reassembled and seeing Whitaker's empty glass, no one commented. Coffee was poured and more conversation flowed, Whitaker's companions leisurely enjoying their small brandies.

Presently, Hamilton enquired if anyone wished for another drink from the bar. He returned with a fresh double for Whitaker. The others, having taken a drink before the meal, and a glass of wine with their food, all declined.

With everyone seated again, Whitaker thought he would need to create a distraction. But fortune favoured him once more. Two more guests, who had been sitting nearby and were now on their way to their rooms, guessed they were fellow symposium-goers and approached their table. Whitaker jumped to his feet to offer his hand and introduce himself, but instead of introducing the rest of his group, he simply sat down again. His companions duly followed his lead, and rose to perform their own introductions. Whitaker again managed to discard his drink without any difficulty.

With the new arrivals gone and everyone seated, his colleagues noted his second empty glass, and although two of them exchanged glances, nobody said anything.

A little later, Mrs French went to the bar, checking first if anyone wished for another drink. She returned with more Scotch for Whitaker. She didn't sit down again, and wished them all a good night.

As he rose to give his own "Goodnight" in response, Whitaker managed to sway slightly and slur his words a little. His colleagues, finishing the last of their coffee, took themselves off to bed soon after.

Left all alone, Whitaker was delighted. 'They all think I've downed six single whiskies. More than enough evidence to prove I'd be incapable of driving anywhere tonight!' He eyed the remaining whisky longingly, but was acutely aware that to actually drink it would lead to disaster. With nobody left to observe him, he tipped the contents of the third glass into the tub.

Shortly afterwards, he made his way out of the lounge, detouring a little in order to speak to the barman. Deliberately placing both hands on the bar as if to support himself, he convincingly slurred out the children's bedtime jingle – "Night, night, Sleep tight, Don't let the bugs bite" – slowly wagging a finger as he did so.

Satisfied with his performance as a typical 'had a few too many' guest, he returned to his room at a little after eleven-thirty. Stone-cold sober, he took stock. So far, everything was running perfectly. The next hurdle was the back door. Would it be unlocked?

He pottered about the room, pacing up and down until his watch showed him it was midnight. Pulling on his dark overcoat, and cramming as much of his head as possible into his black Homburg, the brim low over his eyes, he gathered his car keys, put on his thin leather gloves, and slipped out of his room.

Within a few seconds he was on the stairs. Arriving unobserved at the back door, he saw immediately it wasn't barred. There had been no change of porter, or at least of routine, since his last visit! Wasting no time, he turned the handle and slipped out, experiencing a tiny surge of apprehension for the first time. He dreaded meeting another resident with a 'friend', using the back door for its improper purpose.

There was nobody visible in the street. He walked quickly to his car. Still there was nobody around. Releasing a deep sigh of pure relief, Whitaker set off towards home.

At a deserted spot twenty miles from Bristol, he stopped and recovered the revolver from the spare wheel bay. Whitaker pushed it down into his coat pocket. He fleetingly regretted that it had no safety catch; like most revolvers relying instead on its heavy trigger pull to avoid accidental discharge. He returned to the driving seat.

Nicely ahead of his scheduled time, he arrived on the outskirts of Draycaster. He'd previously earmarked a suitable place to park, within ten minutes' walk of his house and where it wasn't likely the car would be noticed in the dark.

He'd considered the possibility that McNamara might be sleeping in his house, and if so he would abandon his mission. However, as soon as he turned into the cul-de-sac he noted there was no car sitting on the driveway. It didn't necessarily mean McNamara wasn't in the house, of course – he might have parked his car at a distance. But Whitaker nevertheless took the Pilot's absence as a good omen, and abandoned his concerns about his wife's lover foiling his plans.

It was a very dark night, and there were no street lights in Glebe Close. Even supposing someone was watching from the houses opposite, they would never be able to make a positive identification. In fact, there were no lights visible in any house, and trees and large shrubs helpfully concealed the view from his immediate neighbours. So far, so good.

To eliminate all unnecessary noise, he had previously separated the front door key from the many others on his key ring. He slipped it into the lock. The door opened and closed silently.

Inside, the house was pitch dark, but of course he was very familiar with the layout. At the foot of the stairs, he paused to listen. Hearing nothing, he went to the living room and switched on a standard lamp and checked the position of the two cushions he intended to use. The heavy curtains were drawn, and would be unlikely to let much light outside, but even if a nocturnal neighbour should observe this, it would simply reinforce the notion that his wife was entertaining a late visitor. Returning to the hallway, he started up the stairs. The door of their bedroom was ajar, and he could hear Dulcie's steady breathing.

He pushed the door fully open, and stepped inside. Putting on the light, he took a deep breath and bent to shake his wife's shoulder. Dulcie woke with a start and sat up in bed. Before she could speak – much less scream – he identified himself in reassuring tones.

"What on earth are you doing, Robin!" she exclaimed. "Whatever time is it, for goodness sake? And why are you back home?"

"Calm yourself, Dulcie, everything is all right, but I've got some important news and I need to talk to you about it. Put on your dressing gown and I'll explain everything downstairs."

Dulcie stared at her husband for a moment, assessing whether he might be drunk. However, seeing no such signs, she said nothing more. Throwing back the blankets, she slipped out of bed and put on her dressing gown as instructed. She moved onto the landing, and Whitaker switched off the bedroom light as she started downstairs.

In the living room she turned to face him, apparently again checking to see if he had fallen off the wagon. Still doubtful on the point, but at least somewhat reassured, she sat down in an armchair.

"Come on, Robin, what is it? You don't seem to have been drinking, so I have to assume some other calamity has occurred – or is about to occur. Have you knocked down a pedestrian or something?"

Whitaker was walking slowly around the room. He smiled inwardly – a calamity was indeed about to occur – but to Dulcie, rather than an unknown pedestrian. Aloud, he said, "No, no. Nothing like that at all, Dulcie. I do need to say something, but there is nothing for you to worry about."

These were the last, lying, words Dulcie heard from her husband. As he passed behind her chair, he whipped out the revolver from his pocket. Gripping it by the barrel, he used the butt to strike her hard on the side of the head.

Dulcie made no sound, but slumped right down in the chair, semi-prone. Whitaker picked up the cushions earmarked earlier, laid the lower one against her head and, with the muzzle of the gun pointing into the cushion, he pressed the second cushion down on top of it, and fired twice.

The reports sounded very loud despite the muffling effect of the cushions, but he thought in reality the sound wouldn't have been heard far outside the room.

Allowing the cushions to fall to the floor behind the chair he quickly looked around the room, briefly toying with the idea of setting up two glasses, or perhaps coffee cups, to show that a visitor had been present. He decided against this further unplanned action, recognising there was no way a third party's fingerprints could be produced.

Instead, he contemplated removing Dulcie's dressing gown and leaving it discarded on the floor in a manner suggestive of a romantic encounter. He very much liked this idea, but decided it was imperative for him to make his escape as quickly as possible.

He turned out the lamp, paused for his eyes to make the necessary adjustment, then made his way in the dark to the back door. This he unlocked without touching the doorknob, calculating that if anyone checked they would find the last prints on the knob to be Dulcie's own.

By re-inserting his key into the front door lock, he was able to leave as he arrived, making sure the door was properly latched behind him and all without making a sound.

As he stood on the front doorstep, a last-minute thought sent him round to the back of the house again. He opened the back door and left it ajar.

Returning to his car, he started back to the hotel. Anyone intercepting him at this point (nobody did) would never have believed he had just committed murder. He was icily calm. His pulse rate might have been slightly elevated, but he displayed no visible sign of stress at all.

Having begun the penultimate phase

of his scheme, Whitaker again changed his arrangements very slightly, realising his earlier resolution not to use the River Dray a second time was actually a mistake. It occurred to him that if he was remarkably unfortunate, and someone dredging the Bristol docks found the gun – at virtually no distance from his hotel – it could only point to him and not to his patsies. Whereas, if the gun was found in the River Dray, the blame could not be so easily aimed at him, and would certainly cast equal suspicion on his patsies. He stopped the car and ejected the two spent cartridges and the remaining four live ones into the river. The Webley itself followed.

He drove steadily back to Bristol, and parked the car in exactly the same spot as before. Walking back to the hotel he approached the back door, again experiencing a surge of trepidation.

He need not have worried. With gloved hands he gently tried the door. It swung open. Slipping inside, he eased the door shut and paused a moment to listen. All was quiet. He quickly returned to his room. Glancing at his watch, he saw it wanted only a few minutes to half past three. His timings had been spot-on.

The unwinding of tension and adrenalin now swept over him. Dog-tired, he set his little travel alarm clock to wake him at six-thirty. He then undressed, and flopped into bed. Three hours' sleep would, he knew, be totally inadequate, but was certainly better than nothing.

The following morning he forced himself to get out of bed. After a cold bath and shave, he felt sufficiently invigorated and presentable to appear in public, and to ensure that some of his companions and the dining room staff noted his presence.

All went well. He ate his breakfast alone, affecting the poor appetite of someone who had imbibed too freely the night before. Two of the previous night's group sat nearby, and greeted him. Both thought he looked a bit puffy around the eyes, but ascribed this to a hangover from the six scotch whiskies he'd downed before bed. Privately, each suspected he might have drunk even more after they themselves retired.

His breakfast performance concluded to his satisfaction, Whitaker settled his hotel bill and took his case to the car, then walking back to the suite where the symposium was to be held.

The day was one of interminable boredom. But even though his tiredness was a physical and mental drag, Whitaker managed to present a picture of a competent man, interested in the topics covered, and without a care in the world. Shortly before five o'clock, the day's proceedings closed. Before he left, he shook hands with a few of his new acquaintances, and made a point of introducing himself and thanking the main administrator for organising the event.

As soon as he was out of the hotel's front door, his mood became one of utter exultation. He realised the most difficult aspect of the scheme had not been the action in his living room. It was the gargantuan effort required to display the necessary normality when surrounded by people. Actually, though, in terms of 'degree of difficulty', the strain of not drinking the whisky the previous evening ranked higher than anything else.

Realising he would need to be alert soon after arriving home, as without a doubt there would be extensive questioning from the police before he could get any sleep, he decided to pull off the road and close his eyes for half an hour or so.

In fact, he slept in an uncomfortable position for barely fifteen minutes. On waking, he actually felt worse, but reasoned again that even a little rest must be beneficial for whatever came next.

CHAPTER 8

Whitaker would have been highly delighted had he been aware of the events unfolding at his home whilst he listened to the presentations at the symposium.

At ten o'clock, Madge Croft arrived to have coffee with Dulcie. Getting no response from the bell, she was hesitating on the doorstep when Janet Brough, the second coffee-morning visitor, arrived. Old friends, the two greeted one another affectionately and then rang the bell again. This also produced no answer.

Stepping back from the front door, Janet pointed out that all the curtains in the house were still closed.

The invitations had only been issued the day before, and the women agreed it was unlikely Dulcie would have forgotten. Even if she had, it was very odd that she wouldn't have opened the curtains by this time. Janet knew Robin was away; but even if Dulcie didn't rise at the normal time to see her husband off to work, it wasn't likely she would still be in bed after ten o'clock. Belatedly thinking she might be in the back garden, the friends went through the side gate to take a look.

There was nobody in the garden, but Janet noticed the back door was ajar. The two women looked at one another. Without discussion, Janet pushed the door open and the pair went inside.

A loud "Halloo there, Dulcie!" from Madge, elicited no response.

Concerned that their hostess might have fallen seriously ill, the women went straight upstairs. Flicking on lights as they went, and finding nobody in the bedrooms or bathroom, they returned downstairs, and went to check in the living room, still also quite dark because of the drawn curtains.

Janet switched on the light. Immediately, the friends saw Dulcie slumped in her chair. Both had served in Queen Alexandra's Royal Naval Nursing Service, and seen every conceivable injury war could inflict. It was the work of a moment to check for signs of life in their friend – and to discover what had caused her demise.

Stepping back, the women understood they should do nothing more to disturb the scene. Returning to the hall, Janet picked up the telephone, asked for the emergency services, and explained the nature of their discovery.

PC Lomax arrived a little before ten-thirty. Joining the two friends in the hallway, he looked through the living room door. He went no further. From where he was standing he could see the clear wound in the top of Dulcie's head. Asking the women to go into the kitchen, he stationed himself in the hallway, awaiting, he told them, instructions from the detective officer who was already on his way.

Unfortunately, Inspector Wanstall, the assigned detective, never arrived. The constable driving him to the crime scene suffered a massive heart attack while only a few hundred yards from their destination. As a consequence, his car crashed into a wall at some speed. The inspector was catapulted through the windscreen and died instantly. The DC was also pronounced dead at the scene.

Constable Lomax, wondering why the DI wasn't with him within minutes as expected, presently telephoned the station to enquire, at the same time passing on an observation – the visible wound could not have been either accidental or self-inflicted.

It took the best part of an hour for someone in police headquarters to connect the tragic road accident with the missing detectives and the reported murder. The matter was rapidly escalated. When realisation dawned on the superintendent that there was a potential murder case with no local officer remaining of sufficient seniority to investigate it, he quickly got on the telephone to his boss.

The Chief Constable expressed sorrow on hearing the deaths of DI Wanstall and DC

Paine. "Two damned fine men gone. With wives and kiddies, the both of them," he told the superintendent. "Drivers and passengers going through car windscreens – you and I have seen too many of those in our careers, Middleton. You'd think someone, somewhere, would come up with a way to prevent it!"

With his reflections on the waste of life delivered, it took the Chief Constable barely seconds to decide to ask Scotland Yard for assistance.

By noon, arrangements had been made for Yard officers to attend, and the local force was informed the detectives would arrive by three o'clock.

In the meantime, Sergeant Bloy was sent to the house to support Lomax. He took the details of the two ladies, and after telling them to be ready for an interview later in the day, sent them away.

The constable was ordered to remain on guard, Bloy promising he would arrange for a sandwich to be sent round for him.

The sergeant's parting shot was to pass on the superintendent's instructions. Lomax was to explain the situation to the Yard detectives, and then to stay with them to give whatever help he could, "until they send you packing."

****

Chief Inspector Philip Bryce and Sergeant

Alex Haig arrived in Glebe Close a little after the expected time.

Lomax passed on what he knew, including the information about the women who had found the body. He also mentioned what they had said about finding the back door open, and about the husband being away.

"Mrs Brough thinks he's due back tonight, sir," he told the chief inspector, adding, "Superintendent Middleton would like you to call him, whenever's convenient."

"All right, Lomax, thank you. We'll take a look at the body first."

Like both the previous police officers, Bryce stood in the living room doorway, mentally recording the scene. With the light on, he looked carefully all around the room before transferring his gaze to the deceased woman, and shaking his head.

"Poor, poor, woman," he muttered. Stepping aside he nodded at his colleague, "All yours, sergeant."

Only after Haig had taken sufficient photographs did the chief inspector begin his own, close inspection. He saw a slender young woman in her early thirties; auburn haired, with pale freckles scattered across the bridge of her nose and cheeks. A small mole was visible on her collar bone above the scalloped neckline of her green negligee. Bryce could see that, in life, she would have been beautiful.

He eyed the two cushions lying on the floor behind the armchair. One was seriously damaged, with scorching around a rough hole in the centre.

"Shot through a cushion, with the other one used to muffle the sound," he observed. "Did you get pictures of the cushions, too, sergeant?"

"Aye, sir," replied Haig.

"Looks to me like there may have been two shots fired, but we'll have to see what the *post mortem* tells us.

"Lomax, how far away do the two women live?"

"Within a mile, sir, and not far apart."

"Can you drive?"

"Certainly can, sir!"

"Good. Take our car, and go and find them. Bring them both back here to see me, if at all possible."

The constable turned to catch the keys Haig lobbed towards him, and started towards the door, pleased to have a task to perform after hours of inertia.

"Oh, and before you go, Lomax," Bryce called him back. "Jot down the number for your superintendent and leave it by the telephone would you? I'll need to have a word with him before long."

With the constable gone, Bryce took another careful look around the living room before standing over Dulcie and inviting his subordinate's opinion. "First impressions, sergeant?"

Haig gave a sombre response. "Something strikes me as especially cold-blooded here, sir. There's nothing to suggest she was moved after death, so she was sitting in that very chair. Her nightwear is intact, and allowing for the fact she's slumped down, it looks naturally arranged. And apart from her head, she appears completely unmarked. No signs of resistance or struggle – no scratches; no broken fingernails. I'd say she knew who did this to her. Knew him very well, sir."

Bryce nodded slowly. "Yes, I'm sure you're right. While I'm making my call to the locals, take a look at the back door. Any surfaces, on which the last user might have left prints, have a go at lifting them."

As both detectives moved into the hallway, a bell rang out loudly. Bryce, standing nearest, opened the front door and made a snap assessment of the figure on the doorstep. Without any enquiry, he stepped aside, to admit a wiry little man, sporting pince-nez glasses and carrying a small black bag.

With his hand extended as the front door closed behind him, the visitor announced, "I'm Bob Lazenby, police surgeon. You have need of my services, I believe?"

Bryce introduced himself. Haig, already busy in the kitchen dusting the back door, waved in acknowledgement as his boss pointed him out to the medic.

"In there, Doc," Bryce indicated the lounge. "I'll leave you to it for a bit while I contact the local nick. You can open the curtains if you wish, although there's not much daylight left."

Picking up the telephone, he asked the operator for the number left by Lomax. Eventually, he reached Superintendent Middleton. After the usual pleasantries, Bryce was asked if he needed anything further at the house, and confirmed that he didn't.

"As you've presumably heard, our CID department has just lost two members," said Middleton, "and one of our detective sergeants is away. I really can't spare any of my remaining plain clothes men. Constable Lomax is to give you whatever help he can. He's a good lad, but lacking in experience. If you don't get on with him, I'll change him for someone else.

"Bob Lazenby will sort out the PM, of course, and I assume you and he will arrange between yourselves to inform the coroner.

"Oh, and you have rooms booked at the Station Hotel. It's not the Great Western at Paddington, but it's not bad for hereabouts and they'll look after you.

"I'll arrange a room here for you to use as a base, for interviews and so on; just ask the desk sergeant when you come in, and he'll direct you. Finally, any requests or questions at all, you only have to ask."

Bryce thanked Middleton, and put down the telephone.

Haig emerged from the kitchen. "Good prints on the shiny indoor knob, sir; nothing but smudges outside. When the Doc has finished, I'll take the prints from the deceased, for elimination."

The Yard detectives returned to the living room.

Lazenby had chosen to open the curtains, and was kneeling on the floor beside the armchair. "She died sometime between one and three this morning. Shot, as you can see, through the top of the head. I think twice in rapid succession, with a large calibre weapon, but I won't know for certain until I do my examination. I've never heard of such a case before, but I think the bullet or bullets may have passed out of the head and into the neck and onwards. We'll have to see.

"What I can tell you for certain is this. The entry point of the bullets is unusual. Unless the killer is preternaturally tall, she must have been lolling right back in the chair to be shot like that.

Lazenby stood up. "I'm finished here. Are you ready to release the deceased and the cushions to me, chief inspector?"

"Yes, I've seen enough. Make your arrangements please, Doc; and will you also sort out the coroner?"

The police surgeon nodded, "Absolutely; I

can do everything from here; leave it all with me. I'll get the PM done tonight. You'll have my report, addressed to you of course, delivered to the police station tomorrow." The medic went into the hall and picked up the telephone to make his promised calls.

Haig took Dulcie's fingerprints. Making a quick comparison with the impressions on the back door, he advised his chief, "No need to look further, sir. The last person to open the back door from the inside was Mrs Whitaker herself. Looks more and more like she let her killer in."

"Hmmm; does begin to look that way," replied the DCI. Retracing his steps to the kitchen, he opened the back door and surveyed the garden in the dusk. "There's no garage, which makes our search easier. Whilst I'm rootling through paperwork in the study, you take a look around out there, sergeant – particularly in the shed. See if there's anything at all which might interest us. If you can lay hands on a cardboard box at the same time, so much the better. I want to collect up every piece of paperwork on the premises."

Bryce looked around the kitchen as he spoke, and unhooked a calendar. Neat circles were drawn around some of the dates, with initials printed alongside. He held it out to Haig. "Like this. I want everything packed up for us to look at later. When you've finished in the shed, go through all the drawers and cupboards here in the kitchen, and then search upstairs. If you find anything at all which might help us, box it up – diaries; appointment cards; letters; anything at all.

"As soon as Lomax returns with, hopefully, at least one of this morning's visitors, I'll bring them in here for a chat. Not how I'd normally handle a situation like this, sergeant, but I don't want to leave the house before the husband gets back."

Haig nodded his understanding of the unorthodox arrangement. With his usual torch still in the Wolseley, he set about looking for an alternative in the under-stairs cupboard. Happy with the heavy-duty one he found, he made his way to the shed.

Bryce took a quick look in the study, and then saw the headlights of the police car arriving on the driveway. Opening the front door to Lomax, he was pleased to see two women with him. Introducing himself, he led the way into the kitchen and invited the pair to take a seat at the small table, telling the local constable to find Haig and help him.

"Thank you for coming, ladies, and apologies for these rather cramped conditions, but I need to stay in the house for a while, and I didn't want to delay speaking to you."

Between them, Madge and Janet detailed their arrival and subsequent inspection of the house. Both were matter-of-fact in their descriptions of discovering Dulcie. Seeing the DCI looking surprised at their apparent calmness, Madge was quick to explain:

"We were both nurses at Haslar during the war, chief inspector. We saw a lot of horrible injuries, and a lot of death."

"That's not to say we weren't deeply shocked to find Dulcie as we did," added Janet. "She was a very nice friend, and a loss to us both. I shall shed tears for her later."

Madge nodded. "Me too. Please don't think we aren't affected, chief inspector. It's more a case of our previous experiences having toughened us up. We understand how important it is to carry on, and do what must be done."

Bryce nodded, his own wartime experiences allowing him to understand the point.

"Your friend's murder is a particularly callous one, and I need every last scrap of information to find the culprit. Help me, in any way you can, regarding the domestic situation here. And please don't hold anything back. I'll decide if what you tell me has evidential value or not. So, what was the marriage like?"

The women looked at one another. Janet shrugged. "It's not a question of holding anything back; we wouldn't do that. It's more that Dulcie wasn't very forthcoming on the subject herself. She rarely mentioned Robin, and I think neither of us has seen him more than twice. All I'd say is this – I don't think theirs was a very lovey-dovey relationship, if you see what I mean."

Madge was in agreement again, and took over.

"I gathered there'd been a problem with a previous employer, but I've no idea of the details. And it's probably of no interest to you, but I think it was Dulcie with the money. Robin has quite a poorly-paid job in the local museum. I do remember Dulcie giving the impression that he could have done ever so much better for himself."

Bryce raised an eyebrow at this.

"He's got an Oxford doctorate," supplied Janet.

"I see," Bryce smiled encouragingly at the women. "I understand you told Constable Lomax that Mr – or I should say Dr – Whitaker is expected back this evening, after being away overnight at a conference somewhere?"

"According to what Dulcie said yesterday when she invited me to come for coffee today, yes. He's gone to Bristol," said Janet. "To be honest, Dulcie didn't seem too interested, and I suppose I wasn't either, because I didn't ask her what he was doing there. She did say he'd be back tonight."

Bryce glanced towards Madge, who shook her head. "Sorry, I can't tell you even that much. Dulcie didn't mention Bristol, or Robin, to me. The fact is, we three regularly met for coffee mornings, or afternoon tea, in any one of our houses when our husbands were out. Robin could have been in the museum as usual today, as far as I was concerned."

Bryce paused to think over this information. With no further questions, he held out his hand to Janet and then Madge. "Thank you, ladies. I'll need written statements from both of you sometime, but they can wait a day or so. Let me get Constable Lomax to take you back home."

The women simultaneously demurred. "No need, chief inspector," Madge told him. "It's not much more than a ten-minute walk for either of us. Thanks for the offer, but please don't bother."

Bryce escorted the nurses to the front door, noticing an ambulance turning into the cul-de-sac as he saw them out. The late Mrs Whitaker was on her way to the hospital morgue minutes later, and Bryce returned to the study.

Haig was putting a pile of papers into two large boxes, each already almost full. "There wasn't much upstairs, so we came in here to finish up while you were busy, sir. We needed a second box. Heaps of paperwork in the bureau. Not in any order, unfortunately, but there's a diary showing the husband away last night. No mention of coffee today, though."

"Probably because the arrangements

were only made yesterday." Bryce eyed the overflowing boxes and checked his watch. "Lomax, thank you for your help today. It's gone six-thirty now, so grab one of these boxes and take it to the car with the sergeant, then get off home. Tomorrow, come and find us at the police station – say half past eight – and we'll see what we might find for you to do."

Lomax responded with a chirpy "Righty-ho, sir!" He swung a jam-packed box up to his chest as though it weighed nothing, and followed a similarly burdened sergeant to the Wolseley.

When Haig returned he found his boss sitting in an armchair opposite the one used by Dulcie. Passing the murdered woman's chair to sit on the settee, he was surprised he could see no trace of blood anywhere, before realising the cushions removed by the police surgeon must have absorbed what there was, leaving no trace on the cream upholstery of the chair, or the dark maroon carpet.

"I think when, or if, Dr Whitaker arrives, we'll speak to him here in his own living room," said Bryce. "Better than some police station interview room."

The two talked over their findings so far, the DCI passing on the rather sketchy bits of hearsay and assumption provided by the two friends.

Soon after seven o'clock, they heard a car

arriving. By the time Whitaker had engaged his key in the front door lock, both officers were standing in the hallway.

Whitaker immediately stopped short when he saw the detectives in front of him. "Who are you?" he enquired, perplexed. "And I suppose it's your car blocking my drive? Where's Dulcie?"

"That's three questions, Dr Whitaker, and I'll answer them in order.

"I'm Detective Chief Inspector Bryce, and this is Detective Sergeant Haig. We're from Scotland Yard.

"Yes, it is our car outside. I apologise for obstructing your drive."

Whitaker put down his overnight bag and looked from one to the other in apparent bemusement. "I don't understand."

"Before answering your third question, I suggest we go and sit down in your living room," replied Bryce. "We may be some time, and we might as well be comfortable."

Whitaker pushed his way past the Yard detectives, muttering something under his breath about being tired after a long day. Entering the room ahead of them, he waved the visitors towards the settee, and sat down in the chair where his wife had died.

He was privately very proud of his demeanour, and thought it a lovely touch to select Dulcie's chair. It flashed through his mind to wonder what he would have done if her body had still been in the room, or if the chair had been covered in blood. But neither situation applied, and things couldn't have worked out better for him. He looked expectantly towards the DCI, and observed the sergeant take out his pocketbook.

"There is no easy way to say this, Dr Whitaker. I regret to inform you of this, but your wife is dead."

Whitaker jerked upright, staring at Bryce. Then sagged back in his chair, and said, dully: "I suppose I should have realised something serious had happened, with the house full of police. But hang on!" he sat up again. "Scotland Yard detectives – a chief inspector, at that? Something very abnormal has happened, hasn't it?"

"Yes, it has. Your wife has been shot dead. We've only been here a short time, and I can't tell you much. However, it doesn't appear to be the consequence of a burglary. We're proceeding on the basis it was a calculated murder."

Whitaker gaped at him. "Excuse me for a moment," he mumbled, and left the room. Haig looked at Bryce, eyebrows raised, but the DCI shook his head.

A few minutes later, the sound of a flushing toilet was heard.

Whitaker returned, but instead of resuming his seat he stood in visible agitation in the doorway. "Where is my poor dear Dulcie?"

he demanded. "Is she upstairs? In the garden? Where? I must go to her at once!"

Thoroughly pleased that his contrived trip to the cloakroom had given him the thinking time to work out that such questions would be natural – and expected – from a tragically bereaved husband. He paused in the doorway to hear what he had worked out as soon as he had stepped into the living room and seen the empty chair.

"Your wife has been taken away, Dr Whitaker. There will have to be a *post mortem* examination, of course."

Whitaker swallowed and shuddered. Taking his seat again, he begged in an anguished voice: "Please tell me what has happened."

"We're obviously hoping you can help us with information," replied Bryce, "but I can tell you what we know so far.

"This morning, by prior arrangement apparently, Mrs Croft and Mrs Brough visited your wife. There was no response to the doorbell, and they saw the curtains were still closed, even though it was mid-morning by then. They went to the back door and found it open. Concerned, they came inside and found your wife, dead.

"We do, of course need to ask you some questions. I'm happy to do that here, but your wife was killed in this room, so if you'd be more comfortable elsewhere, we can move to the police station."

Despite his fatigue, Whitaker's mind now worked exceptionally fast. Seeing an opportunity to criticise Bryce's tactics, he made his displeasure clear. "An extremely shabby and low trick, chief inspector! I suppose you were looking to see if I hesitated, or baulked or something, when you suggested this room?"

The DCI wasn't even slightly discomfited by Whitaker's rebuke. "Something of the sort, Dr Whitaker," he acknowledged. "You'll appreciate that, in a situation like this, the husband is inevitably a primary suspect."

"I suppose so, yes."

Whitaker's reply was brief. His words, however, accompanied by a small shake of the head and a lifting of his hands in helpless disbelief, were highly effective in conveying acquiescence and co-operation. He now played the part of the shocked husband, bewildered by the hideous situation thrust upon him, but fully accepting the officers' need to eliminate him from enquiries.

"When did this all happen? I've been in Bristol. Left here about three o'clock yesterday afternoon, and Dulcie was certainly alive then! I stayed overnight – plenty of witnesses to that. And, as you saw yourselves, I've only just got back."

It was all most plausibly delivered. Spotting another opportunity to make a natural-sounding response, Whitaker queried the information he'd been given. "You say the back door was open – you must mean broken down, surely, chief inspector? You can't be telling me Dulcie let her murderer in?"

"Let's go through everything slowly," replied Bryce, without answering Whitaker's questions about time, or the back door.

Over the next half hour, the Yard detectives methodically extracted many facts, including something of the couple's history.

Days earlier, Whitaker had decided he would have to be open, or at least reasonably open, about his previous problems. This was based on the principle that it was best for him to tell the police about anything they might be told by someone else, or which they might find out for themselves. He gave the police officers a bowdlerised version of the events at both universities, and the process which led him to his present post.

Likewise, he was fairly candid about his relationship with his late wife – how she controlled the purse strings in order to save him from "a couple of unfortunate habits with alcohol and the gee-gees".

He presented Dulcie's actions as the loyal and devoted support of an angel, rather than how he actually viewed them – the sadistic restraints of an unsympathetic devil.

As he gave his explanations, his voice ragged with the emotions of a man robbed of his one guiding light in life, he was inwardly laughing and congratulating himself for pulling the wool so competently over the eyes of a couple of dozy rozzers.

His marital history complete, and without so much as a hint towards Dulcie's infidelity at this point, Whitaker smoothly moved on to the previous twenty-four hours. He described his arrival at the hotel, and meeting other delegates in the bar.

"I didn't drink before, or during the meal, chief inspector, but I confess I was very naughty in the lounge afterwards. I think I drank quite a few glasses of Scotch. Someone else could probably say. I don't remember much until this morning. I'm very ashamed, of course."

Whitaker named the professor and those with whom he had dined, but only remembered the Christian names of a couple of others who were in his group at the symposium.

"The organiser could no doubt give you a list of the attendees – there must have been the best part of a hundred people there, although not all would have been staying in the hotel. I only spoke to perhaps a dozen. You could get the contact details of those I spoke to and spent time with. I could probably identify a couple more names, if I saw the list."

There was silence for a few moments. Bryce absorbed what he had been told, then asked for details of the hotel and the conference organiser, Haig noting down the information. After another pause, the chief inspector locked his steady grey eyes onto his interviewee's pale blue orbs. "There is one obvious question I must ask, Dr Whitaker. Can you think of anyone who would want your wife dead?"

Whitaker sat motionless and unresponsive, apparently staring at the small rug in front of the hearth. His face was inscrutable but his brain was whirling. This must be the appropriate point to mention his first patsy, and perhaps his second, he thought. But even as he silently revelled in the fact that, stage by stage, his scheme was coming together so marvellously, he suddenly saw a potentially fatal contradiction in what he was about to say.

He had portrayed Dulcie as supremely supportive of him. How could he conceivably reveal her infidelity now, and offer McNamara as a patsy? Surely even the dimmest of detectives would question his earlier claims of her devotion to him? Eventually, he let out a sigh, and looked up to face the Yard officers.

"I think I'm going to have to tell you something else – a couple of things, actually. Please believe me when I say I really should have preferred to suppress this information and let it..." he appeared to wrestle with his emotions again "...let it die with my dear Dulcie. But the truth must come out. She had a lover, chief inspector.

"Brian McNamara. He's a lawyer in the city here. Married, with family. I've met him a few times in the past, but not, I think, since he and Dulcie started to be together."

Whitaker explained how he had discovered the affair, but decided not to mention the steps taken to confirm the liaison. He calculated that when the police confronted McNamara with the little he was about to tell them – the day and time the green Ford Pilot pulled up onto the driveway – the solicitor wouldn't lie to them, or withhold anything. Whitaker belatedly decided it would give his next lie far greater credibility if the details of the hotel the couple stayed at came from McNamara, and not him.

"I never told Dulcie I knew. Perhaps you're wondering why, in the months since I discovered what was going on, I chose to be a *mari complaisant*? The reason is extremely simple, and I only hesitate because I realise many would find it distasteful – probably including yourselves, gentlemen. Indeed, I should have preferred never to speak of it."

Whitaker drew breath and spun out the threads of his freshly conceived falsehood. "My wife was what you might term a 'progressive'." Pointing to a framed print of a Vanessa Bell painting above the mantelpiece, then to another by Duncan Grant above the sofa where Haig sat, he elaborated. "It wasn't only the Bloomsbury

Group's art she admired. She subscribed wholeheartedly to their way of thinking about marriage and relationships.

"You have to understand it was all entirely amicable between us. I chose not to conduct myself in the same way, but I loved Dulcie very dearly, and I agreed before we married that if she found herself attracted to someone else, I would give her complete freedom to pursue her passion. No questions. No recriminations. When the affair ran its course, she and I would pick up where we left off, as though nothing had happened.

"Apart from satisfying my curiosity as to the identity of her most recent lover, I kept my end of the bargain and Dulcie certainly kept hers. She was still utterly, utterly, marvellous to me."

Whitaker paused; he had developed his works of oral fiction exceptionally well so far, but knew he needed to change his expression and tone of voice for his next deception.

Now, he became a man struggling with his conscience – wishing to be helpful to the police, but deeply regretting what he must say. He drew another long breath and assumed a pained expression. "I only mention this, chief inspector, because it occurs to me you are searching for someone with a motive, and I have to wonder if Brian McNamara may be such a person?

"He might have been frightened that Dulcie, taking a completely casual view of their liaison, would speak of their affair, and his wife would hear of it. I can see how he couldn't allow that.

"Or perhaps he was trying to break with Dulcie, and she didn't want the liaison to stop, and threatened to tell his wife." Whitaker shrugged dejectedly. "I'm afraid I really don't know. But with hindsight, I can see a number of ways the affair may have soured between them."

Once again, Whitaker was pleased with the manner in which he had brought out this possibility, taking extra pleasure in the fact that the solicitor was now thoroughly implicated.

Bryce sat quietly again, only interrupting his train of thought to ask if Whitaker knew where McNamara worked.

Haig looked up from his notetaking and gave his boss a break from questioning. "What was the second matter you mentioned, sir?"

"It concerns another illicit affair, sergeant, this one involving our dentist, Keith Forrest. You see, Dulcie is very friendly with his wife Patricia. By an unfortunate coincidence, a few weeks ago I saw Keith in a passionate embrace with some woman or other. I didn't know her name – still don't – but I saw her get out of his car and make a rather lewd display of her legs for him before going into her house. I came home and told Dulcie about it.

"She was upset, of course, because her friend was being deceived." Whitaker, noticing a look of incredulity on Haig's face at this remark, hastened to squash any suspicion of inconsistency in what he was saying. "Under any other circumstances it would be rank hypocrisy, sergeant, since she was doing the same to me. But as I've explained, our marriage was not the usual, exclusive, arrangement, and we were both happy with that. In any case, logic was never among Dulcie's many strengths." Whitaker was extremely careful to deliver this last fabrication about his wife with great affection in his voice, making her alleged deficiency sound a most endearing characteristic.

"Dulcie actually suggested the best thing to do would be to inform Patricia. But then she reconsidered and said it would be better to tell Keith; warn him off, as it were. She said if he stopped the affair Pat might never need to hear about it.

"Whether Dulcie had taken any steps yet, I really couldn't say, as the subject didn't come up again. But if she *had* carried out her threat, and Keith didn't want to give up the affair, or for his wife to find out, it would give him a motive to keep Dulcie quiet for good, I suppose."

Haig asked for the details of the dentist and the address of the alleged girlfriend.

A further silence ensued.

Lack of sleep, plus the physical and mental effort of the last twenty-four hours, was affecting Whitaker. But despite his exhaustion, he was internally jubilant. How easy, how effortless it had been to float his first two patsies to these accepting officers! How cleverly the tables had been turned on the chief inspector and his crude living room trap!

Yes, everything was going as smoothly as he had expected; with the added satisfaction of causing the unfortunate Forrest – he of the myriad public offices and pious persona – to appear an even more plausible suspect than McNamara.

In telling himself that a man of his intelligence and ability could easily outwit these (or indeed any) policemen, Whitaker had already made a bad error. Without any evidence whatsoever to support his assumption, he believed bright people simply didn't join the police force. Therefore, he thought, even the chief inspector would never be able to match his own intellect and artifices.

For the moment, there was nothing to contradict this belief. An extended silence developed as Bryce thought over the information Whitaker had provided. Whitaker happily observed the apparently slow ingestion as proof of a third-rate mind.

Presently, Bryce spoke. "Yes, Dr Whitaker, we'll certainly look into everything you've told us. Obviously, in the meantime, you won't be speaking to either of the gentlemen concerned."

Whitaker confirmed he had no intention

of doing so.

"A couple of final points," continued the DCI. "There will have to be an inquest, of course, although I have no idea when the coroner might open it. You will obviously be a witness. I'm afraid your late wife's body won't be released until the coroner authorises it.

"We've spoken to you, and to your wife's friends, here at the house. But any further interviews will either be at the police station or at the witness's home or workplace. I can't guarantee we won't need to come and look around your house again, but we'll certainly try not to disturb you. We'll keep you informed as far as we're able, naturally.

"By the way, we've removed a great many papers, principally relating to your wife. All completely routine. They'll be examined and returned to you as soon as possible."

The detectives stood, ready to leave. At the front door, Bryce offered his hand, "I'm sorry you'll have to move your car to let us off your drive. But do try and get some rest when we've gone."

Whitaker accepted the chief inspector's hand, and nodded, but said nothing as he made his way to his car and reversed it back into the cul-de-sac.

Bryce signalled Haig should take the wheel and the two detectives climbed into the Wolseley. Haig expertly manoeuvred the big vehicle in reverse past Whitaker's Ford, and courteously paused in the turning circle, so Whitaker could put his car back onto the driveway before the Wolseley pulled out of Glebe Close.

"I don't know this city, and I assume you don't either, sergeant," said Bryce, "but the railway station should be signposted, and hopefully the hotel will be visible close by."

The chief inspector didn't speak again until they reached their destination. Sergeant Haig, who was getting good at understanding when his boss needed uninterrupted thinking time, remained silent, too.

The hotel was more than visible from the station – it was actually built into it, in the fashion of the great establishments attached to some other principal stations such as York, Liverpool Street, and Paddington. Bryce, a devotee of railways and their history, mentally considered other railway hotels he'd either stayed in or read about. This one was perhaps a shade smaller than the one in Perth, he decided.

"Doesn't look too bad," he said, breaking the silence as his colleague parked the car. "Let's see what the rooms and food are like."

Carrying their bags up the steps to the main door (the ground floor of the hotel being effectively one floor above the road level) both were struck by the elegance of the entrance hall. To every visitor it proclaimed *'I was built to be the best within fifty miles, and even though my décor may have faded, no other establishment has overtaken me yet'.*

The receptionist was both charming and very efficient. She quickly sorted out keys, and offered the services of a porter. Declining, the detectives took the stairs and found their rooms on the next level.

"Usual arrangements, Alex," said Bryce outside his door. "Phone calls to our nearest and dearest, then meet up in the bar in about half an hour?"

Haig nodded.

CHAPTER 9

Bryce arrived in the residents' bar first, and ordered two pints of bitter. The barmaid passed him a menu card along with the beer, correctly assuming he would wish to dine. It was a large room, occupied by only a dozen or so patrons – all male, all in business suits, and all seated alone.

He took the glasses and card to a convenient table, and scanned the menu. The choice of food was limited, although not to the extent of no choice at all, as had been the case recently when staying at the Dog and Partridge in Oxfordshire. However, he reminded himself that the set meal at the Dog was excellent. Here, there was a choice of two dishes for both starter and dessert, and three for the main course. All looked very acceptable on paper, but time would tell whether the reality would match up.

Haig arrived, thanked his boss for the drink and sat down. Bryce passed him the menu. Both officers opted for soup, followed by sausage plait with boiled potatoes, cabbage, and gravy. For a change, a shared bottle of wine was agreed and a decent-sounding red burgundy was chosen.

The girl from behind the bar, presumably noting from their expressions or movements that decisions were now made, materialised by their table, notepad in hand. Bryce was pleased to see the efficiency of the hotel staff extended beyond reception. When she had taken the order and gone, Bryce looked at his colleague and sighed.

"All right, Alex. This is one of those cases where I feel the need to break the normal rule. Let's stay informal, but talk over what we have so far.

"Disturbing one, this, guv," replied Haig, appreciating the temporary lifting of boundaries. "I picked up the drift of what he was saying, but I'm looking to you to explain how the doings of the Bloomsbury people ties in with the Whitakers' own marriage. I know they were artistic sorts, but otherwise I'm in the dark."

"The artistic members of the group – the painters and writers – were amongst the most notable, certainly. But intellectuals, like the economist John Maynard Keynes who died a few years ago, were involved, too.

"The connection Whitaker was making was to their rejection of monogamy. Marital relationships were said to be very fluid within the set, with many affairs between them. Twenty or so years ago, the author Margaret Irwin summed it up very neatly in a fictitious

'Gloomsbury', describing it as a place where '...*all the couples are triangles.*'"

Haig responded with a cross between a derisive snort and an amused harrumph. "What did you make of Whitaker yourself, guv?"

"I'm really not sure. I didn't warm to him at all, but that's no reason to think he's a murderer, of course. As an academic – or at least an ex-academic – he's a highly intelligent chap. In his favour, he was pretty open about his fall from grace. And about the fact his wife was involved with another man, too." Bryce took a draught of his pint before adding, "Plus, he was sixty miles away."

"Aye, true enough, guv. But the two suspects he trotted out struck me as being almost too convenient."

"Oh yes; I thought the same. Nevertheless, both do look to be credible possibilities. In the absence of anything else at the moment, we have no choice but to follow-up on what Whitaker's given us."

"I meant to ask something else, guv – who was the Mary Complacent he mentioned? Sounded like something out of Mary, Mary, Quite Contrary. I've not heard that verse, if so."

Bryce, taking another swallow of his beer as Haig made this remark, choked a little as he laughed. "Whitaker's French pronunciation was lacking. It was *mari complaisant*," Bryce gave the correctly accented pronunciation, "a husband who turns a blind eye to his wife's adultery.

"His description wasn't a bad one, actually, if the circumstances of their agreement were as he described. His wife was the one with the money, and she was willing to protect him from himself. Theirs wouldn't be the first marriage where one party heavily supported – or even carried – the other, in various ways.

"Of course, we only have his word that his wife was having an affair at all. Likewise the dentist's alleged affair. We'll have to see both of those men as soon as possible."

Haig set his glass down on the table. "I can't deny that either motive might be enough. Both are local professionals, so they would be concerned about their status, and their family. There would be a huge financial impact if their wives divorced them, on top of everything else."

"Yes, agreed again," replied Bryce. "I think we'll try and interview both men at work. I'd rather not make a fuss at their respective homes if it isn't necessary. Unless one of them is guilty of murder, extra-marital affairs are none of our business."

A waitress came through to report their meal was ready, and led them through to a resplendent dining room. Several dozen guests were already seated, and here there was at least a leavening of females. The principal lighting came from half a dozen chandeliers, supplemented by wall brackets. The linen looked spotless, and the cutlery and glasses gleamed. The officers were shown to a table by the long window, the curtains drawn so they couldn't see outside. Bryce mentally took his bearings, and calculated that the room almost certainly looked down on the station concourse.

Both men were satisfied with the food and service, each comparing the restaurant to the various others they had frequented together over the past six months. Haig remarked that 'away cases' were unwelcome in many ways, but if the accommodation provided by the local constabulary was to this standard, it went a long way towards making the job tolerable. Bryce grinned, reminding his colleague of the appalling hotel to which they had been allocated when dealing with the Hartminster courthouse case earlier.

"I prefer to forget that one, guv," replied Haig with a laugh.

"Indeed, but I fear we'll get worse than the Fitzroy Arms again sometimes. Before you joined me, I'd been parked in some pretty dodgy billets. It's not uncommon to have to share rooms in a B&B, and when the beds are rock hard, the bedding threadbare or damp, and the food inadequate, one's mind can't stay one hundred percent focused on the task in hand."

The remainder of the meal was spent in discussions of the pair's favourite subjects, and continued over coffee in the lounge.

As they climbed the stairs to their rooms, Bryce suggested meeting for breakfast at seven thirty.

****

Whitaker, meanwhile, now master in his own house as well as of his own destiny, was savouring the sensation. During the evening, whilst still sitting in Dulcie's chair, he contemplated going out to a pub. Under his wife's edict, there was absolutely no alcohol in the house, not even medicinal brandy or cooking sherry. However, although his craving was almost overwhelming, he appreciated such a move would be a bad one. News of his wife's death was not yet in the public domain, and whilst he could always drive to a watering hole where nobody knew him, it would look exceedingly bad if it later came out that he went out drinking while his wife lay in the morgue.

An even more cogent reason was that, without Dulcie's beady eye on him, he might get paralytic and start talking out of turn, with equally disastrous results. No; it was essential he remained sober and out of sight.

In making this decision, he didn't find anything absurd in the simultaneous thought ever present in his head – that in a few weeks he would be able to drink again to his heart's desire. He believed that once the police departed, with one of his patsies locked up, or the case unsolved and abandoned, he would be truly free.

In connection with his anticipated freedom, he wondered how long it took for probate to be granted. How amusing it would be to ask McNamara's professional opinion on the point, pretending to be unaware of the affair! He immediately realised this was impossible; the police would no doubt be talking to the lecherous solicitor in the morning.

He sat bolt upright. Before he could obtain probate he would need Dulcie's will. He had always assumed – and indeed her threat to cut him out of it clearly indicated – that he was still the principal beneficiary.

It must still be so, he reasoned. But who was her executor? The couple had never discussed the matter. As far as he was aware, the current will was the one she had executed in anticipation of marriage, ten years earlier. McNamara certainly wasn't in her circle of acquaintances then, and so would not be executor. Dulcie was appointed as executor in his own modest will, and he hoped he occupied the same role in hers.

He got up from his chair and went through to the snug. Dulcie kept various items, including jewellery inherited from her mother, in a deposit box in the local bank. He guessed her will would be there too, but thought it was worth checking if there was a copy in the house.

He lowered the writing slope and found

the pigeon holes empty, only then recalling the chief inspector's parting remark. He was annoyed to realise his own cheque book had been taken along with Dulcie's. He would be demanding its return without delay, as he was already short of cash and would need to make a drawing quite soon in order to buy life's essentials.

He sat down heavily at the empty desk. Something else came to mind, something which he hadn't actively considered before. The house had been purchased when they moved to the city after his first dismissal. Dulcie had read the warning signs very clearly. She alone made the decision they would no longer rent when they moved to Draycaster. Using the inheritance from her aunt, she bought and registered the Glebe Close house in her name alone. He hadn't been in a position to object, of course, but that didn't stop him privately rueing the day (nearly seventy years earlier) when the Married Women's Property Act was passed.

This was all very difficult. With the house beyond his grasp, he recognised he would have to accept there was nothing he could do to get hold of any meaningful quantity of money in the near future.

Putting aside further thoughts of the will and property, he took Bryce's advice and went to bed.

Falling asleep was easy enough, but he

woke up sweating in the middle of a terrible nightmare. Keith Forrest was strangling him for spilling the beans about the dentist's affair. Dropping off again, he was awakened for a second time by a very similar dream – this time with Forrest aiming a shotgun at him. He drifted off again and no further dreams disturbed him, but sleep was intermittent for the remaining few hours of the night.

During his several wakeful periods, he thought some more about the two men he regarded as antagonists. The Scottish sergeant he dismissed out of hand as presenting no threat whatsoever.

The chief inspector he viewed only a little differently. He appeared to have an upper middle-class background, but Whitaker decided the man's educational attainments must be either inferior or very limited. Why else would he join the police? Whitaker's only experience of the police involved constables who would almost certainly never rise even to the rank of sergeant; he could not conceive of any other variety of policeman.

Whitaker was very wrong in his assessment of Haig as some sort of semi-idle appendage, doing little more than acting as chauffeur and scribe for his superior officer. Although without his boss's exceptional level of intelligence and higher education, the sergeant was a bright and thinking individual, already earmarked for greater things within the force. Whitaker was even more in error concerning Bryce, and would not have believed anyone who told him that the chief inspector had a first-class law degree from Cambridge, and was a qualified barrister.

For the moment, though, he remained in ignorance of all this, and confidently believed he could lead the detectives 'all the way up the garden path' and to his own freedom.

CHAPTER 10

Unlike Dr Whitaker, the police officers slept very well. Bryce rose early to take a walk, joining Haig in the dining room to find it did indeed overlook the station concourse. The panorama below was an agreeable one to both men as they enjoyed their breakfast, watching the trains and general bustle of travellers and busy British Railways staff.

Receiving directions to the police station from the hotel receptionist, they made the short journey in the Wolseley, each carrying a box of the Whitakers' papers inside.

The desk sergeant confirmed that a room had been placed at their disposal. Insisting on carrying the DCI's box himself, he led them up some stairs and opened a door half way along a corridor.

"This was DI Wanstall's office – the head of our CID who was killed yesterday. Superintendent Middleton sends his apologies, sir, but we don't really have much spare space here, and I understand Lomax is going to work with you, too.

"This room is a decent size for three, and it's quiet. The Super thought putting in the two side tables and chairs over there will give all of you a space to work, plus there's the extra chair if you have anyone to interview. And you've got a telephone, of course."

Bryce commiserated with the sergeant on the loss of two members of the local force in tragic circumstances.

"In the line of duty, as they say, sir. Although, when that expression was first coined, I hardly think being thrown through a car windscreen could have been imagined. Can I arrange some refreshments for you?"

"Perhaps a bit later, thanks, sergeant." Bryce checked his watch and saw it was almost eight-thirty. "But if Lomax is around, you can send him straight up."

Bryce turned to Haig. "My first job is contacting Messrs Forrest and McNamara. Make a start on those boxes, would you. Dig out all the key documents first, especially Mrs Whitaker's will if it's in there; plus diaries, bank statements, deposit box keys..." Bryce interrupted himself and grinned at his Yard colleague, "You know exactly what to look for, sergeant!

"We'll probably need to go through everything else in more detail later, but if I can get appointments I want us to see these two alleged philanderers as soon as possible."

There was a knock on the door and a

smiling PC Lomax put his head into the room."

"'Morning sir; sarge."

"Hello Lomax, come in and sit down. Before I make my calls, sergeant, tell the constable what we learned from Dr Whitaker.

Haig did a good job of relaying yesterday's interview. Bryce listened, appreciating how his sergeant was developing. He was including all the salient points while omitting more extraneous material.

"I know both those men, sir!" exclaimed Lomax when Haig finished. "Or at least, I know of them; where they work and so on. Mr Forrest has lots of interests – county councillor, for one. He's in the local paper almost every week. It's like he's everywhere.

"And Mr McNamara, he's the senior partner of Hazell, Frobisher, and McNamara; probably the most important firm of solicitors in the city. There isn't a Hazell or a Frobisher any more. At least, not working in the firm," he added.

"Good; very helpful, Lomax. Sit with the sergeant now," Bryce told the young constable. "As he sifts through the paperwork take a note of anything he asks you to, and generally make yourself useful."

Picking up the telephone, Bryce asked the switchboard to connect him to McNamara's firm.

A short pause, punctuated with clicking and clacking, filled the seconds before he heard the ringing tone, followed by a female voice. Identifying himself, he was told the solicitor was engaged. Refusing to accept this dismissal by the receptionist he politely pushed the point until she put him through.

McNamara was no more encouraging himself, and spoke curtly. "What's all this about, chief inspector? I'm extremely busy this morning."

"I'm sure you are, Mr McNamara. I won't ask what your workload concerns, but I'll tell you mine concerns a murder. I'm here from Scotland Yard, and I'd appreciate some of your time today." Bryce's tone left the solicitor in no doubt that he would be seen on his terms, and his terms alone.

There was a short silence. "I see. Actually, no, I don't really see, but still. How about ten o'clock?"

"Thank you. Sergeant Haig and I will call in then."

Ringing off, Bryce dabbled the handset rest and asked the operator to connect him to Keith Forrest's dental practice.

It seemed Mr Forrest wasn't at the surgery, but working from home on other business. When he explained the matter was urgent, he was given the dentist's home number.

In contacting the dentist at his residence, Bryce hoped Mrs Forrest wouldn't answer the telephone, and was pleased when a man's voice reached his ear. Explaining who he was, the DCI asked for an appointment as soon as convenient.

"Bit mysterious," remarked Forrest, his voice a mixture of curiosity and surprised amusement. "A senior Yard officer in our city wanting to speak to me. Can't you tell me a bit more?"

"Not on the telephone. But I will say the matter is delicate, and it might be better to have our talk away from your home. It's up to you, but perhaps you could come to the police station? If that doesn't appeal, we could meet at your surgery, if there's a private room available."

"I see," replied Forrest, his tone much altered. "Even more mysterious – and I have to say concerning." There was a lengthy pause before he continued, "Well, I've done nothing you can arrest me for, so I'm quite happy to come to you. I have no appointments. Whatever time suits you best, chief inspector."

Three o'clock was agreed and the conversation concluded.

"Good, we're all set," said Bryce, as he replaced the receiver again. "Lomax, the sergeant and I are going to see Mr McNamara. While we're gone, I want you to contact the organiser of the conference Dr Whitaker went to."

Haig passed over the information provided by Whitaker.

"Without giving away more than necessary, explain that the police need to contact a number of attendees who may be important witnesses. Ask for addresses and telephone numbers of the four people Whitaker named: Professor Hamilton, Jonathan Armitage, Anita French, and Bernard Harris. We especially need to speak to them.

"Any reluctance to divulge what we need, only then tell them this is a murder enquiry, and that obstructing you in your duty is an offence.

"When you've got the details for all four, start contacting them. Again without giving away information, arrange a time for later today or this evening when they'll be available to take a telephone call from me. Any time up to about eleven pm. Stress the importance of the matter."

Turning to Haig, busily sorting through the first box of papers, Bryce asked "Have you found anything yet, sergeant?"

"Only this, sir," replied Haig, holding up an envelope with the initials 'B.D.B.K.' written on the front, and removing a small key from within.

"Very good! Looks like we have a bank deposit box key. The will, or a copy, may be in the box, but we can't rely on it. Lomax, after you've contacted the attendees, look for a will. If you can't find one, telephone Dr Whitaker and ask if he knows which solicitor might be holding his wife's will.

"If he says he doesn't, draw up a list of every firm of solicitors in the city – including one-man bands, but excluding McNamara's lot.

"We should be back before you've finished. Everything understood?"

"Yes, sir," responded Lomax, cock-a-hoop at having a chance to carry out essential detective work in the investigation, and appreciating the stroke of luck that he happened to be the officer available to respond to the initial report.

Learning from the local constable that the solicitor's office was within easy walking distance, Bryce and Haig set off on foot.

Arriving exactly on time, they were shown straight up to the senior partner's impressive office.

McNamara rose to greet them. Square-jawed, clean-shaven, with a full head of neatly cut hair, he was an exceptional example of masculine physical prime; his powerful build of a type more often seen in active rugby forwards, rather than in desk-bound professional men.

Introductions performed, McNamara invited the detectives to take a seat, but didn't offer refreshments, and dismissed the girl who had escorted the policemen upstairs. As soon as the door was shut he opened the conversation, his manner and tone indicating he felt his time was being wasted.

"You mentioned murder on the telephone, chief inspector. I must assume it's one of my clients, but I've heard of no such thing yet. So please explain – and tell me how on earth you think I can help."

"Of course, Mr McNamara. The fact is that Dulcie Whitaker is dead. It wasn't an accident, nor was it suicide."

The solicitor may have turned a little paler, although neither Bryce nor Haig could have sworn to it.

McNamara responded with an air of detachment and an astonished expression. "Why should such a matter concern me, chief inspector?"

"Do you deny knowing the lady?"

"No; not at all. I recall meeting her and her husband at some university function or other. Whitaker used to be a lecturer, and I occasionally help in the law faculty."

The chief inspector's features and tone both hardened. He addressed the solicitor bluntly. "Please don't prevaricate, Mr McNamara. I think you knew Mrs Whitaker a great deal better than as an acquaintance.

"If it helps you to formulate a more truthful answer, I should tell you this. We have it on good authority that your very distinctive car has been seen on the Whitakers' drive when Dr Whitaker was not at home. Perhaps even more pertinent is the fact that we are armed with more details."

Bryce waited. He realised he was playing a weak hand. Revealing the sparse information Whitaker had given – the date and time the solicitor collected Dulcie on only one occasion – didn't amount to evidence of any sort of intimate relationship between the two. A solicitor could have many reasons for collecting a client in his car, all of them linked to business.

McNamara lowered an elbow onto his desk and pinched the bridge of his nose with a thumb and forefinger. There was a long silence during which he sat completely motionless. "Apologies," he said at last with a huge sigh. "Yes, as you obviously know, Dulcie and I were in the middle of an affair. For the past eight months or so. I didn't realise anybody was aware; actually, I'd have put money on it still remaining secret. We were, I thought, incredibly discreet.

"I realise you can't tell me how you know, so I won't ask. However, I can't think the information came from Ellen, my wife, and I hope, if it's at all possible, she can be kept in ignorance.

"You say Dulcie is dead. Where? And when?"

"I'll tell you in due course," replied Bryce, glad to have the upper hand. "But she was murdered – as you might deduce from the presence of Scotland Yard detectives in your city. And you should appreciate that you're a prime suspect.

"Consider this for a hypothesis: you wished to end the affair; Mrs Whitaker disagreed and threatened to bring matters to a head by informing your wife. You've told us you want your wife to remain in ignorance.

"Or perhaps an alternative: Mrs Whitaker wanted you to divorce your wife and marry her, but you preferred to carry on as you were."

McNamara groaned. "I see your point, of course; how could I not? But neither hypothesis has any grounding in reality. I can assure you we were both perfectly content with the *status quo*. I appreciate you only have my word for it, but it's the truth nonetheless. We were happy the way we were.

"In any case, I'm simply not the sort of person who would ever kill a woman. I can't say I was truly in love with Dulcie, and I don't claim she was with me, although I have reasons to believe I was rather more special to her than she was to me. But if we weren't in love, we had great affection for one another, over and above our mutual physical attraction. I couldn't think of killing her."

"Thank you, Mr McNamara," responded Bryce, his voice as expressionless as his face. "Can you tell us where you were between eleven o'clock on Monday night and say four o'clock yesterday morning?"

"At home, in bed. Reading for the first half-hour or so, and then asleep. And before you ask, no, I have no witness. My wife and I sleep in separate rooms. We both have unfortunate chronic snoring problems."

"As you'll be aware if you have a criminal practice, the police have grave reservations about alibis provided by spouses – so you perhaps haven't lost much in that regard," said Bryce.

"Over the last few days, how many times did you arrange to see Mrs Whitaker?"

"Twice in the last fortnight. I saw her on Monday of this week, and also the Monday before. Last week, she and I went separately to Basingstoke. I drove. She took a morning train. I'd booked into the Cavendish Hotel.

"We never went to the same hotel twice. I booked under my own name. Dulcie wasn't staying overnight so the subterfuge of a false name wasn't necessary – although I'll tell you now I did resort to that from time to time.

"I met her at the station, and took her back to my room. I had genuine business appointments on the Monday and Tuesday, so I stayed overnight, but Dulcie returned to be home before Robin came back from work on Monday. She was only with me for three or four hours."

"Did she appear her normal self?" asked Haig.

"Certainly," answered the solicitor. "Happy to be with me, as she always was. Which was how she was again on Monday of this week."

Sergeant Haig's inclined head and raised eyebrows wordlessly expressed his next question, and McNamara didn't hesitate to provide an answer:

"She'd come into Draycaster city centre to do some shopping. We met, quite by accident, at a small café called The Pantry, in Wymer Street. We'd always been absolutely scrupulous about never meeting anywhere in or around Draycaster, and there we were, accidentally bumping into one another." McNamara shook his head; "bound to happen one day, I suppose.

"Anyway, on the spur of the moment I decided there was no reason why we shouldn't know each other in public. I'd been a sort of colleague of her husband when he worked at the university, and we'd met more than once socially. The café was busy, and we shared a table in a corner at the back, away from the windows. Obviously, we didn't hold hands or kiss or anything, but in other respects we were ourselves, and laughed quite a bit during the meal.

"Incidentally, our waitress might remember us. A rather lovely girl; masses of blonde hair under her cap. She seated us after we'd bumped into one another – and was jolly glad to put us together on the one table when I said we'd share. She might remember us, chief inspector, because apart from the spontaneous agreement about the table, I tipped her rather well. If so, I would hope she would at least be able to vouch for Dulcie being happy."

"Did Mrs Whitaker mention her husband then, or on the previous Monday?"

"No. Dulcie practically never mentioned him, any more than I would talk to her about my wife. Early in our relationship I gathered Robin spent a lot of time 'in beer', as the saying goes. I wondered if that was the reason for leaving his university post so abruptly.

"And she did hint at a betting problem once. But I didn't know for sure and I wouldn't have dreamt of making any enquiries, raking up a load of dirt and gossip. We all have our little foibles, gentlemen, don't we?"

Haig found himself bristling at the solicitor's assumption, and felt a crisp *'No! Not if you mean being unfaithful to our wives, and excessively gambling and drinking,'* on the tip of his tongue. There was something about the solicitor's manner – his calm acceptance of Dulcie Whitaker's murder and the way he almost licked his lips describing the young waitress – which the rather staid sergeant found insufferable. He held his peace, however, and adopted his boss's inscrutable countenance.

Bryce studied the solicitor without speaking for a while. Leaning back in his chair he crossed his legs and folded his arms. "You present me with a difficulty, Mr McNamara. You must remain a leading suspect and your only slight chance of an alibi is if your wife could somehow swear you didn't leave your house in the early hours of yesterday morning. However, aside from the fact that her testimony would be treated with considerable caution, you don't want us to ask her anyway. What would you suggest we do?"

McNamara shook his head unhappily. "I can't offer a solution. I can only repeat that I hope you won't have to approach Ellen. It would seem to be a pointless exercise if you do. She wouldn't be able to tell you anything, and you wouldn't believe her if she did!"

Bryce gave him a thin smile. "I'll have to think about that. Obviously the best way forward for you is if we can find the murderer elsewhere.

"Do you possess a large calibre pistol, possibly a service revolver or an automatic, by any chance?"

"No, chief inspector, I don't. But, as no doubt you'll be checking up on everything, I'll tell you I was issued with a point three-eight automatic during the war. I flew with it over Germany and the occupied territories. Luckily, there was no time when I even came close to using it. I returned it to the armoury at my station on the day I was demobbed, and I think I might have been given a signed chitty to confirm receipt. But whether any record remains today, I've no idea."

Bryce nodded. "You asked for more detail, Mr McNamara. Dulcie Whitaker was shot in her own living room. At least one, and possibly two bullets were fired into her brain from very close range. The *post mortem* examination report will tell me more."

Finally, McNamara looked and sounded distraught. "Oh, Lord. How appalling." He hung his head and fell silent for a moment.

"But what about her husband, chief inspector? If it was he who knew about my liaison with his wife, surely he must be a suspect?" The solicitor's face and voice were both hopeful.

"I can't say anything about who else we might be looking at, Mr McNamara, beyond saying that Dr Whitaker has a much better alibi than you.

"One last question; did you ever act for Mrs Whitaker?"

"No, never. Much later she told me that after she'd decided to buy the Glebe Close house, she asked the owners who would be acting for them. They gave her this firm's name, as they were already clients of ours. So she picked Pemberton's, I believe. They may have handled other work for her, too. Their offices are on the opposite side of this street, a little further down.

"All of that happened before we'd even met. But if we'd been in a liaison by then, I should not have acted for her anyway. Most improper." The solicitor made this last point very firmly; the mere suggestion of breaching professional standards apparently far more serious to him than any private transgression.

"Thank you, Mr McNamara. We won't keep you any longer. If we do decide it's necessary to interview your wife, I'll give you advance warning. Not so you can coach her – I'm sure you, as an officer of the court, would never do that – but as a courtesy so you can, if you wish, tell her about your affair beforehand."

"I appreciate that, chief inspector. I only hope you find the actual culprit sooner rather than later. As I'm sure you understand, being high on the list of suspects in a murder case isn't a pleasant place to be!"

CHAPTER 11

The officers refrained from talking about the case in public as they walked back to the police station. Inside, Bryce told the desk sergeant they were ready to take up his earlier offer of coffee.

Lomax was putting down the telephone as the Yard detectives entered the office.

"Pity you weren't back a few seconds earlier, sir. Dr Whitaker rang; he'd like you to call him back urgently. Very excited, he is.

"When I spoke to him not half an hour ago, he was quite different. I couldn't find a will, so asked him about the solicitors, and he named a firm in Oxford. Said they drew up his will a few days before his marriage, and his wife used the same firm at the same time. He says there's a deposit box at the Home and Overseas Bank, and he reckons if the will isn't with the Oxford solicitor, it might be there. I've written all the details down, sir." He passed a piece of foolscap to the DCI. The information was organised under neatly underlined block capital headings.

"Well done, Lomax."

There was a tap at the door. Bryce,

standing closest, opened it to admit a young constable bearing a tray with the coffees. "I think we'd better see what Whitaker wants, before doing anything else," he said, as he took a mug in each hand and gave them to his subordinates, before taking the last for himself and thanking the waiter.

Lomax gave Whitaker's number to the operator, and passed the handset to Bryce as soon as he heard the ringing tone. Almost immediately, the call was answered.

The DCI introduced himself but was given no opportunity to say any more, Whitaker's voice reaching Haig and Lomax as an excited gabble through the handset.

"Wait a second," instructed Bryce. With his hand over the mouthpiece he enquired, "Lomax, have you seen Mrs Whitaker's cheque book?"

"Yes sir." The constable lifted the book out of a neat pile on one of the side tables and passed it to the DCI.

"I've got it," said Bryce into the telephone. "What? Oh, I see. Well, the last cheque is missing, but there's nothing written on the counterfoil. Are you sure? All right, I'll send someone round straight away to collect it. Please don't handle it any more, although it's probably a bit late to think of that, I suppose. What's his address? Thank you."

Bryce replaced the receiver. "Between your

call to Whitaker, Lomax, and his call back to you, it seems the postman made a delivery. The bank returned some cleared cheques drawn on his wife's account. Whitaker said he wouldn't normally have looked at them. But in view of his wife's death, he felt he should start taking over the running of the household.

"One of the cheques was for two hundred and fifty pounds, and was payable to a friend of theirs. He's sure the signature is a forgery, albeit a fairly good one. In any case, he says, even allowing for the fact that his wife oversaw their finances, she would certainly have mentioned it to him if she'd been contemplating giving, or lending, such a sum.

"So, he's offered a third suspect. Geoffrey Kent, currently unemployed. I've got the address. The theory is that Kent forged the cheque, and killed Mrs W when she found out and taxed him with theft."

"I cannae remember a case before where a suspect volunteered as many as three alternative candidates for the crime in less than twenty-four hours, sir," remarked Haig.

"Same here," replied Bryce, "but they don't seem to be fanciful, it has to be said.

"Anyway, you take our car, Lomax, and nip round to Whitaker's house to collect this cheque. Better take an envelope to carry it in, although on its trip through the clearing house and so on, the chances of any meaningful prints must be near zero. If you don't stop to chat, you should be back in half an hour."

Lomax left, and Haig was instructed to assemble all the bank statements in the boxes. Bryce settled himself at DI Wanstall's desk, and again picked up the telephone. He was shortly connected to Parker, Hargreaves and Paul, the Oxford solicitors.

Explaining who he was, and what he wanted, he eventually spoke to a clerk who seemed to know what he was doing, and promised he would check and return the DCI's call as quickly as he could.

True to his word, minutes later the man rang back and confirmed he had spoken to the solicitor involved in drafting Dulcie Whitaker's will, and the firm did hold the original. On learning that Mrs Whitaker was dead, the clerk hesitated, and said he would have to take instructions. This time he asked Bryce to hold the line. A minute later, another voice came on the telephone. Bryce explained the situation again, adding the information that Mrs Whitaker had been murdered.

"Good grief!" said the shocked voice. "I'm Desmond Hargreaves, chief inspector. I'm Mrs Whitaker's executor. Can you tell me if you've made an arrest?"

"Alas no, Mr Hargreaves. Early days – we've only been here a few hours. Can you tell me anything about the will, please?"

"I think so, although this is all from memory. The actual will is in our storage facility. We're a large firm and storage is in another building, so I should need a couple of hours at least to extract it.

"In the meantime, there was nothing unusual in it, I can tell you that much. The will was written in anticipation of the marriage, as I recall, and the husband is the sole beneficiary. There are no codicils – or at least none that I'm aware of.

"If you don't know of any later version, chief inspector, I'll assume this is Mrs Whitaker's last will. And unless her husband, whom I have never met, is convicted of the murder, he 'scoops the pool', as they say."

"Thank you, Mr Hargreaves. I'll inform the coroner of your position." Bryce was struck by the amount of detail Hargreaves apparently held in his memory, and felt the need to query the solicitor's recall. "I'm astonished you can remember so much, given the will was written ten years ago. I take it wills aren't a large part of your business?"

"As it happens, I remember Dulcie Whitaker – or Fulman, as she was then – particularly because of her uncanny and striking resemblance to my elder daughter. I also knew her father. But to answer your question, I handle a fair few wills, chief inspector. The majority for younger people starting out on married life are exactly like Dulcie Whitaker's – the spouse is the sole beneficiary. I've seen precious few exceptions, and even fewer codicils added to youngsters' wills in the years immediately following marriage. Re-working of wills tends to come much later, after a divorce perhaps, or when children marry someone the parents disapprove of. So you see it's the exceptions which are memorable, and Dulcie Whitaker's wasn't one of those.

"I'll be retrieving the will from our storage facility anyway, and thoroughly checking its content against my memory. That's partly for your reassurance, chief inspector, but also because it has, very regrettably, become a working document for me, and I must have it to hand.

"Will it suit if I telephone you late this afternoon to give you my confirmation – or any correction – to what I've told you?"

Bryce thanked the solicitor warmly, and asked him to leave a message if he was unavailable.

The DCI's next call was to Pemberton's. Once again, he went through explanations to a couple of intermediaries before finding someone knowledgeable. He learned the house deeds, which were solely in Mrs Whitaker's name, were held in the Draycaster office. It seemed the firm also advised Mrs Whitaker on various other matters, but his request for further information about these was refused. Changing tactics, Bryce posed two direct questions. His informant reluctantly revealed that divorce was not one of the 'other matters'. Nor had the firm been involved with the late Mrs Whitaker's will.

Bryce, reassured that the original will was almost certainly the one and only, relayed details of Mr Hargreaves as executor, and ended the call.

Haig caught his boss's eye over the tops of his piles of paper. "There's an envelope with typed bank statements and a few hand written current account balance slips in this lot, sir. All for Mrs Whitaker's account. The cheque book shows the bank's head office, but now we've got the address of her local branch."

"Good!"

Bryce looked across to Lomax's desk. "I wonder how far he got with the conference attendees."

Haig moved across to check. "There's a list of names here. The four we're interested in all have 'phone numbers."

"Excellent. Checking Whitaker's story with them is a job for later. It's getting near lunchtime. I spotted a little café a hundred yards down the street. We'll eat when Lomax returns.

Beating Bryce's half-hour estimate by three minutes, Lomax returned, carrying an envelope; he placed this in front of the DCI.

"Dr Whitaker gave me another four returned cheques, sir, saying we could compare them with the dodgy one."

"Good thinking on his part," remarked Bryce. "I should have thought of that myself."

He shook the five cheques out of the envelope, and using a pencil as an implement pushed them around so they all faced the same way. Haig and Lomax stood looking over his shoulder as he scrutinised the slips of paper.

"I've never understood how handwriting experts can give authoritative evidence," said Haig. "To me, all five signatures are slightly different. Maybe the two hundred and fifty pound one is even more different, though."

"It's certainly a tricky subject. I agree with your assessment. However, perhaps we're subconsciously seeing what we expect to see. What if we'd seen these five cheques, and simply been told one of them was a forgery? Would we still have picked out the two hundred and fifty pound one? What do you think, Lomax?"

"I understand what you're both saying, sir, but I really do think the signature on that one," Lomax pointed at the alleged forgery, "is more different than the differences between the others, and itself – if I'm making sense!"

Bryce grinned. "Clearly none of us would be any use in the witness box, so at some point we may need to employ an expert.

"Dust all these, sergeant – forlorn hope, but still."

Lomax watched with interest as Haig took

out the fingerprinting paraphernalia, and set to work. Bryce sat silently, staring at the ceiling.

"Total jumble, sir; these have all been through so many hands. There are a few clear prints on the suspect cheque, but they could be those of a bank teller, or someone in the clearing house, or anyone."

"Or even Whitaker's – he obviously handled the cheques this morning," said Bryce as he shuffled them all back into the envelope.

"Anyway, let's go and eat. We spotted a café, Lomax, a little way down the street. Okay with you?"

"Oh yes, sir; the food's very edible. Do you mean I'm to come with you?"

"Naturally, you're part of the team."

As the three officers made their way towards the café, Lomax, being in uniform, very much stood out. He was a couple of inches taller even than the DCI, and his helmet exaggerated the difference still further. Bryce found himself almost laughing out loud at the picture of himself and Haig being 'escorted' along the street by the young constable.

****

Refreshed after their meal, the DCI's first instruction on returning to the office was for Haig:

"Your job this afternoon is to take the forged cheque to the bank, sergeant. Push the 'murder investigation' angle as hard as necessary and see what the manager or any of his staff think about the writing and signature.

"Take the deposit box key too. I doubt if the bank manager will let you look in it without a court order, but it's worth a try."

As Haig departed for the bank, the DCI turned to Lomax.

"You did well on those names," said Bryce. "I assume you didn't have time to call any of them?"

"No, sir; that was going to be my next job, then Dr Whitaker rang with his new report."

"I'm going to try to contact at least one of them now. While I'm doing that, take a look through the boxes again. I saw what looked like a diary. Pull it out and see if there are any mentions of more lovers, or anything else which might interest us."

The DCI picked up the telephone again. There was no reply from the Professor's number. Trying Armitage, he found himself speaking to a secretary. Mr Armitage was out of the office, she said, but would be asked to call back when he returned from a meeting, probably within the next half-hour.

Anita French picked up the telephone on the first ring. Bryce gathered Mrs French was a National Trust employee, of some seniority. He explained what he wanted, adding that this was simply a routine procedure to eliminate someone from an enquiry. Mrs French laughed.

"Well, chief inspector, all I can say is this, Dr Whitaker appeared perfectly normal during dinner. As far as I recall he drank nothing. He said something about not drinking and eating. As the meal wasn't marvellous, perhaps he made an error, but still, his choice.

"A group of us went into the lounge for coffee after dinner. He said something about making up for his abstention earlier. I think he drank at least three double whiskies – I bought one of them myself shortly before I went to bed. I suppose he could have drunk more after I'd gone. I would certainly say his speech was a bit slurred when he said goodnight to me.

"Oh, and he looked a little hung-over at breakfast, although he came down for the first service at seven o'clock. He wasn't a speaker or anything in the symposium, and I don't recall he put a question after any of the presentations. But I'm absolutely sure he was there all day."

Bryce thanked Mrs French for her help. He called across to Lomax and asked how he was getting along.

"It's not really a diary of what's happened, sir, more a sort of fixtures list. You know, who's coming for coffee on the twenty-first, or an oculist's appointment on the third, those sorts of things. There's nothing you might call private appointments. No mention of meetings with Mr McNamara, or any other man, for instance."

Bryce nodded slowly and looked thoughtful, the ringing of the telephone disrupting him. Picking up the handset he quickly realised he was speaking to Jonathan Armitage and explained what he was after. He listened for two full minutes, interjecting only with an occasional 'uh huh' or 'I see', before thanking Armitage for calling and ringing off.

"Both Armitage and Mrs French might have been reading from the same script," he told the constable. "Their reports tally exactly. Whitaker certainly had three double scotches, at least, after dinner. Unsurprisingly, he seems to have been tipsy by the time the witnesses retired. On his own admission he is, or has been, an alcoholic, so I can't help thinking that having started, he could have imbibed a few more. As a resident in the hotel, the bar staff could hardly throw him out.

"All in all, I can't see how he could have made a hundred-and twenty-mile round trip to shoot his wife."

The DCI sat back in his chair and stared up at the ceiling again.

CHAPTER 12

Whitaker was in his kitchen. Relaxed and eating a freshly made fried egg sandwich, he mused on his progress, pleased that everything was going like clockwork so far. He would have liked to wash his sandwich down with something stronger than tea, but decided he must maintain abstinence for as long as he was in contact with the police.

Very curious about how the investigation was progressing, he thought it a terrible pity he wouldn't see the facial expressions of his three potential patsies when the police came to call. The idea of watching McNamara was pleasing, but the thought of watching Forrest was even more so. In his capacity of lay preacher, the man stood in his pulpit expounding virtuous conduct as the only way to live one's life – with family paramount. What a hypocrite!

Whitaker thought happily that even if he was unlucky, and all three of his patsies managed to produce alibis, or otherwise avoid conviction, they would still have served to divert attention from him.

Also, and this gave him vengeful satisfaction, all three would be seriously inconvenienced and tainted. With a bit of luck, the marriages of the two philanderers would be ruined. He was happy at the prospect.

His thoughts turned to money. Should he contact Hargreaves & Co at Oxford? He wasn't certain, of course, if they held the will; nor whether they, or he, or someone else, was executor. Although he knew little about probate, he realised that without a death certificate there could be no move until after the inquest. He decided it would be better to wait quietly, rather than appear impatient for the money. The police would no doubt locate anything of interest in their investigations, and tell him about it in due course.

Something else came to mind. He knew there was a deposit box at the bank, containing some jewellery which had once belonged to her mother and grandmother. He assumed, because Dulcie rarely shared financial information since losing his Oxford post, that her equities and bonds would also be in the box. If he could find the key to her deposit box, might he not help himself to the contents and start liquidating some of them? The jewellery could certainly be cashed in quite easily, he thought.

The flaw in this idea came to him almost immediately. If he went into the bank and simply told the staff his wife was dead, they would of course ask to see the grant of probate. At present, he had no standing with the bank. Nor, indeed, regarding the will.

The chance to sell some jewellery was therefore denied him, but he reminded himself that it was better to wait anyway.

His brain ranged over his plan again. The fact the detectives lapped up everything he'd fed them was unsurprising. No policeman could ever match him, after all.

His success so far caused him to question whether he should augment his scheme a little further. Was it not a case of 'the more the merrier'?

Had he been aware of the remark Sergeant Haig made about the three suspects already produced, he would have realised a more apt proverb would be 'too many cooks spoil the broth'.

Ignorant of the sergeant's comment, he spent some time in dreaming up a fourth candidate. However, he didn't really know many people these days. He'd lost most of his few close friends along with his first job, and the remainder with his second. He thought one of Dulcie's cousins might be suitable, and toyed with this idea for a while. He disliked the man intensely, and would have delighted in drawing the toadying little tick into the matter.

Failing to come up with a feasible motive for the cousin, he turned instead to thoughts about a female patsy. Unfortunately, he knew even fewer women these days. He could hardly use Paula Kent when her husband was already involved in a different way.

Or could he? What if it was Paula who, after finding her husband forged the cheque, took it upon herself to eliminate Dulcie? That was surely possible. Who knew what lengths she might go to in order to save Geoffrey from prison?

But was it feasible for a woman to have fired the Webley? It possessed a hefty kick, and she would never have handled such a weapon before. He assumed the autopsy would show that two bullets were fired. Even if a mousy little woman like Paula managed to screw up the courage to do the job, was it likely she would have the guts to fire two separate shots? On reflection, he thought probably not.

In the absence of further candidates with any sort of motive, he reluctantly abandoned the whole idea, telling himself that trying to improve upon perfection was pointless.

His train of thought was interrupted by the telephone bell. He was taken aback when the caller identified himself as a reporter from the local newspaper.

He was unprepared for this, and mentally berated himself as a fool for not realising the news of his wife's death would reach the public domain sooner rather than later.

In fact, the press had heard the news via a circuitous route, but such is the lifeblood of the Fourth Estate. No individual would ever learn the full detail of this particular sequence, but Janet Brough told her husband, who informed his brother, who in turn mentioned it to a couple of other friends in a pub. This conversation was overheard by another man leaning against the bar – who happened to be a stringer for the paper. In the guise of a casually curious member of the public, the stringer managed to ask a couple of pointed questions, and got the name of the dead woman.

Slipping away to find a telephone, he passed on the little he knew to his deputy editor, who was invariably desperate for meaty material. It was nearly closing time when the report, such as it was, arrived, and it was the following morning before a reporter could be assigned. He got nowhere when trying to extract information from the police station, but it took him no time to find an address and telephone number in the directory.

"What do you want?" Whitaker asked sharply when he heard the words 'Draycaster Daily'.

"My paper has heard there's been a murder in the house. Can you tell me anything about it?"

Whitaker hesitated. There was little point in a flat denial, as sooner or later the police, the coroner, or some other authority would undoubtedly make the matter public. He prevaricated:

"How did you hear of such a thing?"

"We have our sources, sir," replied the voice suavely. "Would you be Mr Whitaker?"

Whitaker stood on his dignity and replied with frosty emphasis, "No, I would not be! I'm *Doctor* Whitaker."

"I'm very sorry to disturb you sir, but is it your wife who's been killed?"

"Yes, it is. For obvious reasons, I don't wish to discuss this over the telephone."

The reporter chose to ignore the annoyance in Whitaker's voice, and deliberately misinterpreted his statement. "I quite understand, sir. Could I come round and talk to you face-to-face?"

"Certainly not! I'm not talking to anybody at present."

"Not even the police, sir?" came the impudent riposte.

Whitaker slammed down the handset, furious at the reporter and also at his own unpreparedness.

After a few minutes, and having thought a little more about this, it occurred to him that the press might somehow be employed to his own advantage. He picked up the telephone again, called the police station, and asked for chief inspector Bryce. He relayed the detail of the call to the DCI, remarking that he was unsure of what he should say.

"I see. We've not said anything from here, but these things always slip out somehow. I was intending to make a press statement later today or tomorrow anyway; just haven't got around to it yet.

"I strongly advise you to refuse to comment. Put the phone down if they ring, and don't open the door if they call at the house. If the reporters get too oppressive, let me know and I'll send a policeman to keep them off your property.

"But if you really feel pressed into saying something, it would be in order for you to say your wife was shot while you yourself were away attending a conference. Above all, bear in mind you aren't a completely free agent. You mustn't say anything which might impede our investigation. For example, you certainly can't mention the three possible suspects you've told us about. We've only seen one of them so far, and I don't want the other two warned in advance.

"While you're on the telephone, Dr Whitaker, I have a couple of snippets of information for you, which you'll need in due course. The Oxford solicitors do hold your late wife's will, and at the moment we've not traced a later version. Mr Hargreaves is therefore appointed as executor, and I can tell you I found him helpful and competent. There can be no movement on proving the will until various formalities are complete, of course.

"Similarly, Pemberton's here in the city hold the title deeds to the house.

"I can't tell you about our progress, but my sergeant is with the bank manager as we speak, discussing the cheque. By this evening, we'll hopefully interview another of your suspects. I'll contact you again tomorrow."

Whitaker said he quite understood about the need to be reticent, expressed his thanks, and hung up – smiling to himself.

CHAPTER 13

Sergeant Haig arrived at the Home and Overseas Bank a little before two o'clock. The Draycaster city branch was also the head office for the county and, like the station hotel, built at a time when commercial success was often celebrated in the form of great buildings. Occupying an entire corner of the city's main crossroads, the bank was an exuberant folly of stuccoed columns and Greek pediments. Architecturally, it had nothing in common with any of the neighbouring properties; yet this grandly different and distinguished edifice managed to sit harmoniously amongst them.

Entering through one of the three pairs of double front doors, Haig saw that the bank was busy with customers. All ten cashier windows ahead of him were in service, most with short queues. Spotting the black and white pinstripe trousers and black jacket of a bank floor manager, Haig made his way over to the man and spoke in a low voice.

"Good afternoon, sir, I'm Detective Sergeant Haig from Scotland Yard. I'd rather not flash my identification at you in public; could we speak privately, perhaps?"

If Oswald Keating was surprised by Haig's introduction he didn't show it. He rapidly assessed the man in front of him, and decided he was not a bank robber. With a professional smile, the manager wordlessly led the sergeant to a door on one side of the great hall and then into a large private office. Still without speaking, he waved Haig to a seat as he picked up his desk telephone.

"Ah, Miss Roy, be so good as to tell Mr Ferris to take over from me on the floor until further notice, would you?"

His replacement organised, Keating examined Haig's proffered ID, and spread his hands. "I'm entirely at your service, sergeant, and, I confess, intrigued. How can I help Scotland Yard?"

"It's in connection with one of your account holders, Dulcie Whitaker."

"Indeed?" queried Keating. "A most pleasant lady, and a valued customer. Please tell me you haven't come here about irregularities in her affairs, sergeant!"

"That's precisely what brings me to your bank, I'm sorry to say."

Keating was shocked. He clasped his hands and said nothing.

Haig filled the void. "I was hoping you, or one of your clerks, might look at a few of Mrs

MACHINATIONS OF A MURDERER

Whitaker's cheques for me, and say which of them may be a forgery." Haig took the cheque envelope out of his inside jacket pocket and spread out the contents for Keating to inspect.

The manager bent over his desk and looked closely at the five slips of paper. "I don't want to commit myself, sergeant, it's some years since I regularly handled cheques. I know Mrs Whitaker didn't often write a cheque for more than two hundred pounds, so if one of these is forged I'd suspect the largest first. But I'd also have to say that her current account would bear a good few such cheques – should she wish to write them."

Keating lifted his telephone again. "Miss Roy, send Mr Hinchcliffe in immediately, please."

Replacing the handset, the bank manager smiled at Haig. "I think if anyone can answer your question it'll be young Hinchcliffe. He actually uncovered something similar for us a couple of years ago. A nasty business where a youngster was defrauding an elderly relation. Makes you wonder what the world is coming to, sergeant."

Keating suddenly looked at Haig rather more quizzically. "Which of the cheques does Mrs Whitaker say is forged?"

Haig shook his head and turned down the corners of his mouth. "Mrs Whitaker can't tell us anything, sir. She was shot dead yesterday morning."

The bank manager was horrified, but quickly composed himself as a knock on the door preceded a nervous-looking young man.

"You sent for me, sir?"

"I did, Hinchcliffe. Come round my side of the desk for a moment and look at these cheques. Say if you see anything of concern."

The junior man peered closely and methodically at the slips. Haig watched as his head swung back to the forged cheque again and again.

Presently, Hinchcliffe straightened his back and pointed at the forged cheque. "I don't think the signature on this one is Mrs Whitaker's. There's emphasis – extra pressure on the pen – in several places, whereas you can see she hasn't put the same pressure in the same places on any of the other cheques. And where there's emphasis on the other four cheques, it's consistent over all of them.

"The discrepancies are most noticeable in the signature; but it's pretty good, all the same." He turned to his boss. "I'm not at all surprised this cheque was cleared, sir."

The manager thanked his subordinate and dismissed him. "Can I help you with anything else, sergeant?"

Haig chanced his arm. "I don't have a warrant, Mr Keating, but I do have what I believe is Mrs Whitaker's deposit box key. Is there any way I might be able to have a quick look at what she stored with you?"

Keating weighed up the bank's regulations and his duty to the late Mrs Whitaker and her estate, against his wish to be helpful. He was struck by the considerate way in which the sturdy detective with the mild Scottish accent had approached him in the crowded banking hall earlier. He decided he could offer a compromise.

"I'm willing to take you down, sergeant, and supervise your inspection of Mrs Whitaker's deposit box, on the understanding that I cannot permit you to remove anything."

Haig was happy to agree to the condition, and Keating escorted him to the bank's underground vault. Security gates and guards were negotiated before the two men were allowed into the deposit box area. Keating located the required box and Haig unlocked it.

First to come out were the jewellery boxes, their contents dazzling. Diamond necklaces, bracelets, and earrings, all set with rubies or emeralds, were enclosed in velvet-lined leather cases, embossed in gold with the names of the country's finest jewellers.

A thick sheaf of share certificates lay beneath the jewellery. These bore the names of top firms and registered the sizeable holdings in each.

Title deeds for at least a dozen Oxford properties were rolled up together and tied with a blue ribbon.

"My word," said Haig to Keating. "Quite the wee treasure chest here."

Keating nodded sadly. "All useless to the poor woman now."

Replacing everything and re-locking the deposit box, Haig was taken back up to the main hall again. Thanking Keating for his help, the sergeant took his leave.

Haig returned to the police station looking pleased. He put the key and envelope on Bryce's desk, and sat down, still smiling.

"Why do the words 'cat' and 'cream' come to mind, sergeant?"

The sergeant recounted the details of his visit.

Bryce was also pleased. "All very good. The house alone would be a pretty good thing to inherit, but your description of a sample of the jewels – plus an unknown value of shares and other properties – means Dr Whitaker will do very nicely indeed. However, the detail of what's in Mrs Whitaker's Aladdin's cave is a matter for the executor and not for us; it'll all have to be valued for probate, of course.

"The main outcome from your trip, sergeant, is that we're even more certain that Whitaker is correct, and the cheque is indeed a forgery." Bryce paused to think. "We have Forrest coming to see us very shortly. When we've finished with him, Mr Kent will get a visit at home.

"I've got a few things for you to be getting on with, Lomax, but it'll be good experience for you to sit in on Forrest's interview. Nip down to the front desk and be ready to bring him up."

The young constable, who was rapidly developing ambitions to join the CID one day, nodded happily.

With the office to themselves, Haig and Bryce looked at each other.

"We haven't discussed McNamara, yet. What are your thoughts, sergeant?"

"Don't know about you, sir, but I didn't get any feeling that he's a killer. Yes, he was having an affair with Mrs W, but I think he's a ladies' man, and Mrs Whitaker was just one of his ladies. I thought he was arrogant in his assessment that he was more important to her than she to him."

Bryce frowned slightly and studied the ceiling before replying. "I tend to agree. I can see why Whitaker nominated McNamara, but, unless we find evidence of motive, he isn't the killer. So, he stays on the list, but we look elsewhere for our murderer."

The telephone rang, and Bryce picked up the handset. The call was a very short one, the DCI ending with "thank you very much", before hanging up.

"Mr Hargreaves confirms the detail of the will: Dr Whitaker is indeed the sole beneficiary."

Following a tap on the door, Lomax

returned accompanied by a short, pot-bellied man in his forties, his thinning hair carefully combed over his large bald patch. Whatever attractive qualities Forrest might possess, he was deficient in the good looks usually associated with a Casanova.

Taking the suggested seat, the dentist casually crossed his legs and was entirely at ease. He opened the conversation with a smile. "You've thoroughly piqued my interest with your comment about all this being delicate, chief inspector. I've been racking my brains to think what a Scotland Yard team could possibly be investigating in our city that I could help with.

"Is it something to do with council matters? Someone at county hall pilfering the paperclips, eh?"

"What we're investigating isn't the delicate matter at all," said Bryce soberly, "it's an exceptionally cold-blooded and brutal murder. The delicacy refers to your own position."

Bryce and Haig watched as Forrest's expression became wary and apprehensive.

"A murder? Who on earth has been murdered?"

"Mrs Dulcie Whitaker was shot yesterday, in her own home," Bryce delivered the facts and nothing more.

"Good God!" Forrest displayed genuine astonishment. "I'm incredibly sorry, naturally, but I still don't see what this has to do with me.

The Whitaker's are my patients, but I don't know them other than professionally – and although my wife is friendly with Mrs Whitaker, I haven't seen her or her husband for at least six months."

"Let's come on to the delicate matter, Mr Forrest. We understand you have an extra-marital relationship."

Forrest spluttered indignantly.

"Before you say anything in denial, perhaps I should mention 14, Dial Lane."

Forrest now looked stunned. The detectives waited.

"Oh dear," said Forrest eventually, "I suppose it'll have to come out. Yes, I do have a friend who lives there. She is, as you presumably know, single, but I am married." Forrest gave up the information begrudgingly, clearly very unhappy at having to explain himself. "I still don't see what my private life has to do with this murder, though," he added with a little more spark.

"Very simple, Mr Forrest. We understand that Mrs Whitaker found out about your friendship. It seems she was very upset by what she thought was your hypocrisy – I gather you are a lay preacher among your other activities. She told her husband she intended to confront you with her knowledge before informing your wife."

Forrest raised his voice. "So you think she did speak to me, and I killed her to prevent my wife from finding out? Is that it?"

"In the absence of any other motive for this murder, I'm sure you'll agree the theory has merit," replied Bryce, smoothly.

Forrest was staring in horror at the DCI. He stuttered a few unintelligible words before pulling himself together. "I'm not stupid, chief inspector! I can see what you're saying. I can't deny that the theory might have some merit in the eyes of the police. However, you are absolutely and completely wrong. Mrs Whitaker didn't speak to me. I didn't do it!"

"Very well. If what you say is true, Mr Forrest, you'll want us to look at everything in more detail in order to clear you, won't you? Where were you between the hours of say midnight and four a.m. the night before last?"

Forrest's eyelids flickered rapidly as he mentally weighed up his options. "Do I have to say?"

Bryce gave him a tight smile in response. "No. You don't have to say anything, Mr Forrest. But if I charge you with murder, and you subsequently produce an alibi which you could have given me today, you can be sure no notice will be taken of it."

Forrest seemed uncertain as to whether to answer. Deciding to co-operate, he responded curtly, "Very well. I spent the night with Henrietta Davies. I told my wife I needed to be away on a business trip to London. Henrietta and

I met there by arrangement, and stayed together in a hotel. The Belchamp, in Praed Street. We returned yesterday, travelling on different trains."

"We called ourselves Mr & Mrs Logan. It's a very discreet place, and I got the impression, although we'd never stayed there before, that they make a point of not noticing visitors such as us. But a member of staff might be able to confirm our presence."

"Did you dine in the hotel?" enquired Bryce.

"No; it doesn't have a restaurant. We walked down to Marble Arch, and went to the Corner House – the Maison Lyons."

"Oh, aye," said Haig, "I know it. The place is enormous and always busy. Not much chance of anybody remembering you there, I imagine, so a bit of a problem for you, alibi-wise.

"But here's another problem: there are frequent trains between London and Draycaster, Mr Forrest, and we'll be checking their times with a Bradshaw or an ABC," continued Haig. "You were staying a stone's throw from Paddington. You could easily have travelled to Draycaster before midnight, killed Mrs Whitaker, and got back to London before breakfast. Will Miss Davies be prepared to swear you never left her side?"

Forest looked genuinely shocked at how easily a case could be made against him.

"How can we contact her right now?" interposed Bryce.

"She's a dispenser at Timothy Whites," replied the dentist. She's working today."

"I expect you have the number," said Bryce, pushing the telephone towards Forrest. "Get hold of her if you can, and without saying anything about London, pass the handset back to me."

A very unhappy Forrest carried out the instruction. It took several minutes to get Miss Davies to the telephone. Her lover spoke to her briefly, and then handed the instrument to the DCI.

Bryce explained who he was, and why he – and Mr Forrest – needed her to answer a few questions. Those in the room could only hear one side of the conversation, but it was clear the lady was extremely reluctant to admit anything. Eventually, however, she confirmed she spent the afternoon and night with Mr Forrest, at the Belchamp hotel. She also confirmed they dined at the Maison Lyons.

As Miss Davies sounded very upset, Bryce passed the telephone back to Forrest, and suggested he might care to reassure his friend that, assuming he was indeed innocent and another suspect was eventually charged, nobody outside the room need hear about the incident.

When Forrest eventually put the receiver down, Bryce told him:

"We'll check up on your story, of course.

Before I let you go, do you own or have access to a firearm of some sort?"

"I have a brace of shotguns, chief inspector. I get the occasional invitations to join a shooting party, and I do a bit of clay shooting for sport. Are you saying Mrs Whitaker was killed with a shotgun?" Forrest's voice was bordering on panic.

"I'm saying nothing about how she was killed, Mr Forrest."

"Well, I see my predicament, chief inspector, and I hope you find some independent witnesses to confirm where I was. And before I go I'll say this again: I haven't spoken to, or set eyes, on either of the Whitakers for months. I may have behaved badly in your opinion, but I'm not a murderer."

The interview concluded, Lomax showed Whitaker out. When he returned, Bryce asked "What did you think of Forrest?"

The constable didn't hesitate. "I think he's been a very stupid man, sir, especially given the position and status he has in the city. Matter of fact, and I probably shouldn't say this, I rather hope this does all get out. He'd be taken down a peg or two. I can't say I thought he was lying, though. It could be exactly as he told us. Miss Davies has told us the same story. I suppose she could have been coached by him, beforehand, sir, but from what I could hear I don't think so. All in all, I reckon it wasn't him."

"Aye," agreed Haig, "my thinking, too, sir."

"All three of us, then," said Bryce. "This rather undersized jury isn't ready to convict him. At least, not yet.

"We'll leave the checking at the Belchamp hotel for the time being. And you're absolutely right about the size of that Lyons, sergeant. The chances of anybody being able to swear as to the attendance of any couple must be pretty slim. Let's leave it for now, along with McNamara, and see what joy we can get from Mr Kent.

"You stay here, Lomax, and carry on going through those boxes. There may not be anything more of interest, but there's an awful lot of stuff left, so keep checking carefully."

CHAPTER 14

Sergeant Haig took the wheel, and Bryce navigated with the help of a street map found in Inspector Wanstall's office. The car pulled up at the address provided by Whitaker.

Haig rapped on the front door. Within a few seconds it opened and a man appeared, removing a floral half apron from around his waist as he stood in the doorway. He looked enquiringly at the two suited detectives on the step, each holding out identification. This time, Haig performed the introductions.

Kent didn't seem to take in the 'Scotland Yard' information he was given, and apparently jumped to the conclusion that the police were there to tell him about something dreadful befalling his wife. It took a full minute to clear up this misunderstanding, after which, evidently relieved, Kent invited the officers inside, hanging his apron on the staircase newel post as he showed the way into the lounge.

"Do sit down gentlemen," he said, settling himself on the sofa. "Scotland Yard, eh? What's the problem? I can't think how I can help you, but I'll do my best. Are you sure you've got the right house, though?" Now relaxed and affable, Geoffrey Kent displayed none of McNamara's initial coolness when first approached, nor Forrest's initial amusement.

Bryce opened the questioning without preamble. "Do you have a Post Office savings account?"

As the DCI intended, Kent was taken aback by the question and gave the characteristic gesture of surprise, dipping his chin towards his chest as he jerked back his head a little. "Yes. My wife and I each have separate accounts." His response was unhesitating, the curiosity in his voice as natural as his manner.

"May we see your pass book, please?"

"Yes, I suppose so. I can tell you that since I lost my job a few months ago, the account has been emptied. We're struggling along on my wife's earnings at present, but at last I have a new job lined up, I'm pleased to say."

Kent, smiling over his shoulder at the Yard detectives as he spoke, made his way to the roll top desk. The book was sitting on top of a pile of papers. Returning to the others, he passed it to Haig, who was nearest. Haig opened the book and spent only a few seconds looking at the entries, before nodding and passing the book to his chief. The DCI took a similarly short look:

"Mr Kent, you've told us this account is almost empty. But that doesn't seem to be the case. I see a cheque for two hundred and fifty pounds was deposited on Monday of last week, and thirty pounds was withdrawn from the account this morning."

Before Bryce was able to continue with the obvious next question, Kent was on his feet and moving towards him.

"No, no! There must be a mistake. Show me, please."

Without letting go of the book, Bryce pointed out the two relevant entries. Kent stared at the page for a few seconds, and then returned to the sofa, clearly in need of a seat.

"Impossible," he muttered. "How the hell could that happen?"

"Let me suggest one theory to you, Mr Kent," began Bryce, as he slipped the pass book into his pocket. "You stole a cheque from someone's cheque book, made it out to yourself, and forged the owner's signature. You paid the cheque into your own account. As soon as it cleared, you started to draw on the funds."

"That may be all right in police theory – but it's all wrong in reality!" Kent was thoroughly worked up. He stood again, and almost shouted down at Bryce.

"Wait a minute. You say you're a chief inspector from Scotland Yard. I saw your identification, and I have to believe you. But although I don't know much about police procedures, I can't believe the local force has called you in to investigate an allegation of a forged cheque!"

"You're right, Mr Kent. The Yard doesn't get called in for an odd forged cheque outside – or even inside – the Met's area." Bryce now spoke very firmly, "But when you say the situation is 'impossible', I'm afraid it's you who are wrong, Mr Kent.

"As you've admitted, you can't explain how this money came to be in the account, and I can assure you the cheque paid into your account was undoubtedly a forgery. It's a fact that someone has withdrawn thirty pounds from the account today. And it's also a fact that, were it not for the forged cheque, there would have been no money to be drawn upon."

Before Bryce could say any more, they heard the front door open and close, and a pleasant-sounding woman's voice called out to say she was home.

A moment later, Paula Kent came into the room, much surprised to see two strangers. Bryce and Haig rose politely as her husband performed awkward introductions. Mrs Kent looked enquiringly from one to another as they all sat down. Kent looked towards the chief inspector.

"I'll get straight to the point of our visit, Mrs Kent. We're here about your husband's Post Office savings book."

"Oh..."

"'Oh', indeed, Mrs Kent. I think you have something to tell us?"

Kent, seated next to his wife, was looking at her in astonishment. "What on earth is going on, Paula?" His mouth was suddenly dry and he croaked the words out, greatly fearing what he would hear in reply.

Paula Kent was now on the verge of tears. She gripped her husband's hand in her own. "I didn't mean to do anything wrong, Geoffrey, I really didn't! There were a couple of bills to pay. You'd gone off to the Labour Exchange this morning, and I looked in your book, hoping there might be a little left in the account. When I saw a few pennies over two hundred and fifty pounds, I couldn't believe my eyes!

"I realise it was wrong, and I hope the post office lady doesn't get into trouble for letting me draw from your account, but she knows us both, and as I expected she didn't question it. I'm really sorry, Geoffrey, but where did all that money come from, and why didn't you tell me about it? It's not as if we keep secrets from one another, after all."

Kent put his arms around his wife.

"I'm afraid it's the source of the money which is troubling the police, my dear. Your drawing some of it out is probably irrelevant compared with how it came to be in my account. But I promise you, and these gentlemen, that I have no more idea of the source than you; I've only just been told the money even existed."

Bryce, watching and listening to this exchange very closely, spoke: "You see, Mrs Kent, the money in the account was paid in using a forged cheque. Are both of you still denying any knowledge of it?"

Both, visibly shaken, nodded.

Paula Kent continued her explanation. "I assumed you'd swallowed your pride and asked for a loan after all, Geoffrey, and I thought perhaps you were too embarrassed to mention it."

"I can't tell you how much I wish that were true, Paula," Kent told his wife with great feeling.

"Did you have any particular thoughts as to who such a benefactor might be, Mrs Kent?" asked the DCI.

"We only have one pair of friends rich enough to do something like that for us, chief inspector. The wife is very kind and generous, and the money in their household is mostly hers."

"Yes, true," interjected Kent. "But *think*, Paula; it's inconceivable she'd have given the cheque to me rather than to you, darling; she would definitely have told you, in any case."

"Why not tell us who you have in mind?" prompted Haig.

"Dulcie Whitaker," the Kents chorused.

"I see," said Bryce. "Well, the cheque paid into your account did indeed come from

Mrs Whitaker's chequebook; and the bank is adamant that the signature on the cheque is not Mrs Whitaker's. Dr Whitaker concurs, incidentally."

Bryce allowed this first description of criminal activity to sink in, observing the acute disbelief on the Kents' faces before continuing. "The second, and infinitely more serious matter, is this: Dulcie Whitaker was shot and killed in the early hours of Tuesday morning. No doubt you can now see the answer to your earlier question about the involvement of Scotland Yard, Mr Kent."

The couple were both displaying extreme shock. They sat hugging each other, Paula leaning heavily against her husband.

"But what has the cheque business got to do with Dulcie's murder?" asked her husband at last, as he stroked his distraught wife's head.

Bryce explained. "First we have the facts: someone steals a cheque, makes it out to you, and pays it into your account. Later, someone – whom we now know to be your wife – draws some of that money without asking questions about where it came from."

Paula Kent howled.

"Second, we have a hypothesis: Mrs Whitaker somehow discovers the missing money, believes only you could have taken it, and confronts you. Naturally, you might go to great lengths to avoid the inevitable prison sentence, disgrace, and probable break-up of your marriage." Again, Bryce allowed some time for his words to sink in. Addressing Kent, who was holding up rather better than his wife, he asked, "You see the inevitable connection between the forged cheque and Mrs Whitaker's murder?"

Paula Kent was now sobbing in her husband's arms, tears pouring down her cheeks.

"No, no, no!" muttered Kent. "This can't be happening!"

Everything unfolding before Bryce was leading him to conclude that the Kents were not guilty of any wrong doing. The relatively insignificant matter of Paula's withdrawal from her husband's account might be contrary to Post Office rules, but was hardly criminal. He looked for a way to relieve a little of their distress and anxiety. "Let me ask a question of you both. Do you think, if you'd openly asked for financial help, the Whitakers might have obliged?"

"Yes," gulped Paula from behind a handkerchief as she mopped her face. "I'm quite sure Dulcie would have done so if we'd been desperate; she'd even hinted half as much to me when Geoffrey first lost his job. Robin wouldn't have been involved."

"Do you own a gun of any sort?"

Both looked confused and alarmed at the suggestion. Both heads shook vigorously. Paula Kent began to wail again.

Bryce persisted. "Not even you, Mr Kent, during the war?"

"No. I was a conscientious objector. I spent my time down a coal mine as one of Bevin's Boys. The most gruelling, filthy, and dangerous work imaginable. But to me, far preferable to killing or maiming a fellow human being!"

"Where were you on Monday night, between about midnight and four o'clock in the morning?"

"We were both here, asleep in bed together," said Kent.

His wife nodded, before adding through her tears, "And I'm a light sleeper. I would certainly have noticed if Geoffrey got up and left the bed."

"I fear, my love, an alibi given by a wife for her husband isn't rated very highly by the police. Nor by a jury either," remarked Kent sadly.

Bryce contemplated the couple. His earlier impression that they were not murderers had been reinforced by what he had learned of Kent's war time 'conchie' status. However, he was not yet ready to disclose his thoughts to the pair.

"I'm in two minds," he sighed at last. "There are a number of unusual features in this case which I'm not going into at present. I could arrest you Mr Kent – both of you even – on suspicion of forgery, theft, and murder.

"Instead, what I'll do is this: you're far too upset to think clearly at the moment. I want you to spend some time talking this through. I'm sure you'd be doing that anyway, but I want you to think especially about how someone could have got hold of your passbook, Mr Kent. You'll appreciate that the removal of your book is perhaps key to everything else.

"I can tell you we'll be looking at who paid this cheque in, and at which post office. You should hope that nobody there identifies you. This was a large amount, and the person making the deposit might well be remembered by whoever recorded the cheque."

Bryce stood up, Haig following his cue.

Kent, attempting to disentangle himself from Paula in order to accompany the detectives to the door, was forestalled by the DCI. "No need. We'll see ourselves out."

In the privacy of the Wolseley, Haig was quick with his assessment. "Before you ask, sir, I think something is beginning to smell all the way to high heaven. But I'm pleased we're not bringing the Kents in – I don't think they're the ones who are smelling!"

Bryce, who was driving, negotiated a roundabout before responding with a question. "Did anything strike you about Kent, visually?"

"Nothing in particular, no. Rather an ordinary-looking man, really. At least, he didnae strike me as distinctive in the ways McNamara and Forrest did."

"Agreed. Our other two suspects have

physical characteristics which are easier to describe. It struck me how alike Kent and Whitaker are. About the same age, same hair style and colour. I'd guess them to be very close in height and weight, and they wear similar spectacles. I didn't even discern much difference in the timbre of their voices. What does that tell us?"

Haig was quick on the uptake. "You mean, even if we track down the post office counter clerk who accepted the cheque, and even if he or she recalled the paying-in, it would be almost impossible for them to say if it was Kent or Whitaker?"

"Exactly, sergeant. Which is why I've started to have rather nasty thoughts about our new widower. Mull this over for me: what if he forged the cheque himself? Whitaker's the one with easy access to his wife's belongings, after all. What if he's the one who paid the cheque into Kent's account? And, what if he actually chose Kent to be a suspect deliberately so the counter staff would identify him in a line-up? They wouldn't see both men together of course, because Whitaker wouldn't be a suspect."

"Do you mean there's no point in trying to find which post office it was, sir?"

"Not a lot of point, I think, although we'll still have to do it."

Silence fell between the detectives.

It wasn't long before Haig picked up the

conversation again. "I suppose some would argue that what you said earlier could work the other way, sir. That Kent is guilty, and chose Whitaker for his similarities. They each have access to one of the critical items for the fraud – Whitaker to his wife's cheque book; and Kent his own Post Office book. And they'd each have an equivalent difficulty to get access to the other book in order to make the fraud work. They're even-steven in that respect, aren't they?" Haig didn't want this alternative explanation to find any favour with his boss. He didn't believe it himself, but he knew the preparation for any subsequent court case would need to completely quash such inconvenient possibilities.

"Yes; absolutely. But the reason for Kent's refusal to enlist is a compelling point in his favour. And like you said earlier, something's definitely smelling – and it doesn't seem to be the Kents. I'm going to nail my colours to the top of the mast and say, of our four current suspects, I'm now looking at Whitaker."

"Aye, well, if you'll permit the liberty, sir, while you're up there you can pin my colours at the same time!"

Bryce laughed. "We'll see where the evidence eventually takes us." He guided the car into the police station car park and turned off the engine. "Anyway, let's get inside and have a chat with Lomax before we go back to the hotel."

In Wanstall's office, at a nod from Bryce,

Haig gave the local constable an outline of the visit to the Kents. He repeated the chief inspector's earlier comment that, even if they were correct in coming round to suspect Whitaker, it was going to be a job to prove it.

"The man has a pretty good alibi, seemingly backed up by witnesses. Could anyone who drank at least six measures of Scotch really drive sixty miles, shoot his wife, and drive back again in time to behave normally all through the next day? We'll need to interview those witnesses face-to-face, I'm thinking, sir. Plus the barman. And then try to establish if anyone saw the car being moved at either end."

Bryce nodded. "Yes. We'll prioritise those interviews. And it's occurred to me that Whitaker hasn't been asked the question the other three were asked: whether he owned a pistol. And the way things are shaping up, I'm glad it wasn't asked. It works in our favour a bit that we pretend that we don't even suspect him enough to ask about a gun."

"For the moment, here's what we'll do. You and I will visit Whitaker, sergeant, and reassure him we're making progress following his leads. You can go on home, Lomax, but be back here at half past eight again tomorrow – and you have my authority to come in plain clothes."

****

Turning into Glebe Close, the policemen

could see a huddle of reporters outside the house.

"Drat," muttered Bryce. "I'll shoo them away."

Haig pulled onto the drive behind Whitaker's car. As Bryce expected, several reporters charged after them. The two detectives got out, and the DCI turned to the clamouring pressmen. He raised a hand:

"I'll make a very short statement, and that will be it; I won't answer questions.

"I am Detective Chief Inspector Bryce, from Scotland Yard. Mrs Dulcie Whitaker was shot and killed in the early hours of Tuesday morning. A post mortem examination has been held. These are early days, and all I can tell you is that there are a number of promising leads, which Sergeant Haig and I, with the assistance of the local constabulary, are currently investigating.

"I want you to leave the premises and this area. There is nothing further for you here. However, if you stay away, and come to the police station at six o'clock tomorrow evening, I may be able to make a more extensive statement. Now go, please."

After a couple of half-hearted attempts to put questions, the cluster of reporters dispersed.

Haig was about to knock at Whitaker's front door, but it opened before he could do so.

"I couldn't hear what you said but I was

watching from indoors, chief inspector. I haven't dared to leave the house since I got back from Bristol. Wretched ghouls. Have you ordered them away?"

"I've told them to go, yes. Whether they'll take note, I can't say. We don't have the power to remove them if they're in the street and not causing a public nuisance."

Whitaker invited the officers to take a seat in the living room. They declined his offer of a cup of tea.

"One of the reasons we dropped in was to see you weren't being harassed, Dr Whitaker," said Bryce, deciding this was as good a reason as any to help give the impression that Whitaker wasn't being closely scrutinised. "I'm very sorry if you really haven't managed to get out at all."

"No, I haven't; blast them! After I moved my car yesterday, so you could get yours out, I haven't been outside the house."

Haig tsk-tsked sympathetically.

"Have you come to tell me you've made progress, chief inspector?"

"There are always lots of routine procedures we have to follow in any serious case," began Bryce, his voice and manner both distinctly less alert than usual. "We're tackling those in our own way – no rushing about headlong or willy-nilly. We're looking into the three names you raised, of course, and it's likely something concrete will emerge from those, but it's very early days, and you have to be patient. As do we," he added.

"I can tell you the bank manager and his staff confirm your suspicion – the signature on the cheque wasn't your wife's. So that's a step forward.

"Oh, and several of your symposium colleagues confirm what you told us about being rather the worse for wear by bedtime on Monday evening. I suppose from one point of view you welcome the corroboration, but as a recovering alcoholic you might think differently."

"I suppose so, chief inspector. With Dulcie gone, I'm going to have to try a lot harder."

Bryce and Haig stood up, the DCI extending his hand. "We'll leave you in peace, Dr Whitaker. Hopefully, the press vultures will stay away, but we'll keep an eye on the situation."

Whitaker let the officers out, pleased to see no sign of any reporters remaining at his gate. As he shut the front door he chortled to himself. "What a pair of prize prunes! 'Routine procedures'; 'no rushing headlong willy-nilly!'" He sarcastically mimicked Bryce's voice, amusing himself with the thought of these dunces blundering around in circles, blindly following the false leads he'd laid for them.

Had he been able to overhear the conversation going on in the police car, he would not have been quite so sanguine.

CHAPTER 15

The Yard officers arrived at the police station on Thursday morning well-rested and well-fed. Lomax, dressed in a poorly-fitting, cheap brown de-mob suit (borrowed from his brother), was feeling somewhat self-conscious as he waited for the Yard men in Wanstall's office.

"Sergeant Haig and I are off to Bristol soon, Lomax, to have a look around, and see if the hotel staff can tell us anything useful. It'll take us all of the morning and a bit beyond, but I'd expect to be back by about two o'clock.

"You've got a number of tasks whilst we're away, beginning with the cheque."

Bryce handed over Kent's savings book and gave the necessary instructions regarding a trip to the main post office to identify the branch where the cheque was paid in, and how the local constable should question the staff at both locations.

"When you've done that, come back here. Dig out your list of contact details for the symposium attendees and have it ready."

Bryce picked up the telephone and gave the

number for Professor Hamilton, whom he hadn't reached the day before. "Listen in, Lomax, and you'll understand what I need when you make your calls."

This time, Hamilton answered the 'phone and responded fully to Bryce's prompts, readily describing the events following dinner on the Monday evening. His account tallied exactly with those given by Mrs French and Mr Armitage. Bryce put a further question to him:

"This may sound a little odd, professor, and please think about it very carefully before you answer. Dr Whitaker's three double whiskies; can you actually say you saw those drinks pass his lips? Or could it be you saw the glasses when they held whisky, and then only noticed when they were empty later?"

There was a long silence, followed by the professor clearing his throat. "I see what you're getting at, chief inspector. On reflection, no; I can't honestly say I saw him swallow anything. That's not to say he didn't, of course. However, I do recall at one point a fresh round arrived while we were all standing up to greet a pair of newcomers. When we sat down again I was surprised to see Whitaker's glass was already empty. Didn't give it a second thought at the time, beyond thinking he should go more slowly for his own good."

Bryce gave his thanks and hung up, immediately pressing the receiver rest and asking the operator to connect him to Mrs French's number. Apologising for bothering her, he put the new question.

Like Professor Hamilton, Mrs French needed a moment to bring the hotel scene back into her mind. "Well, I don't know how this helps you, chief inspector, but no, I don't remember seeing him taking so much as a sip. Not even lifting or lowering a glass, actually; just toying with each tumbler on the table."

Bryce was about to thank her and say goodbye, when a piercing, excited squeal caused him to recoil slightly from the handset.

"Of course!" cried Mrs French. "That would explain how he seemed to empty his glass so quickly each time. He never drank it! Chief Inspector, there were several potted palms and ferns around the lounge bar where we were sitting. I'm not saying that's where he poured the drinks away, but I can see how he could have done!"

With the handset replaced, Bryce turned to Lomax, and repeated Mrs French's suggestion.

"I'll leave you to call the other two. Put the extra question about whether they actually saw Whitaker drink anything.

"Another telephone task for you will be the Cavendish Hotel in Basingstoke." Bryce explained what was wanted from this call regarding McNamara and Dulcie's time together. "I don't hold out much hope, but everything has to be followed up. Also, see what you can get out of the Belchamp in Paddington.

"At some point, get round to The Pantry café. Question this attractive blonde-haired waitress, if you can. See if she confirms McNamara's and Mrs Whitaker's attendance and remembers anything about their behaviour. Don't put words in her mouth, though – just let her tell you anything she recalls.

"Any time left over, get hold of some transport and go round to see Dr Whitaker again. Tell him you're checking to see he isn't being harassed. The morning papers have the murder, so it's quite likely there will be reporters again. If so, do what we did and warn them off going on his property.

"That's your reason for visiting, as far as Whitaker's concerned, but I'm betting he'll want an update on what we're doing. Understandable – but don't tell him anything; especially don't say we're in Bristol. Whatever he asks, be as vague and clueless as you like. I want him to feel we're a bunch of under-performing plods." Bryce grinned. "In other words, you have my permission to be anything other than the dynamic plain clothes detective you've become today, constable!"

Happy with the responsibilities he'd been assigned, and encouraged by the chief inspector's confidence in him, Lomax closed his pocketbook and confirmed he was clear as to what he should do.

The Yard detectives made their way downstairs to the Wolseley, Bryce asking Haig to take the wheel. Their first conversation on the journey bemoaned the fact that no England cricket tour was planned for the coming winter. The two men agreed that the 'Commonwealth Team' scheduled to tour India was hardly a substitute, consisting as it did of a collection of Australians and West Indians, and a few Englishmen largely drawn from one of the Lancashire leagues.

After running out of possible further comments on that matter, their conversation was naturally turned towards Isambard Brunel, whose Great Western line was currently almost parallel with their road.

"Extraordinary to think that in the 1830s he surveyed the whole line from Paddington to Bristol, up hill and down dale, almost single-handedly," remarked Haig.

"Yes. And found time to design some superb stations, bridges, tunnel entrances, and so on," said Bryce.

The two men debated which of the great engineer's works were notable successes, and which were failures. They agreed on only one of the latter: the atmospheric railway in Devon.

Bryce insisted Brunel's broad gauge was correct in principle. Superior to lesser gauges in terms of potential safety and stability, comfort, speed, and load-carrying capability; it was only wrong because most of the existing systems were already 'standard' gauge. Inevitably, by the time broad gauge lines were opened, the problems at interchange stations, notably Gloucester, meant that one day there would have to be a single gauge – and it wouldn't be Brunel's.

Haig couldn't accept his boss's view that the Great Eastern steamship had been a failure. He gave a well-argued rebuttal, suggesting the vessel was simply ahead of its time. He also argued (and Bryce conceded) that although the enormous ship proved uneconomic as a passenger carrier, it later found a successful niche as a transatlantic cable-layer.

Good natured disagreements of this sort continued until they ran into Bristol. Having previously consulted maps to check the location of the Arden Hotel, Haig made his way there without difficulty.

They were fortunate in finding a parking space only a hundred yards or so from the hotel, Bryce immediately observing how the lack of hotel parking would be a benefit to Whitaker, with little chance of his comings and goings on foot being as noisy and noticeable as a car engine in the middle of the night.

The detectives identified themselves at the reception desk and asked for the manager. That gentleman, his office door standing fully open nearby, overheard the request and emerged immediately to join them.

"Jeremy Philpott," he announced, shaking hands. "My office is a bit small for three. Let's go into the writing room; it's probably empty at this time of day."

"Thank you," said Bryce. "It would be helpful if you'd bring the hotel register with you."

The receptionist, listening wide-eyed to the exchange, immediately pushed the required tome towards Philpott, who tucked it under an arm and led the way to a room lined with shelves of books. Some winged leather armchairs stood invitingly for patrons wishing to read, with several small tables, each with a chair tucked under, dotted around the room for those who wished to catch up with correspondence. Pulling out padded-back chairs from under two of these tables and assembling them around a third, Philpott invited the detectives to take a seat, and looked at them expectantly as he settled into his own.

"We're investigating a murder, Mr Philpott. Miles away from here, but there's a connection to your hotel, because we understand the victim's husband was staying here at the time the murder was committed. We have several suspects, but obviously we have to check on the whereabouts of everyone connected with the dead woman."

Philpott nodded. "Of course. How can I

help?"

"Can you confirm there was a large group of people staying here on Monday night, and attending a symposium on Tuesday?"

"Yes; there certainly were. About a hundred attended on the Tuesday, and every one of our sixty rooms was taken on Monday night. I believe most were occupied by delegates, and a few of them stayed a further night."

"The victim's husband is Dr Robin Whitaker. Can you confirm he was one who stayed on Monday?"

Philpott opened the register and turned several pages, then swung the book around on the table, pointing out Whitaker's signature to the detectives.

Haig glanced at the page. "The date and signature are clear enough. Do you know what time he arrived?"

"Not exactly, no." Philpott frowned and pulled the register back towards himself. "We were very busy in the late afternoon and early evening, so I helped out in reception. Let me check who booked in ahead of Dr Whitaker, and who did so after him; it may jog my memory."

The manager moved his finger slowly above, and then below, Whitaker's name, before looking up with a smile. "Sir Peregrine Thomas signed two lines below Whitaker. He's stayed here several times before, so I was able to greet him by name. I'm confident he arrived around five twenty-five. We exchanged pleasantries for a minute and I was literally handing over his key when I was summoned to the kitchen urgently. The fish delivery for dinner arrived very late, and a third of our order was missing. Chef was incandescent, pointing at the clock and asking me to contact our fish monger. It was only a few minutes after half past five.

"There was a cluster of arrivals immediately before Sir Peregrine. I should say Dr Whitaker very probably booked in between five-ten and five-twenty. I hope that helps?"

"It does indeed, Mr Philpott," Haig assured him.

"Whereabouts was Mr Whitaker's room?" asked Bryce.

Philpott shook his head. "I can't tell from the register. I'll need to consult other records."

"We'll get back to that in a minute. Talk to us about the various entrances to the hotel. Presumably there are several?"

The manager gave details of the entrances to the front and back of the hotel.

"What happens to these doors at night?"

"The front door is locked at half past eleven each evening. We have a night porter; a guest returning late would ring the bell, and O'Leary would open up. He has other duties, of course. The kitchen doors to the bins and the outdoor stores are secured after the kitchen staff leave. The back door is always kept fastened day and night by a heavy bar which, in emergency, can be slid aside in a trice."

"We'd like to talk to Mr O'Leary; where might we find him?"

"He lives in, chief inspector. He has a room on the very top floor and goes to bed soon after noon, as a rule. If he's in the hotel, he's probably still awake."

"What about the bartender who was in the lounge or residents' bar on Monday evening?"

"Maurice Cole. He works split shifts, usually does three hours around lunchtime, and then from six o'clock to midnight. He doesn't live in, but he'll probably be setting up in the bar very shortly."

"Excellent," said Bryce, pleased. "Take Sergeant Haig with you to ascertain Dr Whitaker's room number, Mr Philpott, and show him the room – not inside, just its general position in the building. If Mr O'Leary is in, I'd like to see him in the lounge immediately."

CHAPTER 16

Constable Lomax was enjoying the variety of his morning. At the central post office it took a little time to find someone who could answer his questions. Once found, the response was positive, and the location – Flixton Street – was given to him.

Without a police car at his disposal, Lomax took a bus to the little branch post office. Here, he wasn't so successful. The sub-postmistress confirmed she would have been present on the day in question, but as she also served sweets, stationery, and a few groceries, she admitted she didn't have a lot of time to notice customers. She confirmed it was her writing in the pass book, and that the cheque was definitely paid in by a man wearing spectacles. Her vague description could have fitted Kent, Whitaker, and many others. She couldn't remember ever seeing the man before. No, she didn't think she would be able to pick him out at an identification parade.

Disappointed, Lomax took a bus back to the city and visited the café. Here, he was far more successful. Identifying himself to the manageress, he inclined his head towards the one waitress in view who resembled the one described by McNamara, and asked to speak to her.

"That's Rita Snell," said the manageress. She pointed across the room. "You go and sit over there, constable, and wait a moment."

Sitting where he was told, Lomax watched the manageress smilingly excuse herself to the customers Rita was attending to, take the girl's notepad, and send her over to him.

Standing to greet Miss Snell, he reassured her. "I'm making routine enquiries, is all. Might you recall a couple who bumped into one another in here this Monday?"

Little more was needed. Lomax's pencil was soon flying over a clean page in his pocketbook. Rita Snell remembered the pair, and the table she seated them at. Without prompting, she ran on for some time, mentioning their frequent bursts of laughter:

"A lovely, happy and polite couple, they were. It's always nice to see because some people are ever so grumpy and rude with one another – and to us girls. Honestly, you've got no idea how people are until you work somewhere like this!

"I remember they both made a point of thanking me as they left – not everybody bothers. Oh, there was a really good tip under a plate for me, too. I hope I'm on duty if they come back again."

The young waitress leaned towards Lomax. Showing no curiosity as to why he was questioning her, she asked instead: "Do you want me to try and remember what they ate?"

Lomax smiled, shook his head and told her she had been helpful enough. He didn't feel the need to tell the girl that she would never see the couple together again. Taking all the necessary contact details, he closed his pocketbook, thanked her, and told her she might be called upon in future.

Returning to the station, the constable placed his first telephone call, to Bernard Harris. Asking the same questions as the DCI used earlier, he was rewarded with much the same answer.

"Now you've mentioned it," said Harris, "and yes...thinking back...I didn't actually see him drink anything at all. No, I didn't. He certainly drained his glass quickly each round, though, I can tell you that much."

Unlike Rita Snell, Harris asked why he was being questioned. Lomax did a good job of fobbing him off.

Jonathan Armitage was also available, and after a moment's reflection made the same observation as his symposium colleagues regarding Whitaker not actually drinking.

Lomax was now ready to move on to his next assignment. Reaching for the telephone to call the Cavendish, he was startled when the instrument rang, and even more surprised when the caller identified himself as Geoffrey Kent, wanting to speak to the chief inspector.

Lomax explained that Bryce wasn't available, and offered to take a message.

"Yes, if you will. And please pass on what I tell you as quickly as possible."

The constable noted the date and time on a fresh page in his pocketbook, realising he was about to hear something important.

Kent gave all the details of the Whitaker's visit on the Saturday evening and concluded: "Robin was alone in our house for over an hour that evening. And then, a couple of days later, he was back in our house again and alone in the living room whilst I was in the kitchen.

"I'm telling you he could have taken the savings book very easily on the Saturday. He could have returned it on the Monday evening.

"Please repeat to Mr Bryce that neither of us is a thief, nor a murderer. And above all," Kent's voice was heavy with emphasis, "please be sure to tell him this – *no one else* has been in our house in the last fortnight."

Lomax promised he would pass on this message, at the same time wondering whether he should try to contact the DCI in Bristol. He had just rejected this thought, when a better idea occurred to him.

"Could you and your wife come to the police station later today, sir, and each make a statement about what you've told me?"

"We'd be glad to," replied Kent. "Paula gets off work at half past three today. Would four o'clock suit?"

"Perfect, sir," replied Lomax. "Ask at the front desk for DCI Bryce. And thank you very much for calling – I have a feeling it's going to be very helpful. Oh, and please don't mention this to anyone else."

A tap on the door brought in a uniformed constable, carrying an envelope which he handed to Lomax.

"PM results from Dr Lazenby for your new boss. I like the plain clothes, Howard," said the officer. "You reckoning on staying in the CID after this case?"

"Be grand if I could, Ted, but there must be others ahead of me wanting the same. This has been really interesting so far – though I suppose most CID work wouldn't be murder cases!"

Lomax picked up the telephone once more, and placed his Cavendish Hotel call. Beyond confirming a booking for the previous Monday and Tuesday in the name of McNamara, no useful information was forthcoming. The manager made the valid point that if Mr McNamara's guest only stayed a few hours, it was most unlikely that any of his staff would have noticed her.

He hoped for better luck with his call to the Paddington hotel used by Forrester, but was equally disappointed. The Belchamp manager did his best to be helpful, and consulted a couple of members of his staff; but in the end all he was able to provide was confirmation that a Mr and Mrs Logan stayed at the hotel on the Monday night of the previous week.

Reflecting on what the chief inspector had said about having no expectations from the hotel calls, Lomax shrugged off his failures and contemplated what to do next. Apart from visiting Whitaker, which he'd deliberately left for after lunch, he'd crossed every other task off his list. He decided to spend the rest of his morning delving into the Whitaker papers which hadn't yet been examined.

His first dip into a box drew out a sheaf of receipts for works done to the house. Many of these were historic, left by the previous owners and relating to improvements and maintenance carried out since the 1920s. He set these aside as irrelevant.

The next item in the box was a small black notebook. It took less than a moment for him to realise he was holding a log showing the odometer readings for the Whitaker's car. At first glance, he thought nothing of it, idly flipping through the pages until he reached the most recent page and entry. Closing the book up, he was ready to put it on his 'done' pile with the receipts, when his *Eureka* moment arrived.

The neat print of the dates, digits,

and journey descriptions, looked very like the writing which he'd seen the day before, on the four cheques written by Mrs Whitaker. He leafed through the log again. No other handwriting was evident, and he intuitively knew this was significant – even if, at that moment, he didn't quite know how. Another shuffle through the box gave him several alternative examples of the late woman's writing with which to confirm his assumption.

He was soon certain the entries in the book were all made by Dulcie Whitaker. He didn't spend long speculating why she kept such a meticulous record of the car's journeys and mileage. At first he thought she may have been checking the car's petrol consumption, but when he found no record showing when the car was fuelled, he realised this was not the purpose of the log. Further reading convinced him that the log was simply a record of who was driving on a particular date, and the distance driven.

Whatever Mrs Whitaker's motivation, Lomax quickly realised that the only thing which mattered was the last reading. This was recorded as two-thirty pm on Monday, after a four-mile round trip into Draycaster, with herself as driver.

Lomax recalled what Bryce had told him about reporters trapping Whitaker in his house. He saw how the last entry in the car log could potentially be crucial evidence – but only if he could get to check the car's current mileage without delay.

This was a problem. One of the CID cars was written off, and he realised the chances of borrowing another were slim to none. He didn't think borrowing a marked car was suitable either, but decided his best way forward was to urgently ask for a lift in one, to be dropped off somewhere out of sight of Whitaker's house.

He bounded down the stairs and explained himself to the desk sergeant, and was soon being driven at speed towards Glebe Close.

There was no sign of any journalists outside the house when Lomax arrived on foot shortly before noon, his uniformed colleague waiting out of sight in the marked police car.

Pleased to see Whitaker's car on the drive, Lomax rang the bell.

Whitaker, assuming him to be a reporter, shouted at him to clear off.

Lomax explained himself in a loud voice to the closed front door. "The chief inspector asked me to drop in, sir, and check the reporters aren't intruding on your privacy."

Whitaker opened up and admitted the constable into the hall. "No; after Mr Bryce told them to go away yesterday, they've given no trouble. In fact, I've only seen an occasional press hound at the gate. Surprising, really, as there's a short piece in the local paper today.

"Anyway, I'm okay, so you can reassure him. Perhaps I'll pluck up courage and go out somewhere later – get a bit of shopping done."

Lomax knew he needed to probe this last remark further. He made a suitably concerned face as he enquired, "Have you really not managed to get out of the house at all since you got back on Tuesday, sir? Not even for a nice little run in your car to get away from it all?"

"No. I was too upset on Wednesday, and every time I thought about going out today there was another gaggle of nosey parkers walking around the Close and looking at the house."

Whitaker changed the subject. "What can you tell me about the investigation, constable? Has anyone been apprehended yet?"

Lomax looked back at Whitaker with what he hoped was a blank expression. "Oooh, I'm not privy to such information, sir. No, no. Much too junior, me. All I can tell you is the Yard boys have several lines of enquiry and are running around every which way pursuing them."

Satisfied Whitaker had been given the required reassurance that he was not actively being investigated himself, the constable took his leave. "If you're happy, I'll get back, sir."

Whitaker let him out and returned to the lounge. He sat with a huge grin on his face.

'Several lines of enquiry' – ha, ha, yes! He'd been clever enough to provide all of those to the police. Once again, he congratulated himself on his sagacity. Without his 'leads', and nothing else to go on, there would have been a real danger the police would have concentrated their efforts on him. His alibi was, he thought, as good as it could be, and well-protected by his patsies. Also, he reminded himself, some of his symposium colleagues had already confirmed the false story of his drinking. Everything was on track.

He must be patient, according to the chief inspector. Well, he could afford to be. He wondered how long a Scotland Yard team would stay on a case if all they could reach were dead ends. He thought a local force would rapidly tire of paying for them with no sign of results. Surely not much more than another week or so? By then, he decided, the police would have charged someone else. Or they would have given up.

If Whitaker had watched Constable Lomax leaving the house, instead of sitting down to gloat, he would have seen the officer peering through the driver's window of the Ford Anglia. He would have seen the officer's pocketbook, and the way he carefully wrote in it.

By the time Lomax left Whitaker's driveway, a five-digit number, together with a precise time and date, were all neatly printed beneath the Glebe Close address already recorded in the book.

CHAPTER 17

Bryce wandered into the lounge of the Arden Hotel and glanced around, noting a sparse sprinkling of people drinking coffee in the large room. Various tubs holding palms and other greenery were dotted around, just as Mrs French described.

Approaching the bar, which was still partially shuttered, the bartender moved towards him.

"Can I get you anything, sir?"

"A pot of coffee for two, please."

"Take a seat, sir; I'll bring it over to you," smiled the man.

Bryce picked a pair of easy chairs against the far wall with a low table between them, and waited.

The bartender soon arrived. As he bent to unload his tray, Bryce deliberately glanced around, leaned forward, and spoke in a conspiratorial semi-whisper even though there was no one nearby. "Help me if you can, with a personal request. Suppose I wanted to bring a good friend to my room later tonight. Not to stay, you understand; only for a visit. Would that be possible?"

The barman did his own check for anyone within earshot. "Not the most unusual question I've ever been asked, sir," he replied with something of a leer. "This isn't my business, as it happens, but perhaps you should speak privately to the night porter – he comes on at nine o'clock. I understand he might be in a position to help you."

Bryce eyed the man not unkindly, and spoke in his normal voice. "You would be Maurice Cole, correct?"

The barman's head jerked up and his face fell. "I've been set up, haven't I?"

"Nothing too serious as far as you're concerned, Mr Cole. I'm a Scotland Yard detective, investigating a murder. My sergeant and I are checking on someone's alibi.

"Another question for you. There were people in here on Monday evening after dinner – hotel guests who were attending a conference the next day. Remember?"

Cole nodded.

"There was one particular group, perhaps four or five men and one or maybe two women. Can you recall them?"

The barman didn't need to think. "Oh yes, sir. That was the only group of more than four people on Monday."

"Ah, good. Can you recall what any of them

were drinking?"

Cole gave this question a little thought. "Single brandies for all of them apart from one; he was on double Scotches. Very uncomplicated order, that group."

"Come and show me, if you can, exactly where they were sitting in the evening, and particularly which seat the doubles drinker took."

The barman needed no time to bring the scene back to mind. He took the DCI across the room and pointed confidently to a larger low table with two sofas and two armchairs, positioned to form a rectangle such that eight people could sit together. It was the only such configuration in the room, the remainder being arranged to seat twos or fours. Cole indicated the whisky drinker's armchair. Bryce noted the large potted plants between the sofas and the chairs at each end of this table – one on either side of Whitaker's seat.

"Did any of the group stand out to you for any reason at all?"

"One of the men – the one on whiskies – drank a lot more than any of the others. When he left the lounge he came to say goodnight to me. He wasn't four sheets flapping in the wind – nothing like; but a bit unsteady, and slurring his words.

"I remember him particularly because he came to the bar to buy a round early on, and told me to take for one for myself. Then last thing, he came up to the bar again. By then he was a textbook happy drunk, really, but not so far gone he couldn't walk, or recite 'goodnight, sleep tight' to me."

"All right – thank you, Mr Cole. I'm hoping to speak to Mr O'Leary shortly. If we find out what we want, the matter of what we might call irregularities aren't really our concern. I won't be telling the manager, but I will say I think you're a fool to yourself to be involved in the business."

The barman looked slightly happier.

"I promise you I never spoke to the double Scotch gentleman about access to the hotel, sir. But I'm sure quite a few people are aware of the arrangement – the ladies of the night in this part of the city, for a start."

Sergeant Haig arrived in the lounge accompanied by a man in his late sixties. They came across to join Bryce, who nodded to Cole that he could go.

"Do sit down, Mr O'Leary," said the DCI, after shaking the night porter's hand.

"There's coffee for you, sergeant. I didn't order for you, Mr O'Leary, because I guess you'll want to get to sleep as soon as we've finished our chat.

"I'll get straight to the point. We're interested in a murder, and we're here solely to check on an alibi. We've no interest in anything else that might go on here – understand?"

O'Leary nodded cautiously.

"Good. We know you have private arrangements for guests to come and go when the front door is locked, without anyone being aware of their movements. Tell us how it works."

The porter hesitated, then wriggled in his seat. He glanced across the room at Cole, who was behind his bar again and watching. Bryce couldn't see, but Haig saw Cole shrug his shoulders and then nod. The porter made his decision.

"The back door is unbarred at about ten o'clock, sir, well before the main doors are locked for the night at eleven-thirty. Guests can leave the hotel without passing reception, so no-one gets the jitters at the desk if they aren't indoors again when I shut up shop for the night.

"I put the bar back at four-thirty sharp. Anyone who's come in must either leave by then, or stay until the morning and leave by the front door – but that's not wise."

"How many people are aware of this arrangement, Mr O'Leary?"

"I dunno – could be hundreds, I suppose. It's worked good for a dozen years or so."

"Do you only unbolt the door on request, or is it done automatically every night?" asked Haig.

"Automatic. Every night. That's 'cause we have quite a few regulars; they've come to expect to use the door without having to ask first."

"So on Monday evening this week, did anyone come to ask for the door to be open?"

"No, guv – it's quite a while since that last happened."

"What's in it for you? A small contribution to your pension fund, as it were?"

O'Leary became defensive. "I've never asked nor expected! But from time to time a few people might be...*grateful*...to me afterwards, and express themselves with a bit of a present for me."

Bryce and Haig both eyed the old reprobate.

"I see no reason to talk to Mr Philpott about this at the moment. I do see every reason to point out that your side-line might cost you your job and home at the same time. You should ask yourself if you think it's worth it.

"As for the purpose of our visit, I can't guarantee you won't be called as a witness if there's a trial. For now, we just need a quick written statement from you."

Bryce turned to Haig. "Get writing, please, sergeant. A few lines will do."

Haig pulled a foolscap pad from his case. It took only five minutes to compose the statement. Haig read out what he had written and Bryce nodded his satisfaction. O'Leary agreed to sign it, rejecting the opportunity to alter or add anything, and then took himself off to bed.

As soon as the night porter was out of earshot, Bryce drew Haig's attention to the potted plants across the room. "It seems Whitaker sat in that chair," he said, pointing. "Very convenient for pouring away any drink which you might want people to think you'd swallowed. In a minute, we'll get Cole to make a simple statement about where Whitaker sat."

Bryce poured more coffee for Haig, and refreshed his own cup. "When we get up, scrape some of the soil from various parts of the pots on either side of the chair. Bag it all up and we'll get the analyst to see if either contains any of the chemicals in Scotch, or alcohol. I know the stuff evaporates very quickly, but maybe it leaves some sort of residue." Sipping at the surprisingly good brew, he asked Haig to report on his travels around the hotel.

"Whitaker's room is on the first floor, at the far end of the corridor. The back staircase is only feet away. Down one flight, and the back door is straight in front of you. From his bedroom door to the street would take thirty seconds maximum. Not much doubt in my mind that's what happened, sir."

"Hmm. His plan was really very simple, but the set of false leads and suspects he arranged made it look more complicated." Bryce drew Haig's pad towards him and, based on what Cole had said, began to write a statement for him.

When completed, the barman was called over. Expressing himself happy that the statement was true and fair, he added his address under his name at the top, and signed without making any changes.

"Half past twelve," said Bryce as they left the hotel. "Let's get going, sergeant. We can find somewhere to eat along the way.

****

Fortified by lunch at a roadside hostelry, the detectives talked over the case as they headed back to Draycaster.

"What do you reckon, sir; is there actually enough to convict Whitaker?" queried Haig from behind the steering wheel.

"A weak point for us is the gun. I think the chances of finding it are nil. Too much deep water in Draycaster and Bristol, so a priority will be asking Inspector Lessing to dig into everyone's wartime career – Whitaker's first," said Bryce, mentioning the colleague he'd relied on in previous cases to look into the service histories of suspects.

"And I'm still concerned about the three 'hares' Whitaker set running for us to chase after. Although you and I don't have a feeling for any of them being guilty of murder, that's not evidence.

"We have to prove every case 'beyond a reasonable doubt', and this one is no different.

This case is rather complicated, though, inasmuch as we have some evidence which might be sufficient if Whitaker were our *only* suspect, but which might not be sufficient when three alternatives are being touted by the defence. The insufficiency is compounded by the fact we don't actually have any cast-iron evidence against our preferred suspect – it's all circumstantial."

"What do you think would happen if we arrest Whitaker and charge him with what we've got so far?" asked Haig.

"I think the prosecution would have a difficult decision to make from the start. For example, should they call one or more of Whitaker's three stooges as prosecution witnesses?

"It would be a very risky move in some ways. They'd basically be parading McNamara, Forrest, and Kent as alternative murderers for the jury to choose from. The judge would no doubt tell the jury that these three men are not the ones on trial – but, inevitably, the defence would contrive to suggest that one of them might be the murderer."

Haig groaned.

"Another problem is never knowing how someone is going to perform in the witness box until the pressure's applied to them. Even if only one of those three men was unconvincing under cross-examination, the prosecution's pretty much given the case to the defence."

"Better not call them at all then, you think?" asked Haig, pleased to spot an obvious and easy way around this potential hurdle.

"Not really, sergeant, no. If those three *aren't* called for the prosecution, the situation is probably worse."

Haig's startled side-long glance drew a further explanation from his boss.

"As you know, neither side 'owns' a witness. The defence might well call them – if necessary requesting a witness summons to get a reluctant one into court. Defence counsel would certainly manage to let the jury know how the police were told about these three at a very early stage, and would ask, rhetorically, *'why didn't the Crown call these witnesses?'* You can see how it would look bad for the prosecution.

"And the ultimate problem which may sink us if we go to trial with what we've got, is that the defence doesn't even need to call McNamara, Forrest, and Kent. Whitaker's barrister could sit quietly, like the cat at the mouse hole, and wait until the prosecution case is closed. Then call his client. Whitaker would immediately say he told us about three alternative suspects. He would name them, as he could safely do without fear of a slander action, and detail his allegations.

"The judge might – almost certainly would – allow me to be recalled to the witness box.

I'd have to agree I was aware of the three other suspects. The best I could say is that we didn't find them viable.

"The defence would have a field day; I'd be made to look as though I were hiding something, and attempting to scapegoat Whitaker because I couldn't gather enough evidence against one of the other three.

"After all that, a jury might very well think there was 'reasonable doubt', and acquit Whitaker," said Bryce ruefully. "And frankly, sergeant, if I were on the jury, in those circumstances I might well concur!"

Haig looked glum. "We need to really sharpen up the case against Whitaker, then?"

"Yes. If we could show that he knew how to handle a pistol, it would be a step in the right direction. But we must also do everything to show why each of the alternative suspects fails – and I'll tell you, sergeant, I'm not sure that's possible."

Haig could only remember one other case where he'd heard his boss consider the ins and outs of court proceedings so pessimistically. The remainder of the journey was completed in silence, each man processing his own thoughts.

CHAPTER 18

Somewhat subdued about the prospects of a conviction, the Yard officers found Lomax looking very excited when they returned to the office.

"Lots to tell you, sir!" the young constable almost gabbled.

"Calm yourself, man, sit down, and take your time."

Lomax made a visible effort to obey, but remained animated. He picked up Dulcie Whitaker's car log, and brandished it at his colleagues before handing it to the chief inspector.

"Good lord – she was keeping tabs on her husband," said Bryce. He looked at the recent entries. "Her shopping trip on Monday is recorded as 13,174." He passed the book to Haig. "She returned at two-thirty – Whitaker must have left for Bristol not long after. There would be practically no time left for either of them to drive anywhere else before he left for Bristol."

"Yes sir!" said Lomax, the excitement in his voice mounting again. "That's exactly it! So I got round there as quick as I could this morning after I found the log, and I noted the car's current mileage. Dead easy on the Anglia – you can see it from outside the car, no trouble.

"It read 13,413 today, sir. 239 miles driven after she returned from her last journey. That's definitely two round trips between here and Bristol!"

Bryce looked at Lomax almost affectionately and smacked the palm of his hand down on his desk blotter. "Excellent work, Lomax! Not only for spotting the book, but for having the sense to go and check the current reading immediately."

The young constable, hugely pleased with this praise, continued. "That's not all, sir, Whitaker says he hasn't been out at all since he got home on Tuesday. So he can't say those extra miles were put on since then."

"Nicely done, Lomax, very nicely done," approved Bryce. "Remember, though, this isn't cast iron on its own. Given we all now believe Whitaker is an out-and-out liar, we must constantly expect more of the same from him. He could say, for example, that after he got to Bristol he went on a little sightseeing trip."

"About a hundred and twenty miles, in the dark?" asked Haig, grinning widely and feeling much more cheerful about securing a conviction with this new evidence. "And if he did go sightseeing, he could never have arrived around five-twenty to check in, and get back in time to meet Professor Hamilton in the bar at quarter to seven. Cannae see a jury liking that one, sir!"

"Perhaps not," agreed Bryce. "What about disputing the accuracy of his wife's record? He might suggest she misplaced a digit somehow."

"Well, I've heard of a Devil's Advocate, sir, but with respect I don't think many jurors would swallow either of those suggestions."

"No; but his counsel would be bound to put them forward if so instructed – and anything which could distract the jury from unfortunate facts is helpful to a barrister.

"The extra mileage on the clock is certainly an enormous plus for us, of course. But I still think it isn't cast-iron. I can see the defence arguing about the admissibility of the book. At the very least, we're going to have to prove the entries are in Mrs Whitaker's writing, and hers alone.

"You said you have 'lots' to tell us, Lomax. What else?"

The constable reported the details of his visits to the central post office and the café, and the outcome of his phone calls. He handed the *post mortem* report to Bryce and said, "There was another unexpected thing, which I also thought was very important, sir: Mr Kent called." Lomax recounted the detail of the telephone call, adding that he had asked the couple to come in at four o'clock to make statements.

Sergeant Haig smiled as the DCI beamed again. "You'll make a fine detective, Lomax!"

Breaking the seal on the *post mortem* envelope, Bryce took out the papers and quickly scanned them. "No surprises, gentlemen," he reported. "Mrs Whitaker died instantly, two bullets, ·455 calibre, were fired into her head from above. A contusion on the side of the head was inflicted before death. The shots were fired through a cushion, as we saw. Both bullets passed down through the neck and were recovered from inside the body. Dulcie Whitaker was otherwise in excellent physical shape."

Bryce looked up at the clock on the wall. "About fifteen minutes until the Kents arrive."

"Are you feeling we're in a better position now, sir, than you did after lunch?" asked Haig, hopefully.

Bryce shook his head. "Earlier, Lomax, I was discussing with the sergeant the problems likely to arise when the defence alludes to three other possible murderers, whom we'll have to admit we tried to investigate, but haven't been able to definitely clear. There's one thing you must never lose sight of in these cases – juries like to have *one* defendant in front of them. They still find it difficult enough to decide on that one's guilt – especially in a capital case. If they have a few other candidates paraded in front of them..." He spread his hands.

"Yes, I understand, sir. But if I was on

Whitaker's jury, I'd think the evidence against him was more than enough to convict!" said Lomax earnestly.

Bryce and Haig both laughed.

"Aye, at this moment, I'm sure Mr Bryce and I would, too," said the sergeant. "But you haven't heard the defence barrister's merciless cross-examination of our witnesses – including you, Lomax – nor his impassioned closing speech!"

"All too true," agreed Bryce. "Anyway, while we're waiting for the Kents, you two should crack on with your own statements covering today's events."

The chief inspector used the time to contact Inspector Lessing, his old friend at the Yard, who was liaison officer between the police and military.

****

The Kents were punctual. Taking turns, they repeated their theory about how the savings book could easily have been purloined on the previous Saturday, and how it could have been just as easily replaced on Monday with the new deposit paid into it.

Satisfied he was hearing the truth, Bryce asked the couple to write out their own statements, Haig helping them to avoid opinion and speculation.

An hour later, both statements were

signed.

"I promise nothing," the chief inspector told the couple as he stood to see them out. "But rather than accusing you, we're now moving in a different direction. Go home, and try not to worry."

"Hard to comply with that advice," said Kent. "Being wrongly suspected of murder – and still being under some suspicion – isn't something you can simply clear from your mind! Actually, I was wondering about seeing a solicitor to get advice about suing Whitaker for defamation or slander or something."

"I understand why you might feel so inclined, of course. But I suggest your position is rather like a cricket captain who's won the toss. As you probably know, the old saying is: 'Bat first. If in doubt, think about it. Then bat first'.

"In your case, I think the corresponding default position is 'do nothing'. Think about it by all means. However, doing more and starting legal proceedings would be unwise, in my view. Don't underestimate how highly stressful and very costly it would be, for a start."

"I expect you're right, chief inspector. As Paula is against the idea, I doubt it would have got far off the ground anyway."

The Kents departed hand in hand, both in far better spirits than when the Yard officers left them the day before.

Bryce leaned back in his chair. "Well,

gentlemen, I think we have enough material to make a move.

"Lomax, by convention a local officer should make the arrest if possible. But with respect, I don't think your seniority is adequate. I'll check if Superintendent Middleton is still here, and suggest one of us makes the arrest, with you in attendance."

Middleton had gone home, but the operator had his home number. The subsequent conversation was quickly concluded, with the outcome clear to Haig and Lomax before the DCI replaced the handset

"That's all agreed then. I'll toss you for the dubious honour, sergeant." Bryce pulled out a florin. "Heads I go, tails you go," he said, as he spun the coin and captured it on his forearm.

"Tails. Okay, he's all yours, sergeant. Arrest him on suspicion of murder – never mind about the forgery and so on.

"The custody sergeant will know the ropes about getting him a solicitor when you get back.

Haig and Lomax left, the latter excited by his next role. He had seen very few arrests – and those only for minor assaults, shop thefts, and the like. To be present today was an experience which he realised might never be repeated in his career.

Bryce pulled the list of attendees towards him and started telephoning the same four witnesses yet again. He was successful in contacting all of them. He first asked each one if he or she could confirm the time Dr Whitaker left the hotel. Armitage couldn't say, but the other three were adamant that they'd shaken hands and said 'goodbye' to Whitaker at five o'clock or soon after.

Bryce warned each witness that he would arrange for someone from their local police force to take a formal statement. All were even more curious as to the reason for all the questions. Bryce felt able to explain that he was investigating the murder of Dr Whitaker's wife, but declined to elaborate further.

These witnesses were of course intelligent people. At the end of their conversations with the chief inspector, each mentally reviewed the questions asked. Given the question about whether anyone actually saw Whitaker drink any alcohol, each independently came to the same conclusion – their erstwhile colleague was suspected of killing his wife.

Satisfied with the result of his calls, Bryce found a foolscap pad and started drafting out the points he wanted the four hotel witnesses to include in their statements.

Almost immediately, he was disturbed by the telephone. The desk sergeant informed him of the arrival of two reporters, saying they were expecting a statement at six o'clock. In the next breath the sergeant reported three more press men had arrived.

Bryce, who had forgotten his promise, made his way downstairs and found seven reporters were now waiting. He greeted three, from national newspapers, by name. The desk sergeant was eyeing the group with disfavour, and Bryce asked if there was anywhere he could take the men to free up the foyer.

"I suggest the mess room, sir, if you don't mind one or two other officers being present?"

Reassured this wasn't a problem, the sergeant led the little procession along a corridor and ushered them into a large room. Three constables, chatting over their break-time cups of tea, looked at the newcomers in surprise and interest.

"I'm about to make a statement to these reporters. Ignore us, please, gentlemen."

Far from ignoring the proceedings, the three bobbies gave him their full attention as he turned back to the press men.

"For those of you who don't know me, I'm Detective Chief Inspector Philip Bryce, from New Scotland Yard. Detective Sergeant Haig and I, with considerable help from Constable Lomax of the local force, are here to investigate the murder of Mrs Dulcie Whitaker. She was shot in the early hours of Tuesday morning, in her own home. The weapon has not yet been recovered.

"We have been following a number of leads over the last two days, and have interviewed a number of people.

"As a result of our investigations, I can say that a man is helping the police with our enquiries. I have nothing else for you at the moment."

There was an immediate clamour from the group around him."

"Can you give us a name?" "Is he actually under arrest?" "Was the victim known to him?" Is he related to the victim?" "What was the motive?" All these questions came in the first few seconds after Bryce stopped speaking.

"Sorry, gentlemen; I'm not answering any questions tonight. I strongly suggest you ask again at noon tomorrow – there will be nothing else before then."

He shooed the still-grumbling group back through the foyer, and out into the street.

Having almost pushed the last one out of the door, he returned to the desk, where Haig and the duty sergeant were standing, grinning.

"There are occasions where a first-rate investigative journalist can be helpful to the police," scowled Bryce, "but this isn't one of them. I'd forgotten I agreed to make a statement today, and of course I'm still not really ready."

Looking at Haig he asked, "Have you brought Whitaker in, sergeant?"

"Aye, sir, all booked in and whisked away to the cells. Said nothing when I told him why we'd come; and he didn't speak in the car, either.

"He took his pick of the three solicitors he

was offered, and plumped for a Mr Egerton, who's been contacted. I assumed you weren't in any hurry to do Whitaker's interview tonight, sir, so Egerton will come at eight o'clock tomorrow morning."

"Very good. You're quite right to let Whitaker sweat overnight. Where's Lomax?"

"He watched the processing; then I sent him upstairs to carry on with his statement writing. Sergeant Bates here told me you were with the press; I was waiting for you to emerge."

Turning to the custody sergeant Bryce said, "I hope Whitaker doesn't cause you any trouble overnight, Bates. We'll give the solicitor a bit of time to talk to his client tomorrow, and come along about half past eight."

The Yard officers took the stairs to Wanstall's room, where the local constable was diligently writing. He started to rise as the detectives came in, but Bryce signalled this was unnecessary.

"Pack away your statement until tomorrow, Lomax. Haig and I are off to the hotel and it's time you went home, too.

CHAPTER 19

Whitaker lay on his uncomfortable bed in his police cell, thinking furiously. It was barely two days since he'd offered Messrs Forrest and McNamara as likely murderers, and only thirty-six hours since 'discovering' the forged cheque and suggesting Kent as a third suspect.

Then there was the matter of his own, convincing, alibi. Surely, he thought, the police could hardly have started their investigation, and certainly couldn't have eliminated every one of the patsies, and destroyed his wonderful alibi too? It simply wasn't feasible, especially in the timeframe.

No, he reasoned, this must be a bluff. Perhaps he'd been arrested to lull one of the patsies into a false sense of security? A smile replaced his angry features. Yes! This was clearly the way of things.

Happy with his interpretation, he rather wished he'd refused the offer of a solicitor; it was clear he didn't need one.

His once first-class brain was not working as it should – Indeed, apart from the occasional flash, it hadn't done so for several years. Otherwise, it might have occurred to him that although the concept of lulling a patsy was indeed a possibility, the police would never lock him up in a cold cell without an explanation – and his agreement.

However, he was, as always, completely satisfied with his own reasoning, and consequently laughed and joked with the officers who came at intervals to feed him and escort him to the toilet. He thought they probably weren't 'in' on why he was there, and so made no attempt to discuss his arrest with them.

The officers, in their turn, marvelled that a man arrested for such a shocking crime could even manage a smile, and privately marked him down as a cold-blooded killer.

Which was exactly what he was.

****

Bryce and Haig spent another quiet evening in their hotel, and were again quite happy with the food and drink available.

In several recent cases, Haig had seen the DCI extract admissions from suspects, simply by bombarding them with unassailable facts. During the evening, he asked if his boss thought Whitaker would confess in the morning.

Bryce shook his head. "This was all thoroughly organised. Arranging the three suspects for us was cleverly done; and the hotel alibi – complete with witnesses – was precision-planned from start to finish. Whitaker's definitely the type who believes he can outwit us, so no; I don't think he'll confess tomorrow.

"He'll want a jury to decide. As helpful as everything Lomax has produced is, I still think the verdict could go in Whitaker's favour, given a competent defence team sowing enough doubt in the jurors' minds. A lot might depend on the tolerance of the judge as to what he allows to be brought in. But, of course, it's usual in capital cases to allow quite a bit of leeway.

"Incidentally, it might be a bit of a rush to get him before a magistrate tomorrow, so I fear it's another night here for us. Presumably there's a Saturday morning remand court, so we should be homeward bound before lunch. I think you can safely ring Fiona, and tell her she and Rosie will see you the day after tomorrow."

CHAPTER 20

The Yard officers arrived back at the police station a few minutes after eight-thirty the next morning. Bates was off-duty, and a new desk sergeant reported that Mr Egerton was in an interview room with the prisoner.

"Good," replied Bryce. "Is there any reason why we can't do the interview in the office upstairs?"

"Can't think of one, sir," replied the sergeant.

"Good, again. Get someone to tell Mr Egerton we're ready to carry on when he is. Then have him and his client escorted to Mr Wanstall's old room."

Upstairs, Lomax was working on his statement. Bryce told him to find a fifth chair from somewhere, and park it by the door, explaining this would be where the constable would sit, acting as observer and door guard.

"There was a telephone message for you a few minutes ago, sir, from Scotland Yard." Lomax took out his pocket book.

"Inspector Lessing. He said to tell you

Whitaker was commissioned in the army in October 1939. The records can't say for definite, but the inspector says his information is that he would definitely have been issued with a sidearm."

Lomax supplied the details of Whitaker's early transfer into Bawdsey. "Mr Lessing says not to bother to ring back to thank him, but you do owe him a pint, sir."

Bryce grinned. "Thank you, Lomax. Useful information, as you'll appreciate."

Almost immediately there was a knock at the door. A uniformed constable entered with Whitaker in handcuffs. They were followed by a slim man in his late thirties, well-dressed, but looking less than happy.

"All right, constable, you can remove the cuffs and leave Dr Whitaker with us," instructed the DCI.

Introductions were performed.

"Not particularly spacious in here, but larger and more comfortable than most police station interview rooms," Bryce remarked.

"True enough," agreed Adrian Egerton, "and lacking the usual unpleasant smell, too.

"If I may kick off, chief inspector," the solicitor continued, now using his courtroom voice, "Dr Whitaker informs me that he has only been arrested to lull other suspects into a false sense of security. If so, I would have to query why my time has been wasted."

Bryce and Haig exchanged a quick 'told you so' look.

"You've been misinformed, Mr Egerton. I believe Dr Whitaker will have very urgent need of your services – and in due course those of counsel. That being so, and assuming you will represent him, I'll refer to him as your client.

"Last night, your client was arrested on suspicion of the murder of his wife, and cautioned. He said nothing after caution, but we'll repeat it, so you can be sure the formalities have been complied with. Sergeant?"

Haig issued the caution again.

Whitaker didn't speak. Egerton looked at him, and muttered: "They seem to be very serious. Do you definitely want me to represent you?"

"I suppose so," replied Whitaker ungraciously, "but this is all a complete farce."

"Let's see how we get on, Dr Whitaker," said Bryce.

"Before we start in earnest, though, I'm going to apologise again that you've been troubled by the press since you got back home on Tuesday evening. We cleared them away once, but I know how the press are. Have you been able to get out of the house at all?"

"No – I haven't even dared to go into the back garden, and certainly not out of the front door. I hardly dare pick up the telephone either. But, as I told your officer yesterday, I'll have to get out to do some shopping very soon."

"Very well, let's move on. Can you please describe how you went to Bristol on Monday – what time you left, what time you arrived, and so on?"

Whitaker paused for so long his listeners thought he wasn't going to answer at all. At last, he responded witheringly. "I suppose we have to play your silly, silly games. I went by car. I left home around three o'clock. I arrived at my hotel around five-fifteen. I parked a little distance away, as the hotel has no car park."

"And then?"

Whitaker truthfully described his arrival, and how he became acquainted with fellow symposium members.

"And were you together with this little group for the rest of the evening?"

"Yes. We all got along, and agreed to dine together in the hotel. After dinner, we went back to the lounge – more or less the same group, as I recall."

Whitaker's next words were sarcastically laboured. He addressed Bryce as though he were an idiot. "That's when, as I told you before, chief inspector, I made a fool of myself. I hadn't taken any alcohol before or during dinner, but in the lounge afterwards I succumbed to temptation and drank far too much."

Whitaker turned and spoke to his solicitor rather more politely. "I must explain, Mr Egerton, that I'm a recovering alcoholic. I shouldn't have drunk anything at all – certainly not the three or four double whiskies I consumed."

"On Tuesday, you gave us some names of people in your little group. For the record, can you repeat those, please?"

"Yes, although I don't see why they should be dragged in. There was Anita French – she works for the National Trust, although I don't know where. Very nice woman. A fellow called Armitage; director of a minor museum in Manchester, I believe. Then there was a retired professor, name of Hamilton. Good chap. Oh, and a man called Bernard Harris. No idea what he does, but one of those 'life and soul of the party' types."

"So you had a number of drinks. Did you buy any of those yourself?"

"I bought a round, certainly – I'm not a sponger!"

"What time did you go to bed, Dr Whitaker?"

"I'm not sure. I think there were only three of us at the end. We were residents, of course, but I seem to remember talking to the barman before I went to my room. I suppose it was a bit before midnight." Whitaker was sparing with his details and made no mention of his little recitation to Cole, correctly understanding he should not pretend his memory was excellent whilst also claiming he was drunk.

"You probably slept very well, given your doses of Scotch," remarked Haig.

"Yes, I did, sergeant. The proverbial log. Although I don't remember going back to my room at all." Realising here was an opportunity to embellish something which couldn't possibly be refuted, Whitaker added: "When I woke the following morning I was ashamed to find I hadn't even undressed properly."

"What happened on Tuesday?" asked Bryce.

Whitaker again supplied the necessary information from breakfast onwards, truthfully claiming, "I drove home after the symposium, and unexpectedly found you," before falsely concluding "and a terrible tragedy, waiting for me."

"Yes, indeed," agreed Bryce, now ready to question Whitaker about McNamara, Forrest, and Kent. He shifted his gaze to look directly at the solicitor. "Mr Egerton, what you're about to hear next isn't technically privileged, but as we go along you'll appreciate that some of it is rather sensitive. I'm sure you won't allow it to get outside this room, unless it becomes necessary."

Egerton made a small 'whatever you say' gesture with his hand.

"Let's look at the two men you named as possible suspects on Tuesday evening, Dr Whitaker, and also the third man you named the following morning."

"You told us Brian McNamara was having an affair with your wife. You also told us she was unaware that you knew."

Egerton sat forward. The name of a fellow solicitor raised in proceedings was immediately concerning to him. His voice was disapproving as he asked "How can an alleged affair be relevant?"

"Be careful, Mr Egerton," Bryce warned him sharply. "It's unprofessional and potentially damaging to your client to use the word '*alleged*' to describe something your client has stated to the police as fact!

"The relevance is this: Dr Whitaker suggests that his late wife might have threatened to inform Mrs McNamara about the affair. He further suggests two viable reasons why such a thing might have happened. His conclusion is that McNamara killed Dulcie Whitaker, to prevent her from 'spilling the beans'.

"We have interviewed Mr McNamara. The affair is admitted."

"There you are!" interjected Whitaker with satisfaction. "Everything exactly as I told you."

"Yes. However, we've looked closely into the matter of Mr McNamara. We're satisfied, with corroboration from an independent witness, that he and your late wife were on very good terms as recently as Monday lunchtime of this week. That was of course only a matter of an hour or so before she brought the car home, and you left for Bristol. Such a serious dispute could hardly have occurred so shortly after they parted so fondly. Indeed, McNamara could hardly have planned and carried out the murder in such a short time. He has been removed from our list of suspects.

Whitaker glowered. "So what about the others, then? It must have been one of them."

"Well, there's Mr Forrest. Again, he admits adultery. But he and his lady friend were in a London hotel on Monday night, and we have been able to verify his story."

"You might say Forrest could have slipped back to Draycaster, carried out the murder, and got back in time for breakfast. We've looked into the possibility. His friend denies that he left her, of course, but also the timings would be tight to impossible. In fact, we believe it would be much easier for you to do the job from Bristol. Consequently, Mr Forrest has also been struck from our list."

Whitaker sat, scowling, but remained silent. Egerton, whose eyebrows had shot up again when Forrest's name was mentioned, stared down at his legal pad.

"Then we come to Mr Kent," Bryce continued. "The cheque was indeed forged – the matter isn't in dispute. However, the Kents are certain they can identify the date and time when the passbook was taken, and when it was returned. They believe it was you on both occasions. We have their statements."

Whitaker looked apoplectic. His solicitor laid a hand on his arm and spoke quietly to him, advising him to say nothing.

"No!" shouted his client, shaking off the restraining hand. "I will speak. It's a calumny, chief inspector. It's vile! I shall sue them for slander."

Egerton looked pained.

"We note everything you say, Dr Whitaker," said Bryce, pointedly glancing over to where Sergeant Haig sat, recording the interview. "We've found where the forged cheque was paid in – the Flixton Road post office. In due course, it might be instructive if we put you in an identification parade, to see if the postmistress picks you out."

Whitaker looked dumbfounded.

"The Kents said, and we believe them, that your wife would have lent or even given them money, if they'd asked. There was no reason to resort to forgery, theft, and murder. They too have been crossed off the list."

There was complete silence in the room. Bryce kept his eyes on Whitaker; Whitaker kept his on the edge of the desk.

The chief inspector delivered the inevitable conclusion. "So you see, Dr Whitaker, we are left with you as our sole suspect. Before re-examining your position, I'll ask you a question: what military service did you do?"

Whitaker hesitated, admitted the facts of his war record, but without mention of the Webley.

"I see; so on receiving your commission you were issued with a sidearm, yes?"

"I have no memory of such a thing."

"Really?" queried Bryce. "Let me help your memory out then. This is what I learned yesterday." Bryce drew forward Lomax's pocketbook and repeated the details supplied by Stephen Lessing. "I suggest you took advantage of the chaos at the time you were demobbed, and hung onto your pistol."

"I did not; and you can't prove I did!" retorted Whitaker. He was shocked to learn his military records could be dredged up so easily – but still confident the Webley never would be.

"Let's leave that for the moment, and move back to your alibi, instead. Your stay at the Arden Hotel on Monday of this week wasn't your first, was it?"

"No. So what?"

"Perhaps nothing. Or perhaps, what you knew about the hotel from your previous visit led you to select it again this time."

Whitaker spluttered, genuinely speechless with indignation. This was not the truth of the matter at all! But he could hardly say he'd booked his room months before he decided to kill his wife.

"We've spoken to the symposium delegates you socialised with on Monday evening. You'll no doubt be pleased to hear that none of them contradict your story. The hotel manager confirms your time of arrival, and one or more of your new acquaintances confirms your teetotal behaviour before and during dinner, as well as your changed behaviour in the lounge afterwards. Your presence at the symposium is similarly confirmed, as is the time of your departure on Tuesday."

"There you are, then," scowled Whitaker, "confirmation of everything I told you. I'm vindicated! Why are you still going on about this?"

Bryce regarded Whitaker with expressionless indifference as he delivered his next blow. "What none of your witnesses is prepared to state is that they saw you drinking anything apart from coffee after dinner. One of your witnesses suggests you tipped your drinks into the potted plant tub beside where you sat."

"Sergeant Haig and I visited the hotel yesterday. We've taken soil samples from the pots beside where you were seated during your claimed post-prandial excesses. I confidently expect one or both to show traces of whisky. There can't be many hotel guests with reason to tip out expensive liquor – and certainly not in the quantity we believe you did."

Egerton leaned forward and muttered in

Whitaker's ear again. Whitaker shook his head, but this time didn't speak. The solicitor sat back and made another note on his pad.

"Here's a recap of one or two points, Dr Whitaker. You've told us, very clearly, that you drove straight to Bristol, and straight back after the symposium closed. Since returning, you've claimed – in the presence of three police officers and your solicitor – that you haven't left your house at all. Correct?"

Whitaker nodded sullenly.

"The sergeant will record that you nodded your agreement to the question.

"So, between your wife returning after lunch on Monday, and last night when you were arrested, your car has made only one journey to Bristol, and only one journey back. That's it?"

"Yes," growled Whitaker.

"Is there a point to this?" asked Egerton.

"A very good one, Mr Egerton." Bryce drew the log book out from a desk drawer. "The late Mrs Whitaker made meticulous recordings of the car's mileage readings after every journey, however short. She also recorded the date, destination, and duration of each and every trip, and who was driving. We know the reading when she came home on Monday after having lunch with Mr McNamara. We also know what the current reading is.

"Perhaps your client would care to explain how the distance recorded – between his wife arriving home at lunchtime on Monday and now – is twice that for a single round trip between here and Bristol?"

Egerton looked alarmed, and turned again to his client, who for the first time showed signs of understanding how serious his position was.

"Dr Whitaker, I strongly recommend you say absolutely nothing further!" said the solicitor, not bothering to lower his voice, and speaking with unmistakeable, urgent emphasis.

His client finally appeared to grasp the wisdom of the advice and pursed his lips.

"Sergeant Haig will note that your client made no reply when the matter of the mileage was put to him."

"I assume you propose to charge my client, chief inspector?"

"Oh yes, Mr Egerton. But I'd like to say something else to him first.

"I imagine you were unaware your wife checked up on you to the extent that she did, continuously recording the odometer readings in the car after every journey.

"It's certainly ironic, and possibly unique, that written evidence provided by the victim herself before her own death will be a key element of your trial.

"Robin Whitaker, I charge you that between Monday October 17th, and Tuesday October 18th, at 11 Glebe Close in the city of Draycaster, you murdered Dulcie Mary Weston

Whitaker, contrary to Common Law."

A thousand thoughts were clattering in his head, but Whitaker made no movement and no sound.

"You'll want to talk to your client in private, Mr Egerton, I'm sure.

"Lomax, handcuff Dr Whitaker again and take him down to an interview room. Tell the custody sergeant he's been charged, and ask for someone to take over from you. I'll go down and sort out the paperwork later."

"Egerton, get me the very best barrister there is. I'm a rich man," said Whitaker as his hands were cuffed.

"Not exactly true," interjected Bryce. "Certainly, your late wife was prosperous. And, assuming the will held by Hargreaves in Oxford remains current, you are indeed her sole beneficiary.

"However, there's another very sensible bit of Common Law, known as the Forfeiture Rule, which precludes a murderer from benefitting from his crime. I think every country in the world has something similar. Our plain-speaking American friends call theirs the 'slayer rule'. Unless by some miracle you're acquitted, Dr Whitaker, you have nothing but your own finances to rely on.

"The nature of your crime will, of course, be attractive to counsel hoping to make a name for themselves. So yes, Mr Egerton may be able to brief a first-class representative who is prepared to forego their usual fee. But I doubt whether you'll be able to reimburse a top KC who expects a retainer of five hundred guineas and a hundred guineas a day in refreshers.

"Take him away, Lomax."

CHAPTER 21

Constable Lomax returned a few minutes later and found Haig alone, the DCI having left the room for a moment.

"That was really something, sarge; what an experience!" he burst out.

Haig looked up from his writing.

"Aye, it was indeed, laddie," he agreed. "Even though I've seen the Chief demonstrate his interviewing skill several times, I know I still could never equal it. You won't be aware of this – and we never ever discuss it, by the way – but he is a barrister himself."

Lomax goggled.

"Anyway, I'm sure you'll remember this case."

"Certainly will, sarge. And I've got more new experience to come, in giving evidence at the Assizes. Hope that goes okay, and I don't accidentally make a hash of things."

"Try not to worry about it. Your evidence is straightforward, and might not even be challenged. You'll manage either way, I'm sure."

Bryce returned. "I've been to inform

Superintendent Middleton of the current position." He resumed his seat and crossed his legs, thoroughly relaxed compared with his sharp alertness when dealing with Whitaker and Egerton. "I also took the opportunity of telling him that your conduct over the last few days has been exemplary, Lomax.

"I mentioned in particular that it was you who spotted the key piece of evidence. I've suggested, as the force has lost a detective constable, you might be given the opportunity to join the CID. That recommendation will also be in my official report to the chief constable. It's up to your superiors, of course, but I've made clear what my views are."

Lomax's face was a picture. He'd always worked hard and given his best, but today was the first time he'd been told his potential had been raised with the higher ranks. "I don't know what to say, sir. Thank you very much indeed!"

"All merited, Lomax," smiled Bryce. "Take a seat; I need to explain a few things to you.

"The county doesn't have a prosecuting solicitor available, so I've been asked to present the case before the magistrates tomorrow. Although you won't be required, I suggest you come along – in uniform again.

"Whitaker will be remanded until committal proceedings can be held, probably in a fortnight or so. We'll be back here then, and you, Lomax, or your statement, will be required.

"Depending on the court cycle, it might be a couple of months or more before Whitaker actually comes to trial.

"Apart from statement-writing, we still have several outstanding tasks, and a couple of those are for you, constable. The first is a little trip to Hendon with the soil samples. You can take our car; the sergeant will give you directions.

"We need short statements from the symposium people. It's potentially contentious to write a statement for someone else, but I'm drafting something for each of them anyway. When you get back, I want you to contact the local police in the area they live, and dictate the suggested wording over the telephone. Get a local officer to go round to the witness, and each person can say what he or she wants – but there'll be my template to help them."

Lomax nodded. "Got all that, sir."

"We could get statements regarding the forged signature from the bank manager and his teller. However, since Whitaker himself told us it was a forgery, there really isn't much point in getting anyone else to say so, and neither of those two is a handwriting expert.

"Actually, for the act of forgery to be any use to us, we need to go a bit further if we can – and see if we can prove that the signature is most likely to be Whitaker's work.

"I seem to remember seeing a cheque book

on Dr Whitaker's own account in our boxes. But we probably need to see if there are any better examples of his writing – some of his own returned cheques would be ideal. Take a look, Lomax, and see if you can find anything.

"A back stop might be to acquire the signature he used when checking into the hotel, but I think more examples would be needed.

"Then I'll consider getting an expert to give an opinion as to whether the signature on the forged cheque is likely to be his work.

"That leaves the official at the central post office, and the one at the little post office. To be quite honest, I'm not really sure how much they can help. I know I mentioned an identification parade, but it's a double-edged sword – there's every chance she couldn't pick him out. Although that certainly wouldn't be fatal to our case, it would be another chance for the defence to muddy the waters. However, I think we'll have to hold one, if only to prevent adverse comment from the defence if we don't.

"There's another point here. It's quite possible that Egerton will advise his client not to co-operate with a parade. If so it then becomes a double-edged sword for him instead, because at trial the prosecution will make every effort to imply that Whitaker was afraid of the postmistress identifying him.

"I guess Egerton will still be here, so pop down, Lomax, and ask him. If he agrees, we'd better try to fix the parade for this afternoon, before tomorrow's court hearing – after which Whitaker will be taken off to jail and we'd need a production order.

****

Lomax returned fifteen minutes later and reported on his mission. "I spoke to Mr Egerton outside the interview room, sir. He was clearly in favour, and went to discuss the matter with his client. I couldn't hear what was being said, but there were raised voices. After about five minutes he came out again, and announced Whitaker wouldn't co-operate."

"Okay – include in your statement the fact that he rejected the offer to hold a parade." Bryce mused aloud, "Either side could try for a dock identification, of course, but that's fraught. Actually, I doubt if the prosecution will call the postmistress anyway, and I can't see the defence daring to do so. Still, the good news for us is that Whitaker was given his chance and rejected it."

Lomax resumed searching through the Whitakers' papers whilst he waited for the sergeant to finish preparing the samples for the Hendon laboratory.

"Everything's ready to go to the lab, sir," said Haig presently. "All clearly labelled, and I've enclosed a note telling them what we're looking for." Haig turned in response to an excited yelp from behind him. "It looks like Lomax has come up trumps again."

The constable was waving two sheets of paper.

"I can't find any returned cheques, sir, and in fact the last cheque in Dr Whitaker's book was apparently issued six months ago. This is a sort of letter, from him to his wife. Dated about four months ago. Basically, it's a promise to toe the line, to not drink or gamble."

"Excellent; good work again. We'll take it back to the Yard with us when we leave, and I'll consult our in-house expert. He'll say whether it might be worth asking an independent expert witness.

"Okay, Lomax, are you all set?"

The constable nodded, clearly eager to go.

"Despite the sergeant's note, I'll do a belt and braces job, and call Hendon to explain you'll be arriving this afternoon, and what they must look for. Off you go, then. Oh, and by the time you get back we may have gone to our hotel. If we're not here, bring the car to the hotel and ask for us there."

The Yard officers spent the next few hours drafting statements, calling witnesses to explain what was happening, and in Bryce's case preparing a report for the chief constable.

At noon, as he had promised, Bryce went downstairs and again made use of the mess room to dictate a statement to the press reporters. This time he named the arrested man, but refused to give more than the basic details of the crime.

The Yard officers had a basic but sufficient lunch in the same room a little later, and afterwards they continued with their paperwork.

At three o'clock, Superintendent Middleton arrived, and enquired whether the Yard men would be in for the next hour or so, as the chief constable wished to pay them a visit.

The top local officer duly arrived unaccompanied. A short man, white-haired and somewhat red in the face, he was the archetypal middle-ranking ex-military officer. However, he looked very intelligent, and alert. After brief introductions, he took a seat.

"Apologies for having to give you poor Wanstall's office," he remarked, "but it's by far the best we could do, short of turfing Middleton out of his room!

"Anyway, I wanted to congratulate you on getting to the bottom of this case so quickly. I gather you've been contending with a lot of deception from Whitaker. You'll be letting me have a report sometime, no doubt."

"It's actually written already, sir, and if you don't mind it not being typed you can have it now," said Bryce. "There will have to be a supplement in a day or so, as we haven't quite finished the work."

"No, no; leave it until you're ready, man.

You needn't bother about getting it typed – as long as your writing is legible!

"Now, I understand we can't locate the county prosecuting solicitor, and as the prosecuting sergeant has no experience of this sort of matter we're prevailing on you to present the case in the morning. It's asking a bit much – are you happy?"

"It's not a problem, sir. I don't anticipate any difficulty."

"Ah, I've just remembered – when I called to request the Yard's services, your AC told me you double as a barrister, so you're used to courts. I don't suppose you'd save us a bit of money, and agree to prosecute at the Assizes too?" he joked.

Bryce and Haig both grinned.

"So," continued the chief constable, "how strong do you think your case is? Is it proof against some wily defence counsel bamboozling the jury?"

"With respect, sir, one can never foresee every eventuality. Let's say I'm cautiously confident – I wouldn't have arrested him otherwise."

"Good; well, I've no doubt the Crown will use one of the top Treasury counsel – hopefully a KC we've been pleased with before. This is going to be a high-profile case, without doubt, and there's no point in spoiling the ship for a ha'porth of tar. We'll put up the best we can.

"By the way, Middleton tells me you're pleased with one of our young constables."

"Yes, sir, PC Lomax. I've suggested to Mr Middleton that Lomax might be given the chance to fill the post your unfortunate DC held. I've put the same recommendation in my report to you."

"I don't know the chap other than by sight. But Middleton backs up your judgement, and the matter's in hand as we speak."

"Thank you, sir; I'm sure you won't regret it."

As the door closed behind the chief constable, Bryce sighed. "Let's call it a day, Haig. I need to talk to the custody sergeant, and this evening I need to get ready for court tomorrow. It's a long time since I presented a case before magistrates."

As they walked down the stairs, Bryce raised a question. "Have you thought of applying for the detective inspector's job here?"

"Crossed my mind, sir. But I'm not sure I'd really enjoy working away from the smoke. Fine for this sort of 'away' case, but maybe not permanently. And I'm sure Fiona doesn't want to move again."

"Fair enough – you'll get your chance in the Met sometime."

At the front desk, as Bryce completed the formalities with the custody sergeant, it suddenly occurred to him that he didn't know where to go the next day.

"Where is the courthouse, sergeant?" he asked, "it's obviously not attached to this building."

"About half a mile away from here, sir; but as you're staying in the Station Hotel, the court is even closer. Turn left instead of right when you leave the hotel, and the courthouse is only a couple of hundred yards along Hurngate Street."

CHAPTER 22

Whitaker was now more unhappy than at any time before, even when his wife was making his life a misery. He was forced to accept that his position was, to say the least, precarious.

He was shocked that this situation could ever have arisen. His planning had been meticulous. Everything was ready. Even if the three patsies failed – as he'd known they might – his personal alibi was perfect.

Except that his devious witch of a wife had kept a detailed record of the car's movements and mileage readings! God, wasn't that absolutely typical of her controlling behaviour?

And he hadn't even been aware of the log's existence. The police obviously found the book among the papers they took from the study. It galled him excessively to realise he might have found it himself – and shoved it straight into the Rayburn.

He considered what his solicitor told him – the log would be challenged as to its accuracy. Perhaps even better, challenged as to its admissibility – it would be a point for his barrister to consider. He cheered up a little. If the judge refused to allow the log book to be produced in evidence, surely the rest of the case against him must fail? Everything else was circumstantial, and much of it was hypothesis; leaving the hotel by the back door, for example. There was no actual *evidence*.

Whitaker was also shaken by Bryce's remark about the Forfeiture Rule. Egerton had emphatically confirmed that the chief inspector was correct in law. But in any case, for the time being he would be unable to get his hands on any of Dulcie's money to pay for his defence.

Egerton also explained the 'cab rank' rule barristers operated, and outlined the exceptions to the rule – which included the ability of a client to pay reasonable fees.

A clerk in chambers would offer his case to the selected barrister. The solicitor thought acceptance was pretty much assured on the basis the chief inspector suggested – valuable exposure for the barrister in a high-profile case, despite the necessity of a reduced fee. The solicitor held out hope he might be able to brief a very competent barrister on this basis. He explained about the possibility of a King's Counsel, although necessarily there would be the expense of a junior barrister as well. KCs didn't demean themselves by appearing alone, he learned.

Whitaker knew that Egerton would be

representing him in the magistrates' court the next day, and was assured nothing would happen which would require legal decisions. Whether the barrister appeared for the next hearing – the 'committal' – was a matter to be discussed after counsel was briefed.

Whitaker wondered whether Egerton was up to the job. He hadn't chosen the man – merely picked him out at random from a short list offered by the custody sergeant. Suppose the police chose men for the list according to their pro-police attitudes? Or suppose such solicitors deliberately performed badly to ensure that the police continued to recommend them?

Whitaker's brief moment of near elation rapidly reversed into depression.

His thoughts turned to Egerton's proposal to co-operate with the identity parade. Of course, he hadn't admitted to his solicitor that he was guilty as charged. He was vaguely aware that to do so would seriously limit the actions his legal team could carry out on his behalf. But he was pretty sure Egerton believed him to be guilty.

Nevertheless, he simply couldn't have agreed to attend the parade. If the wretched postmistress identified him, it would be the end. He had struggled to understand Egerton's explanation of the risks of not taking part. Regardless of that, Whitaker was sure his was the correct decision.

Even now, after being charged with a

capital offence, he didn't accept his action was wrong. It was Dulcie who was at fault, in taking her intransigent attitude. No husband should have to put up with such restrictions on his liberty.

****

The following morning, Bryce and Haig walked to the Draycaster magistrates' courthouse. Dating back to the 1880s, it was built in the grand style much loved by civic dignitaries commissioning public works in an era when the ostentatious display of a community's wealth was the norm. Lomax, back in uniform, was waiting for them.

Inside, an usher indicated the only courtroom in use.

Arriving in the designated room, Bryce introduced himself to the elderly clerk, and explained why he would be handling the Whitaker case.

The clerk looked at him closely. "My goodness me," he exclaimed. "I've read about you, chief inspector. Anyway, I assume you are simply asking for a remand this morning?"

Bryce was just confirming this, when Adrian Egerton joined them. He was evidently a regular in the court, and was in fact appearing in another case following Whitaker's.

"We only have four remand cases today, so it'll be a very short morning. However, we'll call your case on first, gentlemen, as the most serious – and only the third capital case I've seen here in twenty years as justices' clerk."

Various people came and went around the front of the court. The press table was already full, and the public gallery was also filling rapidly.

"Never seen a crowd like this for a Saturday remand court," remarked the clerk. A uniformed sergeant arrived and introduced himself to Bryce.

"I'm prosecuting the other cases in this court today, sir – and I can tell you that I'm very pleased you're taking the murder charge. I've never even seen one of those!"

Bryce smiled. "I'm expecting it to go smoothly, and be finished inside five minutes," he replied. "Who's sitting today?"

"Mrs Blount, sir. Nice lady; highly experienced and thoroughly competent. Odd taste in hats, though," laughed the sergeant.

At two minutes to ten o'clock, the clerk disappeared through the rear door, and moments later a female magistrate followed him back in to a call of "all rise".

Formal bows completed, everyone resumed their seats apart from the clerk.

"The first case is Dr Robin Whitaker, your worship. I've asked for him to be brought up."

Almost at once there was a rattle of keys, a sullen Whitaker came into the dock, accompanied by a police officer.

"Are you Robin Blythe Whitaker, of 11 Glebe Close?"

"Yes."

"You have been charged with the murder of Dulcie Mary Weston Whitaker."

The clerk turned towards the bench again. "Madam, Dr Whitaker is represented by Mr Egerton, and the prosecution is in the hands of Detective Chief Inspector Bryce. May the defendant be seated, madam?"

"Yes, sit down." In three short words Mrs Blount sounded every bit as efficient and effective as the prosecuting sergeant had described. "No doubt Mr Egerton has explained the purpose of today's proceedings, Dr Whitaker – this is a preliminary hearing prior to a more formal hearing, probably in a few weeks' time. The matter you are charged with can, of course, only be dealt with in a higher court."

She looked at Bryce. "Yes, chief inspector?"

Bryce rose. "Thank you madam. I ask for this matter to be adjourned to a date when a committal hearing can be held. My application is for a remand in custody. I can say that the prosecution will be ready in seven days. My friend may require rather longer."

He sat down again, and Egerton stood up.

"I am at a disadvantage, madam; we have not yet had time to instruct counsel. I should not wish to commit to a particular course of action when counsel might, at a later date, think a different course would have been preferable. However, if a date is set, say three weeks hence, I'm sure we will be ready. I do not wish to make any other application at this stage, but I make it clear that my client strenuously denies the charge."

"Thank you Mr Egerton."

The magistrate consulted with her clerk regarding dates.

"Stand up, Dr Whitaker. I am going to put this matter off until Monday November the 14th, when the court will expect the committal proceedings to go ahead. Mr Egerton will explain what that entails.

"In the meantime, you will be remanded in custody."

Whitaker's burly custody officer motioned him out of the dock, Egerton whispering to his client as he went that he would come to the cells to speak to him later.

The chief inspector stood to bow, before relinquishing his place at the prosecutor's table to the sergeant who was preparing to present the next case.

Haig and Lomax joined him as he left the courtroom. As soon as they entered the foyer they were surrounded by the half-dozen reporters who were, like the officers, only present for the one short matter.

Bryce held up his hand in the traditional

'stop' fashion.

"I can tell you nothing further, gentlemen. And I'd remind you that the editor of a British newspaper – one represented here this morning, I see – was imprisoned earlier this year for contempt of court, having imperilled a trial by publishing material which he shouldn't!"

He pushed past the pressmen, and the three policemen left the building.

"Thank you for your help, Lomax," said Bryce outside. "Get your statement prepared as soon as possible. A prosecuting solicitor will no doubt speak to you in the next day or so, and collect it. We'll be back the day before the committal, I expect, and we'll see you then.

"Come on, sergeant, we'll get our things from the hotel, and see what life is like back in London."

CHAPTER 23

In the cells beneath the court, a very unhappy Whitaker was talking to his solicitor.

"Why didn't you ask for bail?" he raged.

"Absolutely pointless," replied Egerton. "No magistrate would ever grant bail in a matter of this nature – and the one sitting today is the toughest on this Bench."

Whitaker, still grumbling, subsided a little.

"So I've got to stay in here for another three weeks?"

"You won't be here, you'll be taken to prison. But you'll be in the remand wing of the prison, not in with convicted criminals."

Whitaker muttered something about how he doubted it would be much better.

"As the magistrate suggested, I'll explain the next stage. When you're brought back here, the bench – sitting as examining magistrates next time – will hear more about your case. They will hear from witnesses.

"It won't be for the magistrates to say whether or not you're guilty. Their only task is to decide whether there's sufficient evidence on which to commit you for trial before a judge and jury."

"I understand," replied Whitaker. "It seems very complicated."

"Yes, it is," agreed Egerton. "But it does allow a defendant, if he so wishes, to test evidence, and maybe get some thrown out. The ultimate aim is to show that there isn't sufficient evidence to put before a jury."

Whitaker instantly brightened. He would somehow ensure the case was thrown out before it got to the judge and jury stage!

Egerton, spotting the signs of misplaced euphoria, brought his client back down to earth. "I should warn you – for a single, capital charge, that would be a very rare occurrence. Also, refusal to commit is not the same as an acquittal – the prosecution can have another go later."

Whitaker cursed.

"I put in some calls to barristers' clerks yesterday afternoon," continued the solicitor, "and I expect to hear back on Monday morning. We'll get someone very competent to represent you.

"It's early days, and we'll have to see how counsel advises us to proceed. I'll visit you again as soon as I have firm news."

Egerton made his escape. The solicitor was used to dealing with clients of all types; with some he could get a rapport, and with others he couldn't. This one looked like being firmly in the latter category. They would certainly have numerous meetings over the next few weeks, and the prospect didn't appeal.

Egerton was a careful planner, always looking ahead and anticipating likely eventualities. He thought very briefly about a probable last meeting with Whitaker. It would be after the prison governor brought the news that no reprieve was to be granted. No doubt the appointed barrister would do the talking (what on earth could one say to a condemned man?), but Egerton supposed that his own presence would also be expected. He rapidly banished this ugly vision from his mind, reminding himself that Whitaker was not yet convicted. He must, of course, believe in his client's innocence.

Not an easy matter, given what the chief inspector had said in the police station.

****

On Monday, Morton Reynolds, an up-and-coming 'junior' in his late thirties, agreed to accept the brief. Confident that he would take silk in the next five years, Reynolds, a man with half a dozen impressive acquittals under his belt, had never led in a capital case. This one would certainly attract national headlines. Win or lose, his name would certainly become even more widely known.

Ten days later, and armed with the

statements of most of the prosecution witnesses, Egerton travelled up to London to discuss the brief with Reynolds in his chambers. The two lawyers had not met before, and Egerton was surprised to see – as Reynolds emerged from behind his desk to greet him – that the barrister wore a very built-up boot on one foot. This didn't quite compensate for the shortness of his leg, and as Reynolds moved across his office to pour out two dry sherries, he walked with a pronounced limp.

"Well, Egerton, I have to say this brief is a bit thin," complained the barrister. "As far as I can see, we don't have a single witness we can call. Our client obviously thought all those in the Arden hotel would help him – but now they'll certainly be called by the prosecution. And from what I can see, his four fellow drinkers are all educated people who won't easily crack under cross-examination.

"Then, we have the three men named by the client as suspects. I imagine they'll also be called by the Crown. If they aren't, I don't think we dare do so."

"Suppose the client insists we call them?" asked the solicitor. "After all, apart from his alibi, he made the case to the police that one of those three was the killer. It would be quite a change to his story if he doesn't stick to it, and the jury might think it odd."

Reynolds pondered this. "An interesting

hypothesis, Egerton. I think we'll have to play it by ear. If the Crown calls them, it's going to be tricky enough to cross-examine as it is. If Whitaker insists we call them, they'll hardly be friendly witnesses to say the least. I assume you haven't seen any of these people yourself?"

"No, none of them. No property in a witness, of course, so do you want me to sound them out?"

"I think not. Their statements are damning, and I can't see what helpful material we could glean from these people.

"The postmistress is even more dangerous – I doubt if they'll call her, but I can't see that we can either. We'll never know whether she might have picked him out at an identification parade. But once the police proposed to hold one, I think he should have followed your suggestion to appear in it – risky though it would have been. As it is, it won't be hard for the Crown to imply that he was scared to appear in a parade.

"Any chance of scraping together another witness or two?"

Egerton shook his head. "Best option would be if he'd smuggled a prostitute into his room, and she was prepared to swear he was with her between say one o'clock and two o'clock."

Reynolds gave a humourless smile.

"What about insanity?"

"I've seen no sign of anything of the sort.

He's a highly intelligent man, of course, DPhil and so on; and we've all heard the old saying about genius being one step from insanity. But all the planning done here in order to avoid being found out..." Egerton sighed. "I don't see how any medical man could ever say he didn't know what he was doing – or didn't know it was wrong."

"However, insanity may be the only option in the end," said Reynolds, his voice as serious as his face. "I'll come and see him the day after tomorrow and make my assessment then. Also, of course, whether to call him in his own defence. What's your view?"

"I'd expect him to come across well giving evidence in chief. How he'd fare under cross-examination by top Treasury counsel is another matter."

"I see. But if we get that decision wrong, he'll likely swing."

Both lawyers reached for their glasses and fortified themselves with the pale liquid. The enormity of their responsibility was daunting.

"Well," said Reynolds as he set down his glass, "I think there are only three other matters to discuss today.

"First, we'll have to question the admissibility of some of the evidence, as you've suggested in your brief. This log book thing is potentially damning; we have to move heaven and earth to get it excluded, but at the moment

I don't see on what grounds. Also, although we don't have a statement yet, this business of the soil sample from the flower pot – it needs to be kicked into the long grass. As for the statement from the porter chap, there's nothing there to incriminate Whitaker.

"Second, there's the question of junior counsel. From what you've told me, our man hasn't enough money of his own to feed you and me, never mind a third mouth. But anyway, this case isn't really so complex that a third brain is needed; nor for an additional person to relieve me of some of the cross-examination. Unless you have strong contrary views, Egerton, I suggest you don't look for anyone else."

"No, I completely agree."

"The final matter is the question of the committal. Do we fight, or not? You know your local Bench – any views?"

Egerton hesitated. He was not expecting the question, having assumed that counsel made such decisions alone. He was aware this was Reynolds' first time as leader in a murder trial, but he himself had never been involved in a capital case either. "I've done twenty or more committals at this court in the last few years," he said at last, "and observed others.

"All I can say is, where there are multiple charges, the magistrates occasionally throw one or two out. But when there is only a single charge, I don't recall any instance where the magistrates have refused to commit. It isn't a very high threshold that they have to cross, after all."

"No, true. I have to admit, Egerton, I've hardly ever handled a committal – in the cases I deal with at Quarter Sessions or Assizes, the earlier work is nearly always done by the solicitor before I come on the scene."

The barrister thought for a moment.

"I can't see any point in trying to get this thrown out by the examining magistrates. Realistically, it's never going to happen. So, I think it best not to give the prosecution witnesses a chance to polish up their act by doing a dress rehearsal in being cross-examined. I don't intend to give Whitaker the option on this point.

"So, you do the committal, Egerton. Try to get the evidence about the log book excluded, but otherwise sit tight, listen to the depositions, and reserve our defence."

CHAPTER 24

Three weeks later, Bryce and Haig returned to Draycaster, ahead of the committal hearing the next day. Arriving at the police station late on Sunday afternoon, they were shown to the same office as before, Inspector Wanstall's replacement still not in post. They found a grinning Lomax, now officially appointed as a detective constable, waiting for them. Also present was a short, swarthy man, with very little hair but a remarkably bushy black beard. He introduced himself as Simon Grady, the county prosecuting solicitor.

"Sorry you got lumbered with the initial hearing, chief inspector," apologised the lawyer. "My wife and I were staying with her parents, and while there I was taken ill. However, I've since learned you're a barrister, so it wasn't too onerous a task, I imagine!

"Well, to business, gentlemen. I think you'll be pleased to hear we have Malcolm Livesey leading Jeremy Frith for the Crown. The defence has retained Morton Reynolds – on his own. It might look a bit one-sided; two appearing for us and one of those a KC. But by the time we'd heard about Reynolds appearing solo, our two were already arranged.

"Incidentally, I gather another Treasury counsel, Angela Lacon, was considered for Frith's role, but she felt she was too close to you." Grady's statement sounded more like a question.

"Absolutely right," smiled Bryce, delighted to hear that Angela had been in the running ahead of Frith. "I've known her for years. She and her husband are my closest friends. However, I also know all three of the men you've mentioned.

"Anyway, what's happening tomorrow morning, Grady?"

"Reynolds isn't coming down for the committal hearing. Egerton will handle it. Livesey isn't going to be here, either, but Frith will prosecute.

"The good news is that Egerton has indicated he won't be asking questions. Consequently, Frith proposes to depose only the minimum number of witnesses to guarantee the magistrates will agree to commit. I'm inclined to agree with his policy.

Provisionally, he's calling you three officers, and maybe two of the four conference delegates. He's definitely not calling any of what we might call the three dupes as witnesses at this stage. An interesting decision, but Livesey has approved it.

"The thinking originally was this: if

Reynolds tried to raise the three alternative suspects before the magistrates tomorrow, you could have deposed that you looked into all of them and eliminated them from your enquiries. That scenario isn't going to happen now – but we're still warning McNamara, Forrest, and Kent, to be available for the Assizes. Livesey will decide nearer the time whether to actually call them.

"You and your sergeant are experienced witnesses, but Lomax here isn't. I've already spent some time explaining that he has just two crucial bits of evidence to give: the log book, and the mileage reading he actually saw on the car. I'm sure he'll do us proud!"

Concluding his input with a friendly nod for the young detective, and citing other urgent business, Grady gathered up his papers and hurried away.

Bryce and Haig looked again at Lomax, who was still smiling.

"A word of warning," said Bryce. "What happens in the witness box tomorrow is rather different to a trial. The speed is likely to be very slow in comparison, as the clerk has to take everything down, probably in longhand."

"Aye. It all feels more relaxed compared with a trial, but you need to be equally alert. Be sure to read your statement many times, so you're as word perfect as possible," advised Haig. "Knowing you have everything on the tip of your tongue is a great help with any nerves you might have."

Bryce agreed. "I don't know what you may have in your pocketbook which isn't in your statement, constable, but you should assume you won't be granted permission to refresh your memory from it."

Lomax nodded, appreciating these nuggets of experience and wisdom from the Yard officers.

"We're back in the same hotel – would you care to join us there for dinner this evening?"

"Very kind, sir; yes please!" replied Draycaster's newest detective.

"Half past seven, then."

****

A few minutes before nine o'clock the next morning, Bryce and Haig arrived at the courthouse. Haig spotted Lomax across the concourse, and went to sit with him. Seeing Egerton and Grady talking with his old acquaintance Jeremy Frith, Bryce strolled over to say 'hello'. Observing the tradition of the bar, he didn't shake hands with his fellow barrister.

"What do we know about the magistrates today?" asked Bryce.

Grady smiled. "Committal proceedings in murder cases aren't exactly common here. I hear most members of the Bench wanted to sit. Apparently, the Bench chairman has refused to allow more than five. He can't be here himself, so today's chairman will be Mrs Blount, who dealt with the first remand hearing, I gather. She's handled committals before – some of yours, Egerton, I recall."

Egerton nodded. "It is quite amusing, though – a single justice could deal with this, and we're to have five. I do hope they don't spend a lot of time discussing their findings. I've seen seven sitting here before, for licensing and so on, and it doesn't make for rapid decision-making!"

"True," remarked Grady, "although I suspect the outermost four are often 'yes-men or nodders', to borrow Wodehouse's delightfully descriptive words."

The other three men smiled.

"Ah, well, at least I don't have to tog myself up today," laughed Frith. "Assuming Whitaker is committed for trial – and you don't seem to be opposing committal, Egerton – do we know which judge is on this circuit at present?"

"I hear Urquhart is starting in Winchester towards the end of January," said Grady. That means he'll be in Salisbury, where this case should go, a couple of weeks later. I doubt if he'll do the whole circuit, but he'll probably get as far as Exeter before handing over to someone else."

There was silence for a moment, as all four men considered what they knew about Mr Justice Urquhart. 'Tough but fair' was an epithet used perhaps too freely to describe judges and magistrates, but the expression matched Sir

David Urquhart perfectly. Both prosecution and defence were content.

****

The next few hours came as a complete anti-climax to Lomax.

Bryce was called first. As soon as he finished, and Egerton remained in his seat, the prosecution knew the matter would go to trial.

There were only two moments of dispute. Haig gave evidence of collecting a sample of soil from the plant pots, and Egerton bounced up to say that this evidence should not be admitted, as whatever the result of any analysis might be, there could be no evidence linking anything in the pots to his client.

Mrs Blount, after consulting the clerk, brushed the objection aside, saying it was a matter for the trial court, should the case be committed.

Egerton was even more vehement during Lomax's evidence, when the constable referred to the log book.

"This exhibit really isn't admissible, your worships!" he exclaimed. "There is no evidence to show it was created by my client's wife, and even if it was, it may be that accuracy in some key area is lacking."

"What do you say, Mr Frith?" asked the magistrate.

"Simply this, madam. At trial, evidence

will be called to prove that every entry in this book was written by the late Mrs Whitaker. Technically, it is a document rather than an exhibit, and a document is of course anything containing information – which the log book undisputedly does, and we are therefore entitled to put it in. In my view, it is certainly admissible at trial, and as you have already observed, it will be up to the trial judge to make a contrary ruling if he disagrees. To that extent, I respectfully suggest it is not a matter for your worships sitting as examining magistrates."

After quickly consulting with the clerk and whispering with her colleagues, Mrs Blount agreed with Mr Frith's view.

Egerton played no further role in the proceedings until the second of the symposium witnesses finished, whereupon he stood up again and announced that Dr Whitaker reserved his defence.

Without retiring, the magistrates again quietly conferred. Seconds later, Mrs Blount announced that the defendant had a case to answer, and he would be committed for trial.

Frith requested a remand in custody, pending appearance at the next Salisbury Assizes. Egerton made no application for bail, and Whitaker was duly remanded.

Bryce spent a few minutes talking to the lawyers in the courtroom, and then joined his officers who were now standing with the symposium witnesses in the foyer. He introduced himself to the four witnesses, as although he had spoken to them on the telephone, this was the first time he'd actually seen them. He found that Mrs French, one of the two not called, was not only a feisty lady but was already convinced of Whitaker's guilt.

"You must hang him, chief inspector," she exclaimed, almost as soon as Bryce spoke to her. "He really tried to use us so he could get away with killing his poor wife."

She wasn't alone in her view, her three companions all agreeing.

"As I'm sure you know, Mrs French, it's not my job to hang anyone. My job is to investigate a crime and arrest the person I think is responsible. It's the prosecuting counsel's job, using the evidence I provide for him, to convince the jury to convict – despite the efforts of the defence counsel to persuade them otherwise. The judge's job is to see fair play, and, if the jury convicts in this case, to pass a mandatory death sentence. Finally, the Home Secretary, doing an unpleasant task which has caused at least one holder of that office to decline a second term, decides whether or not to recommend a reprieve. If he refuses, then the public executioner does the necessary."

"Yes, chief inspector, you're right of course, and I apologise. I spoke without thinking."

"But you're quite correct on your other point – Whitaker certainly tried to use the four of you. And he went much further than just reinforcing his alibi. You'll hear at the trial that he actually named three separate men, all of whom he said had reason to kill his wife. We are, of course, completely satisfied they didn't do it – but a jury might worry about convicting him if alternative candidates are trawled in front of them."

"How appalling! You can't think he'll get off?" Mrs French almost wailed.

"Obviously, I hope very much he won't," replied Bryce, "but trials are very unpredictable."

"We understand you are a barrister yourself, chief inspector," said Harris, speaking for the first time. "Why were only two of us called today?"

"Mr Livesey, the KC who will be the lead prosecutor at the trial, and Mr Frith, whom you saw today, decided that to put up all four of you at this stage was unnecessary. In fact, there are at least nine more witnesses who are not even here. Any, or all of them, may be called at trial.

"Actually, I believe Mr Grady, the instructing solicitor, drew your four names from a hat to decide the order. Mr Armitage came out first, followed by Professor Hamilton. When they'd been heard, Mr Frith decided not to go any further down the list. However, I'll be astounded if you and Mrs French aren't called at the trial."

"No chance of Whitaker doing the decent thing and putting in a guilty plea, I suppose, chief inspector?" asked Hamilton.

"In a capital case, rarer than a hen's tooth, although not without precedent," replied Bryce. "Mr Reynolds could put forward a guilty but insane plea, but the presence of you four would, in my view, suggest that Whitaker knew exactly what he was doing.

"Yes," said Armitage, "dashed poor show all round."

"Anyway, lady and gentlemen, thanks for coming today; I'll no doubt see you again."

Saying goodbye to Lomax, and wishing him well over the next few weeks, Bryce and Haig returned to their car and headed back to London.

****

Whitaker had sat through the committal proceedings feeling less and less comfortable. As he heard the evidence piling up – including the production of the log book and the demolition of his carefully-arranged alibi – it all seemed much worse than when he was reading the various statements.

Having been doubtful about his solicitor from the outset, during the morning he started entertaining doubts about his barrister too. Why hadn't Reynolds bothered to appear?

It was obvious that the log book must be excluded, but Egerton had only made a token effort to do so – and failed miserably in the attempt. Surely his barrister would have made a better fist of it?

Also, the solicitor had made no effort whatsoever to question any of the witnesses and shake their testimony, even though he'd originally indicated this was a possible – and likely – action.

These and many more feverish thoughts raced through Whitaker's mind. By the time Egerton came down to his cell, he was in a foul temper.

"As good as we could have expected, Dr Whitaker," his solicitor began cheerfully.

"Rubbish," snarled Whitaker. "Why didn't you attack those lying witnesses? Why let the court think you agreed with them? And why didn't Reynolds come himself?"

"There was absolutely no point in 'attacking' the witnesses today," replied Egerton calmly. "Like it or not, there were ample grounds for the magistrates to send you for trial, and nothing I could have done would have made any difference. Nor could Mr Reynolds. Cross-examining witnesses here simply prepares them for the next round. Far better to leave them out of it at this stage, and give them a searching cross-examination at trial."

Somewhat mollified, Whitaker subsided for a few seconds. Then he shot upright again. "Well, I'm far from satisfied. You'll need to convince me that during the trial Reynolds will really tear into these people – rip them apart.

"Anyway, what about Kent and the other two? You didn't call them today."

"We reserved our defence, Dr Whitaker; it wasn't my place to call witnesses in committal proceedings. However, we need to consider very carefully indeed whether we should bring McNamara, Forrest and Kent into the arena next time. And the postmistress, come to that.

"Mr Reynolds will have a serious discussion with you, a week or so before the trial starts." Egerton cleared his throat. He knew his next remark would not be well-received. "This morning you saw how two witnesses you expected to help you were called to give evidence against you. You must brace yourself for the possibility of the Crown also calling McNamara, Forrest, and Kent – as witnesses for the prosecution. You need to appreciate that, and give it some thought."

Whitaker said nothing. After his lawyer left, he was taken back to a remand prison cell and did indeed start to think.

In his heart he knew his solicitor was right. Two of the witnesses expected to back his story had actually done their best to destroy it. He'd seen the other two come into court later, when it must have been decided they didn't need to go into the witness box. The inference was clear – all four would testify against him.

The witness list also included three hotel employees. It seemed they would say how he could have slipped out of the hotel.

But surely all such evidence was circumstantial? The overwhelming threat to his alibi was Dulcie's wretched book. Could he rely on Reynolds to get the thing thrown out at the trial? If not, what could he himself do to discredit it?

And what exactly did Egerton mean about 'giving thought' to the prosecution calling McNamara and company? If his alibi failed – as it surely must if the log book was allowed in evidence – and the patsies weren't to be called as possible murderers, what was left?

Whitaker shivered. For the very first time he allowed the prospect of being convicted to cross his mind.

CHAPTER 25

As forecast, Mr Justice Urquhart was to preside at Salisbury. He had decided to deal with two other matters on the opening day of the Assizes, and a starting date for Rex v Whitaker was set for the third day. A duration of five days was provisionally allowed.

A month earlier, having received the news about Urquhart, Malcolm Livesey called a meeting in his Holborn chambers. Frith, Bryce, and Grady all attended.

"I didn't expect to be involved today, Livesey," said Bryce.

"I'm not interviewing you as a witness of course – nor even discussing your own evidence. But I hardly think the Bar Council could object if Frith and I avail ourselves of your advice on other matters, to supplement that from Grady here."

Knowing Livesey was a bencher of his Inn, and also a member of the Bar Council, Bryce privately thought the chance of anyone raising an ethical objection was vanishingly small.

"How many barrister police officers are there in the country, Bryce?" asked Livesey. "You must be pretty well unique!"

"Not unique," replied Bryce. There's a detective superintendent in Yorkshire – but he read for the bar while serving as a police officer. There's an inspector in the Met who followed a similar route to me, and will go far – but he wishes to remain in the uniformed branch. There must be a handful of others around the country. After all, being a non-practising barrister is a good way of getting on in other fields – as a member of Parliament for a start. And there are certainly several other Met officers who have law degrees, but haven't read for the bar or for the Law Society exams."

"Ah well," said Frith, "your decision to leave the bar has probably helped me; if you'd remained, it might be your name on this brief rather than mine!"

Everyone laughed, and Livesey called the meeting to order.

"There are a number of decisions to be made, gentlemen. I make it clear that those decisions will be mine, and whatever the outcome of the case I'll be responsible for them. However, I confess to being in some doubt, and the combined experience of you three fellows will be helpful."

There was a muttering of agreement from the others.

The four men spent the next two hours discussing the case – its weaknesses and pitfalls.

The bulk of the time was given to discussing which witnesses to warn, and provisionally which ones to call. How best to use the expert witnesses was also given close consideration.

"I've come across the soil analyst, George Burton, before," said Frith. "He's a very experienced scientist, and authoritative in the witness box."

"I've also met him, and I agree he presents very well," said Bryce. "Reading his report, it seems pretty clear – the trace residues he mentions could only have come from certain Scotch whiskies – including the variety Cole says Whitaker was drinking. No doubt Reynolds will press hard to debunk that interpretation, but Burton will be able to withstand cross-examination.

"The more difficult job won't be Burton's, though – it'll be yours, Livesey. You'll need to overcome Reynolds' inevitable and quite reasonable suggestion that even if there are traces of whisky in the soil, there's no evidence to show the defendant put it there."

The performance of the handwriting expert, Bailey, was raised by Frith. "I've seen him in court several times, and of course he's truly independent, happy to work on either side of the fence. He also performs competently in court, despite usually being faced with cynicism from judges and opposing barristers regarding his trade."

"Very true," agreed Bryce. "Even if graphology doesn't have a universal seal of approval, it's been around as a field of study for a very long time; Bailey's a crucial witness for us. I don't see how Reynolds can challenge the cheque's status – Whitaker himself told us it was a forgery. So Bailey won't need to say much on that. But he will say the signature and other writing on the cheque definitely wasn't Kent's – and could have been Whitaker's. Reynolds will have to destroy Bailey's evidence in cross-examination, and probably also produce his own expert.

"Also, of course, it's absolutely essential for Bailey to nail the fact that all the log book entries were made by Mrs Whitaker."

"Agreed," said Grady. "I do worry, though, what argument the defence might offer as to why the whole book should be inadmissible. The examining magistrates said it was a matter for the trial court, but in reality the solicitor never actually put forward his case on the matter."

"Yes," agreed Frith. "It was a very half-hearted attempt, which was never going to succeed in that forum. We'll have to wait and see what they try and spring at trial. However, I'm blessed if I can see how they can ambush us. My call is Urquhart will rule the log book admissible."

Livesey looked pleased at this. "These four people who attended the symposium. You've seen two of them in the box, Frith – opinion?"

"Both excellent. Highly educated, intelligent people. Came across very well in the box, although neither faced cross-examination. I didn't interview them beforehand, of course, and I haven't spoken to the other two, but Grady tells me they are equally erudite and articulate."

"I spoke to all four after the committal, and I agree," added Bryce. "Mrs French was particularly incensed about being 'used' by Whitaker, and told me I have to hang him myself!"

"A barrister-executioner really would be a first," laughed Livesey. "Very well. We go with all four. Although if the first two or three pass muster, we can always shorten the list.

"What else do we need to consider?"

"As yet, the defence hasn't made any noises about the possibility of pleading insanity," said Grady. If they do, we'll need to get a really good man to examine him beforehand, and something from the prison medical officer too. In fact, I think I'll arrange something now, rather than wait for the other side. Can't do any harm."

The others nodded.

"Reynolds will have a job pushing for that verdict," remarked Frith. "Unless complex planning and ruthless cunning imply insanity."

Bryce smiled at the suggestion.

"Very well, gentlemen," said Livesey, "that seems to be all for today. Frith and I will deal with the other preliminary matters, order of witnesses, and so on. When we know what witnesses Reynolds is going to call, we'll also decide which of us will be cross-examining them."

"Actually," interjected Bryce, "I'm prepared to have a modest bet – if he calls any witnesses at all, they'll be handwriting or psychiatric specialists."

"You don't think he'll put his client in the box, then?" queried Livesey.

"Not voluntarily, no. I've interviewed Whitaker, and I assume Reynolds has done so too, by now. He must realise that his client would be sufficiently arrogant to think he could outwit you, Livesey, in an oral argument – just as he thought he could outwit the police. I think Reynolds will worry."

"I take your point. Of course, he doesn't have to decide until we close our case. I have to say that I hope he does call his client. I'll enjoy drafting my cross-examination anyway, in case it's needed!"

Bryce grinned. "I wonder if Reynolds follows Marshall Hall's practice of giving his client a written note with *'I wish to give evidence'* and *'I do not wish to give evidence'* – and inviting the client to return the slip with one option struck out."

Livesey smiled. "I don't do defence work these days, but I always gave defendants the choice as to whether they wanted to take the stand. Not quite so formally as Hall, though; all mine ever got was an oral question!"

CHAPTER 26

A few days later, Reynolds and Egerton met at Whitaker's prison and held a similar exchange of professional opinions whilst waiting to be escorted to an interview room.

"This has to be said, Egerton," remarked the barrister, "possible defences are thin on the ground. Some tricky decisions must be made."

"Indeed," replied Egerton. "Will you let him make them?"

"May not have much choice, old chap. Even if I can get the judge to throw out the wife's log book – and I'm not at all confident about that – his hotel alibi has more holes than the proverbial sieve.

"As for his three alternative killers, I'll admit to you, privately, that they were produced far too conveniently. I gather the police have looked into all of them thoroughly, war records included, and not found anything against even one. All three are on the prosecution's warned list already, you know."

"Yes, and the handwriting expert I consulted is of no use," said the solicitor. "Bailey's statement says the writing on the forged cheque is 'more likely than not' Whitaker's, and my expert wasn't prepared to give a contrary opinion. Hopeless to call him."

Reynolds made no response to this depressing news.

"Will you call Whitaker?" asked Egerton.

"God knows," replied the barrister. "Given his academic lecturer background, he should make an excellent witness, capable of standing up to tough cross-examination.

"On the other hand, how would he come across on the stand? And what evidence could he give anyway? By the time he gets in the box, a string of what he thought were his alibi witnesses will have just about destroyed the alibi. If he tried to stick to the alibi it would come down to a dispute between him on the one side and four eminently respectable people on the other – not to mention his wife's log book. Not good odds."

"I suppose our client hasn't suggested any other witnesses?" asked Reynolds, hopefully.

Egerton shook his head. "No. Not even a character witness. He seems a singularly friendless individual."

A warder arrived to escort them. Both men looked unhappy – and not only because of the depressing surroundings.

For Whitaker's benefit, though, Reynolds switched on a smile as he greeted his client.

"How are you keeping, old boy?" he enquired.

"Damn silly question," retorted Whitaker. "The bed – if you can call it that – is uncomfortable, the food is rotten, there's nobody of intelligence to talk to, and there's nothing to do. I expect you two to get me out of here!"

There being no answer to this tirade, Reynolds didn't attempt one. Instead, he asked if Whitaker had given thought to the problems outlined at their last meeting.

"Yes, of course – not much else to think about," replied Whitaker ungraciously. "But what's to decide? Whatever those liars at the hotel are saying, I was too drunk to drive at the time. And all you have to prove is that one or other of McNamara, Forrest or Kent, killed Dulcie. Probably Kent, even though at least he wasn't having an affair like the other two reptiles."

Reynolds sighed silently. Egerton, not for the first time, rued the moment he agreed to represent this obnoxious client.

"Well, Dr Whitaker," said the barrister, "I think it's time we spelled out a few blunt facts. You can take them or leave them, as you wish.

"First, no one can get you out of here before your trial. That's simply how it is with a charge of murder.

"Second, the four witnesses from the hotel – and you saw two of them at the committal hearing – will not support your contention of being drunk.

"Third, your late wife's log book will destroy whatever possibility might remain about your alibi, unless at this late stage you can put forward some convincing reason for the one-hundred-and-twenty-mile discrepancy. I shall obviously try to have the document ruled inadmissible, as Egerton did earlier, but I have no legal grounds, and therefore no real hope of succeeding.

"Fourth, the prosecution will certainly call one of your own suspects to give evidence against you, and may call all three. The clear inference is that the police have checked them, and ruled them out. We'll come back to this in a minute.

"Fifth, you said Mr Kent forged your wife's signature on a cheque. The cheque was paid in at a small post office away from the town centre. You refused to take part in an identification parade, at which the postmistress accepting the cheque would have been asked if she recognised you. The Crown will undoubtedly say that you were the man who paid in the cheque, and were frightened in case she picked you out. They will also say that the forger was quite probably you yourself.

"Sixth, the Kents have put forward a very credible story as to how you could have taken, and later returned, Mr Kent's post office book. Circumstantial evidence only, of course. But, like the position of your hotel room being – the Crown will say – conveniently close to an unlocked back door, it all accumulates in the mind of the jurors.

"Finally, there is the matter of the weapon used to shoot your wife. The prosecution has done a lot of digging. They will be able to prove you were issued with a service revolver, of the right calibre, at the beginning of the war. They also intend to show that when you were transferred, the army more-or-less forgot about you. They will suggest that at the end of the war, you did what it seems many other officers did, and retained your revolver. There is no evidence for that – but no evidence to show it was handed in, either. At the very least, your war record shows you knew how to handle such a weapon."

Reynolds paused. Egerton, who thought the barrister had painted the damning but necessary picture very well, waited for another outburst. It wasn't long in coming.

Whitaker stood up and started shouting. "You think I did it and you've given up! You're useless. You're supposed to get me acquitted, not cave in to all these lying witnesses and corrupt coppers!"

He ranted on in the same vein for a full minute. The two lawyers sat impassively. When at last he subsided, and sat down again, Reynolds spoke:

"What we think doesn't matter in the

least. At the end of the day, the only relevant thing is what the twelve jurors believe.

"My job is to do the very best for you at trial. And, with due modesty, I'm considered one of the finest advocates in my field.

"I've explained all these points because it is absolutely essential for you to appreciate the strength of the case being put up against you – and indeed the inherent weaknesses in what you have given us so far. I can't emphasise that too much.

"Now, you must tell us how you want to proceed. Do you want to continue with your alibi?"

"Yes, of course I do. It's too late to change direction at this stage!"

The lawyers said nothing, but both noted that the remark hardly proclaimed 'it's a genuine alibi'.

Egerton made a note.

"Okay, then," continued Reynolds. What about McNamara, Forrest, and Kent; do you still want to float any or all of them as possible murderers?"

Whitaker thought for a moment.

"The more the jury has to choose from the better, I should have thought. On the other hand it might look better to pick one," he said. "Which has the weakest alibi?"

Reynolds barely managed not to groan out loud. "It's not so simple," he replied. "Originally, in interview, you explained how all three had reason to kill your wife – and indeed how you could not have done it yourself. The prosecution will undoubtedly mention all that. You will need to be able to produce a reason why you're backtracking on two of the three. Nor, incidentally, are we in a position to compare the strengths of the alibis."

"Yes, yes; I do see. All right, I want to continue to accuse all three."

Egerton made another note.

"Mr Egerton has recorded that, despite my warning about the strength of the prosecution's case as far as the various witnesses are concerned, you still choose to maintain your original case. So be it.

"Only one matter remains, which I can advise on but only you can decide. Do you wish to go into the witness box and give evidence yourself? Remember that such a course is not compulsory – indeed not long ago a defendant wasn't even allowed to do so."

"Of course I want to say my piece. But what's your advice, then?"

Reynolds hesitated.

"Where the prosecution has a weak case, and the defence has been able to give a spirited rebuttal through cross-examination and with a number of credible defence witnesses to put forward, it's often the case that the defendant is better off not giving evidence. It's all too common for an arrogant defendant to think he's cleverer than the barrister on the other side, and lose the case all by himself.

"However, we do not have a good case. Moreover, you haven't suggested any witnesses other than those we've mentioned – and none of those are likely to help us.

"So, frankly, appearing yourself may be the better course."

"Then yes, I want to give evidence," said Whitaker resolutely.

"Oh, by the way, the prison medical officer has been talking to me a lot, asking silly questions and making lots of notes. Then yesterday some other doctor arrived, and spent a couple of hours asking me the same sort of questions. I didn't object, because it was something to relieve the boredom. I assume they're looking to see if I'm insane, aren't they?"

Reynolds and Egerton avoided glancing at each other.

"Well, I rather think it's the reverse," replied Reynolds. "I think the prosecution is pre-empting any move by us to argue that you didn't know what you were doing, or that it was wrong."

The lawyers expected another furious outburst, but this time it didn't come. Instead, Whitaker sat looking at the table.

Eventually, he spoke calmly for the first time. "I suppose you'll have to consider presenting that argument, and get another expert in to look at me."

"Stop there!" commanded Reynolds. "The only way that can be done is if you were to admit killing your wife – and you must not tell us such a thing. If you were to do so, I could not present the defence you have given us. I hope you understand what I'm saying."

Whitaker nodded.

****

The lawyers stood outside the prison and again exchanged opinions.

"I'm not sure whether to laugh or cry, Egerton," said Reynolds. "I'm beginning to dread the thought of our man under cross-examination by someone like Livesey."

Egerton nodded. "Quite. Whether or not he's guilty, saying he wants to stick to the alibi simply because he can't change direction now – that's hard to take.

"Anyway, assuming he doesn't change his instructions, do you want me to investigate anything else? I could find some of the other symposium delegates, for instance?"

"No point, I think," said Reynolds. "He admits he stayed dry before and during dinner, and we already have all the witnesses for the period afterwards. So anyone else could only confirm what he himself has, perhaps foolishly, already stated."

"What about an independent analyst to look at the soil sample?"

"Again, I think not. Burton is unquestionably the best in the business, and nobody we might find would be likely to persuade a jury he's wrong. No, the only thing to do there is try to get the evidence excluded. The default position is to hammer home the undoubted fact that there isn't a shred of evidence to attribute the whisky to Whitaker."

"Have you changed your mind about my seeing the postmistress?"

"No. It's a tricky one, but I simply daren't call her. Even if we got Kent into court somehow, and got her to identify him, I think she'd alter her testimony as soon as Livesey suggested there was someone else in the room who fitted the bill. Mind you, I don't think the Crown will call her either. No, best leave her be."

"We have to fight every inch, naturally, but his remark about getting our own psychiatrist to examine him doesn't exactly suggest he himself is very confident! Oh dear, oh dear."

"Can I give you a lift to the station?" asked Egerton.

"No, thanks; it's only a short walk, and I really need the exercise. You'll see Whitaker a couple of times a week, I suppose – let me know if he says anything useful."

CHAPTER 27

A little over three months after the murder, Bryce and Haig travelled to Salisbury by train, on the day before the trial. Their mutual interest in railway history inevitably sparked a discussion about the awful accident at Salisbury station in 1906, when twenty-eight people died as a boat train was derailed at the eastern end of the station.

"Never been proved what caused it," remarked Haig. "Far too fast on the curve, of course, but why? I don't buy the theory about some rich American bribing the driver to get into Waterloo early. There's no evidence that the new driver coming on at Templecombe ever spoke to a passenger – they'd all have been asleep, for a start."

"Agreed, Alex. What seems odd to me, over forty years later, is that no post mortem was ever held on the driver or fireman. It's all very well theorists later suggesting one of them suffered a heart attack, and while attending to him the other didn't realise where they were – there's no evidence for such a thing either.

"But the speed was certainly in excess of seventy, on a curve with a limit of thirty – since then reduced to fifteen, and in fact today all east-west trains are required to stop at the station anyway."

"I tend to support the theory that a contributing factor was the new Great Western cut-off line through Castle Cary, which would have made the London and South Western's boat train route less competitive. It seems a strange coincidence that the cut-off was completed the very next day, knocking about twenty miles off the GWR route."

"Aye, I'm with you there, guv – and the LSWR Plymouth boat trains stopped running not that long afterwards, so the GWR won.

"Another odd thing," he continued, "is the arrangement for changing engines and crews at Templecombe. I've often wondered why they didn't go on a few more miles and change at Salisbury – so eliminating any risk of speeding on the curve."

"True," replied Bryce, "but there's quite a nasty rising gradient on the east side of Salisbury. I know stopping trains have to get up the bank from a standing start, and having to restart a heavy boat train might have involved quite a struggle back then. Maybe they'd have to put on a more powerful locomotive, or provide a banking engine."

"A lot of bravery shown by many people

that night, guv. Nowadays the fireman of the stationary engine the boat train crashed into would have got a George Medal at least. Not a nice way to go, scalded with the boiling water from your own engine, but still trying to help others."

The officers were silent, each thinking of another fireman, blown up during the recent war when his own munitions train exploded, and posthumously awarded the George Cross – the highest possible civilian award for bravery.

At Salisbury, they were met by a beaming DC Lomax, who had also arrived by train, in his case from the north rather than the east.

"Let's get to our hotel, gentlemen," said Bryce. "Then we'll have a bite to eat, after which I have a meeting with Mr Grady. I suggest you two go along to the Guildhall – it's in the market place. Go into court to observe for an hour or so. You in particular, Lomax, need to see what happens – the proceedings and the whole atmosphere will be quite different from a magistrates' court or even quarter sessions."

The hotel, selected for them by Grady, was rather better than Bryce anticipated – and a great deal better than Haig and Lomax expected. The lunch was more than adequate, and Bryce suggested they dine there in the evening.

In answer to a question from Lomax, Bryce said he expected the trial to last at least four days.

"There's the three of us, four conference

delegates, the pathologist, the Kents, and the experts Bailey and Burton. I reckon that's two full days, allowing for cross-examination.

"Then there's three members of the hotel staff – say an hour between them.

"After all those, we have the big unknown. If either Livesey or Reynolds decides to call Forrest and McNamara, then the best part of another day is gone.

"However, there don't seem to be any more defence witnesses, so I can't see this going beyond a fourth day. Frankly, I'm worried that Reynolds has something up his sleeve."

"But that's not your concern, sir, surely?" suggested Lomax.

"Quite true, strictly speaking," agreed Bryce. But a detective's reputation is built on winning cases – as you'll discover soon enough. If a defendant is acquitted, when I'm sure he's guilty, then that would normally reflect badly on me – chances are I haven't provided evidence to plug some loophole. A couple of losses in high-profile cases, and bang go your promotion prospects!"

"Not always the detective's fault, though, is it sir," said Haig. "What about those two cases a few months ago – one where the police surgeon made an error, and the other where the prosecuting counsel messed up a winnable case? Nobody could, or would, blame you."

"Perhaps not," replied Bryce, "but it was

fortunate that neither of those cases were high-profile ones. Mud sticks!"

****

Over dinner, Lomax shared his first impressions of the Assize court. Haig and Bryce were familiar with the flummery, and smiled as Lomax enthused about everything.

"It'll get better tomorrow morning," promised Bryce. "You'll hear the ancient proclamation about 'His Majesty's Commission for Oyer and Terminer and General Gaol Delivery'!"

"Read about that, guv – wonderful bit of tradition."

"Yes, and of course there's a lot more. You may have noticed a little bunch of flowers in front of the judge. It's called a nosegay. He carries those to ward off the smell – and the risk of catching gaol fever from the defendants in court. Typhus, as we know it now. The nosegay may have helped with the smells, but I doubt if it ever had the slightest effect on the disease. Judges always carry one at the Assizes, though. Another thing judges of the High Court carry is a black cap – actually a simple square piece of black silk.

"Don't forget, Lomax, when giving your evidence, you obviously look at whichever barrister is asking the question. But as far as possible, look towards the judge when you give your answers.

"And remember the correct form of address in this court is 'my lord', or 'your lordship', as appropriate. A judge of the High Court isn't actually a lord – he's given a knighthood on appointment – but it's another piece of tradition."

****

Next morning, the three officers walked the few hundred yards to the courthouse. As they crossed the market place, Bryce admired the outline of the Guildhall they were about to enter. A triglyph frieze supported by six Doric columns formed the entrance portico. Although he had never before visited the city, Bryce had read about the Guildhall, which dated from 1795. A mere hundred and fifty years of history in this building, he thought, but there had been courthouses in this square since the early fourteenth century.

The three policemen sat down outside the courtroom to wait. They were soon joined by the other witnesses – all called by the prosecution.

The chief inspector was the only person present who knew all the witnesses (including the two experts with whom he had been involved in previous cases), but he made no attempt to introduce those who didn't already know each other. Consequently, most of the sporadic conversations that took place avoided the subject which had brought them all together. The only reference Bryce made to the case was a remark addressed to everybody, suggesting that some of them might have a very long wait – almost certainly until the next day at least – before being called. This revelation caused a couple of groans, and Mrs French said it was a pity they couldn't spend the time in the court room observing.

"Better hope you're called sooner rather than later, then," said Bryce. "After you've given evidence you'll be able – indeed will be expected – to sit in court."

Inside the court, the judge took his seat. The prisoner was brought up into the dock via a door in the floor, and after confirming his identity was told to sit down.

Unusually, it was Reynolds who stood first.

"My lord, I have an application to make in the absence of the jury, and perhaps it might be more convenient to hear me now, rather than having to send the jury out later."

"Do you know about this, Mr Livesey?" asked the judge.

"I can guess what my friend is going to say, m'lord."

"Very well, Mr Reynolds."

Reynolds addressed the judge. "In due course, my friend is going to refer to what we might call a log book, containing records of mileage readings allegedly made by the deceased, and referring to the defendant's car. He will seek to produce this book as evidence. My application is that the production of this book should not be allowed, nor should there be any reference to it. The relevant reading may not have been made by my client's wife; it may not have been an accurate reading when it was made, and indeed we do not know exactly when it was made. It is unfairly prejudicial to my client, and I ask you to exclude it, my lord."

"What do you say, Mr Livesey?"

"We shall be calling expert evidence to show Mrs Whitaker was the sole writer. We shall show how the last recorded reading fits in with the recent and known journeys of the vehicle. We shall also call evidence to show the mileage reading on the car after the defendant's return. The discrepancy will demonstrate that the defendant's statement about distances travelled in the critical period is unambiguously untrue.

"As your lordship is aware, all relevant documentary evidence properly obtained is admissible. This document quite clearly relates to the facts of the case. It was, I need hardly say, properly obtained, and my friend doesn't suggest otherwise. I confess that I don't see on what grounds my friend seeks to bar it, and I ask you to allow it."

"Well, Mr Reynolds," said the judge, "I assume you are acting on instructions. If the courts were to bar the admission of evidence simply because it was prejudicial to a defendant,

I really don't know where we should be. The application is refused."

Whitaker's expression was furious, but he managed to contain himself and say nothing.

A jury was brought in, and sworn. The judge said a few words to them, and then motioned to the prosecuting counsel.

Livesey rose to inform the judge (actually to inform the jury and public, as the judge was already aware) that he and Frith appeared for the Crown, and Reynolds for the defendant.

The clerk told Whitaker to stand.

"You are charged that between the 17th and 18th of October this year, you did feloniously and with malice aforethought kill and slay Dulcie Mary Weston Whitaker. How say you – are you guilty or not guilty?"

Whitaker firmly announced "Not guilty" and was told to sit down again.

Livesey opened the case for the prosecution. His voice was neither loud nor hectoring, but mellow and well-modulated. He made clear statements which he said would be backed up with evidence later. He used words and phrases which the members of the jury, whatever their background, could follow.

First, he explained to the jury that it was the defendant's own wife whom he was charged with murdering, in the early hours of the morning. "You will hear from the police surgeon regarding the time and cause of death."

After telling the jury that police officers would give evidence about the defendant's suggestions of three alternative killers, Livesey continued:

"The senior Scotland Yard detective and his colleagues looked very carefully into the defendant's suggestions. You will hear the results of those investigations from the officers concerned. The Crown does not propose to call two of those men, both supposedly having affairs. Suffice it to say that the police are satisfied that neither is guilty of any criminal matter. Although their names will inevitably emerge, we see no necessity for them to be further embarrassed here. My learned friend may of course choose to call them himself."

(Every listener could infer from Livesey's words – and his tone – that he thought it would be sheer folly for his friend to do any such thing.)

"But we shall call the third person named by the defendant. You will hear from this man and his wife – and from an expert witness – how the defendant's allegation is totally untrue."

"Livesey then explained which other witnesses would be called for the Crown, and gave an outline of what each would say.

"I am near the end of my opening, ladies and gentlemen, but there is one more crucial piece of evidence.

"Officers will describe the finding of a book, detailing the journeys made in the defendant's car. You will learn how this record was made by the victim, with the last entry being made on the afternoon before she was killed.

"You will hear how this simple document destroys the defendant's claim about his own movements around the time of the murder.

"Finally, ladies and gentlemen, the prosecution is not required to suggest a motive, but we shall do so anyway. Evidence will be brought to show that Mrs Whitaker was very comfortably off indeed – whereas the defendant, having lost two jobs because of the addictions which you will hear about, earned comparatively little and possessed no capital of his own. Money is therefore an obvious motive.

"But perhaps there is more. The log book shows how Mrs Whitaker kept tabs, shall we say, on her husband. You will also hear that, in interview, the defendant said that she did not permit him to consume alcohol, either inside or outside the house. You may think that he wanted to escape what he thought was her tyranny, and become master in his own home.

"You will also hear a little more about Mrs Whitaker's affair with another man. The defendant stated in interview that he knew about the affair, but told the police it was in his interest not to let his wife know he knew. You may come to a different conclusion – perhaps he was beset with jealousy, and killed his wife for making him a cuckold.

"But regardless of possible motives, the facts of the case will speak for themselves. When you have heard all of the evidence for the Crown, there can be no doubt as to your verdict – that the defendant deliberately shot his wife in cold blood.

"I call Dr Robert Lazenby."

CHAPTER 28

After the police surgeon finished giving his short but rather harrowing evidence, the trial progressed steadily. Dulcie's two friends followed the doctor, and then the DCI took the stand. He spent almost an hour in the witness box, but to the surprise of most in the court, Reynolds did not rise to cross-examine. Sergeant Haig's evidence also went unchallenged – to the barely concealed fury of the defendant.

The judge looked at the clock – it was now a little after twelve thirty – and observed to Mr Reynolds that Dr Whitaker seemed to wish to speak to his legal advisors. "It would seem a convenient time to break for lunch. "We'll reconvene at two o'clock," he decreed.

Reynolds, who along with Livesey and Frith had been expecting an invitation to lunch in the judge's lodgings (a fairly palatial establishment, infrequently occupied), resigned himself to a less pleasant lunchtime venue. As too did the prosecuting barristers, as they couldn't expect an invitation in the absence of the defence.

In the cells there was a blazing row. Whitaker ranted about the failure to exclude the logbook, and about the lack of challenge on everything said by Bryce and Haig.

Egerton asked Whitaker which specific bits of the evidence so far he thought should have been challenged.

"Nothing in particular, but as much as possible, so it doesn't look as if everything they say is gospel!"

Whitaker paced around restlessly.

"I followed your instruction regarding the logbook," said Reynolds, "although I was fully aware there was no hope of excluding it. Indeed, you may have noted the judge's remark about assuming I was following instructions?"

Whitaker nodded curtly.

"The judge was letting me – and the rest of the court – know that he realised I should never have made such a frivolous application on my own initiative.

"You employed me to do my best for you, and I've been doing so. But I must use my professional judgement at each step regarding how, and indeed whether, to cross-examine witnesses. I saw no point in questioning irrefutable facts."

Whitaker wasn't impressed, and continued to scowl and swear.

A short silence followed, after which he suddenly announced, "I'm dismissing you both. I can do as well or better on my own. You'd better go and tell the old fool in court."

"On your own head be it, Dr Whitaker," replied Reynolds evenly, betraying no hint of his feelings. "Nevertheless, and I continue to represent your best interests here, it might be better if I don't repeat your description of the judge to him. But I will indeed pass on your decision."

The two lawyers returned to the courtroom. The judge had, as they thought, left the building. They decided to snatch a quick lunch.

Returning half an hour later, Reynolds found the court clerk, and asked him not to call up the prisoner, and not to bring the jury back into court, until he was able to address the judge.

At two o'clock Urquhart took his seat again, and Reynolds made his announcement.

"My lord, I have to inform you that the defendant has dispensed with my services – and also those of my instructing solicitor. He believes he can do as well or better himself. I would concede that this case contains no legal complexities, and certainly he is an extremely able man, but you might still think he is unwise."

Reynolds sat down.

"What do you say, Mr Livesey?" asked the judge.

"Aside from sympathising with my friend and his solicitor, I express no view on the matter."

"No. Well, this is a fine kettle of fish. I can't think of a precedent in a capital case. I think I'd better have him up, still in the absence of the jury. Stay where you are for the moment, Mr Reynolds, if you please."

Urquhart signalled to the clerk, and Whitaker was brought back into the dock.

"Your counsel informs me you have dismissed him, and that you wish to continue the trial without his services. Is this correct?" asked the judge.

"It is," replied Whitaker. "I couldn't do any worse."

"In your opinion, Dr Whitaker. Perhaps, though, you have heard the old adage, 'a man who is his own lawyer has a fool for his client'?"

"It's new to me, my lord; but it sounds like an advertising slogan coined by a lawyer drumming up business for himself and his associates!"

Mr Justice Urquhart gave a thin-lipped smile. "The origins of the expression, probably going back to the Middle Ages, are lost in time, Dr Whitaker, but it does seem Abraham Lincoln used it, and he was a lawyer. Many lawyers have quoted it since then – including me now.

"You are of course perfectly entitled to represent yourself. But be warned of this. You have been represented up to now by one of the ablest young barristers in the land. If you decide to dispense with him, your decision will be irrevocable."

Urquhart's tone was as grave as his expression. "If for any reason you decide later to change your mind, under no circumstances will I agree to abort this trial and allow you to restart with new counsel. What do you want to do?"

"I shall manage on my own," replied Whitaker stubbornly.

Reynolds sighed. He stood, hitched his gown up onto his shoulders, and bowed to the bench. With his table top cleared and everything already safely stowed in his briefcase, he limped out of court, followed closely by Egerton.

"You can have as much paper as you need, Dr Whitaker, and pencils and so on. If a witness is going too fast, you may ask me to slow him or her down, so you can take whatever notes you need. The courts make every allowance for someone conducting his own defence. Nevertheless, you are expected to follow procedures."

Urquhart quickly outlined how Whitaker should behave, and then called for the jury to be brought back.

"Ladies and gentlemen, Dr Whitaker has decided to continue with his trial without the assistance of his lawyers. That is his decision alone. It is also his absolute right. You must not speculate on his reasons for making the decision – it has nothing whatsoever to do with your coming eventually to a verdict. Let us continue."

Detective Constable Howard Lomax was called, and sworn in.

Frith carried out the examination in chief. Livesey, seated beside him, took no active part.

Although nervous initially, Lomax gave his evidence effectively, Whitaker making no objections.

When Frith finished, the judge thanked him.

"Dr Whitaker, this is your opportunity to ask your own questions of this witness. Stand up, and carry on."

Belatedly, Whitaker realised he didn't have the least idea about how to cross-examine. The courtroom waited. After what seemed like an eternity, he blurted out a question. "How do you know the entries in the book were made by my wife?"

Frith was about to jump to his feet to object, and the judge was minded to rule the question out of order anyway, but Lomax, quick as lightning, forestalled them both. "I don't," he replied. "It's not for me to say. I understand another witness will give evidence to say who made the entries. When I found the book I was entitled to make a reasonable assumption about its origin. Based on my assumption, I went to your house to see what the reading was in your car."

'Nicely done, Lomax!' thought Bryce to

himself.

"But you can't possibly say the figures in the book are genuine," persevered Whitaker.

"Depends on what you mean by 'genuine'," replied Lomax, displaying great acumen. "Those are real numbers written in the book. The last entry was made by your wife recording her shopping and lunch trip very shortly before you drove the car to Bristol. You told me you hadn't driven anywhere after you came back from Bristol. But when I read the odometer it was clear to me that your car had travelled about a hundred and twenty miles further than you say it did – which would be the same as an extra round trip between Bristol and your home."

With some difficulty, Bryce resisted the urge to smile. The young detective had, most articulately, delivered a damaging blow to Whitaker. Reynolds would never have given Lomax the leeway to get that lot in!

The judge was having identical thoughts, but for the time being decided against suggesting that the defendant should change his line of attack.

Whitaker realised he was losing the skirmish, and changed tack anyway.

"You say you went to the central post office with the forged cheque, and you learned it was paid in at another post office in the city. You've said nothing about that. This matter never came up at the hearing in the magistrates' court. Did you go to this other post office?"

"Yes. I spoke to the postmistress who accepted the forged cheque. She gave a rough description of the man who paid it in."

"Did that description fit Geoffrey Kent?"

"It could have done," replied Lomax, "but it could equally well have fitted you!"

This was almost too much for Bryce and Haig, both finding it difficult to stop themselves from chortling out loud. Livesey and Frith could also hardly believe the extent to which the defendant was making his already bad case even worse.

Whitaker blundered on regardless. "Are you going to call this woman as a witness?"

"It's not for me to say; I don't make the big decisions. But when I offered your solicitor the chance for you to appear in an identification parade in front of her, he turned it down because you told him to."

The prosecuting barristers were delighted. No need to find a way to put in this piece of evidence after all – the defendant had done it for them!

Whitaker scowled at Lomax. Understanding he wasn't helping himself, he sat down abruptly.

"Any re-examination, Mr Frith?" asked the judge.

With a lightness of tone which fully conveyed his underlying meaning, the junior barrister replied, "I think it would be impossible for me to adduce anything more useful from this witness than the court has already heard, my lord. I'd like to call Reginald Bailey."

The renowned handwriting expert was sworn in, and gave the court details of his qualifications and experience.

Before Frith could ask his first question, the judge intervened.

"Dr Whitaker, Mr Bailey is put forward by the Crown as an 'expert witness'. That means he is able to give his opinion on matters within his field of expertise – unlike other witnesses who are only allowed to testify as to facts known to themselves. At this stage, you have the right to challenge Mr Bailey's expertise. If you don't, or if your challenge is unsuccessful, then when Mr Bailey has given his evidence you will still be able to question him on his findings."

"I can't challenge his expertise, my lord," replied Whitaker.

"Very wise," muttered Livesey *sotto voce* to Frith, "given he's the world's foremost authority!"

Frith took Bailey through his evidence. The expert, an old hand in the box, avoided technicalities as far as possible. His evidence showed that, in his opinion, the cheque was a forgery, most likely written and signed by the defendant. He firmly stated that the cheque was not written or signed by Geoffrey Kent; and that the log book was entirely written by Dulcie Whitaker without any amendments.

"Now, Dr Whitaker," said the judge when Frith sat down, "Do you wish to dispute any of Mr Bailey's findings? If you do, remember you can only do so by asking him questions of your own."

Whitaker was almost panicking. He fully understood the importance of the handwriting expert's evidence. He knew it was damning, because of course Bailey's opinion was nothing less than the truth. It was hardly surprising that no question sprang to his mind with which to attack the veracity of the testimony. He sat numb and silent for a while, then shook his head.

Mr Justice Urquhart felt uncomfortable. This situation was unprecedented in his experience. All eyes in the courtroom were upon him, those of the legal professionals particularly curious as to what he would do. After a moment's hesitation, he asked the jury to retire while a legal matter was discussed. When the door closed behind them, the judge leaned forward.

"Dr Whitaker, you made the decision to dispense with your learned counsel. You are representing yourself. I don't dispute that you are an intelligent and highly educated man. But, as far as I know, you have no experience whatsoever in cross-examination.

"The Crown has produced a witness who has – and you should note my bluntness – been very damaging to your cause. If you do not succeed in breaking down his evidence, the jury is entitled to take everything he said as fact. It doesn't bode well for you."

"I understand, my lord," muttered Whitaker dully. "But I don't believe my lawyer could have done any better, and I'll stick as I am. When I get in the witness box myself, the jury will believe me."

"As you wish, Dr Whitaker.

"Thank you, Mr Bailey, you may step down." Signalling to the usher the judge said "Let's have the jury back, please."

Geoffrey Kent was the next witness, and was followed by his wife. Frith took both through their evidence very quickly, repeating for the benefit of the jury Bailey's evidence – that Kent was not the forger – and that this expert opinion had not been challenged by the defendant.

Whitaker studiously avoided looking at the Kents while they were in the witness box, and declined to cross-examine either of them.

Livesey rose. "My lord, we now propose to call seven witnesses regarding the alibi which the defendant put forward in interview. Looking at the clock, perhaps you might prefer to adjourn now, so all seven can be heard on the same day."

"Yes; I suppose we'd only have time for one more witness today. Very well, we'll adjourn. Be back here at ten o'clock tomorrow, members of the jury."

CHAPTER 29

Sitting in his cell, Whitaker reviewed his position. Even after hearing the evidence given in the committal proceedings, he had still convinced himself all would be fine at trial. He would have his day in court. He would be believed. The full extent of the danger he was facing only really began to sink in when he listened to the opening address by the Crown's barrister. But it was the judge's observation that matters did not 'bode well' for him, which enabled him to realise a fresh strategy was essential, before it was too late. Unlike his first plan, evolved and honed over months, there was now very little time.

He'd seen and heard more than enough already to realise it would be a waste of time to try and break down any of the witnesses who were yet to be called. In all probability, such a move would only reinforce the idea of his guilt in the jurors' minds.

No – what was required was an all-out attempt to get sympathy from those twelve unprepossessing people who held his life in their hands. He must continue to appear helpless – defenceless – against the might of the criminal justice machine. He must expose the injustice of his situation: one little man of the people; unfairly pitted against two heavyweight barristers, a solicitor, and three police officers. He must make the jurors realise he was being put through a travesty!

Feeling a surge of relief now he had some sort of substitute plan, Whitaker sat back in his cell and waited to be taken back to prison. But by the time the van arrived he was already picking holes in his newly-formed strategy. The wretched judge had spoiled things for him, by emphasising to the jury that it was his own decision to dismiss his lawyers. Worse, they'd even been told to ignore his lack of representation when they eventually considered their decision.

Also, and it was a bit late to think about this, the weight of the evidence against him remained. How much sympathy would be required to overcome it?

The answer seemed to be *far more than he was likely to get*.

It was at this depressing moment that he suddenly remembered one crucial fact – for a conviction, a jury must return a unanimous verdict. So only one juror needed to be sympathetic. Yes, of course! This was his way forward to freedom.

He resolved to look over the jurors in the morning, and select one who might be suitable. When giving his own evidence, and making his closing speech, he could maintain eye contact with his chosen juror, and convert him or her.

He instantly corrected himself. No, no! Not 'her'. A female juror probably wouldn't be very sympathetic in a case involving a dead wife. It must be a man.

While the jurors were being sworn, Whitaker had idly glanced at the seven men and five women. Since then, he hadn't looked towards the jury box once. He belatedly realised this might have been a mistake, and made another resolution. From tomorrow he would look frequently towards the jury, and appear friendly.

Whitaker really didn't have a clue.

Unbeknown to anyone in court, some members of the jury were already strongly against him. Despite the judge's standard exhortation about trying the case based on all the evidence they would hear, and on nothing else, some members believed that further proceedings would be a waste of time.

Three jurors hadn't understood that nothing in Livesey's opening was evidence, and had assimilated everything he had said as if it were proven fact. Unsurprisingly, Whitaker was already convicted in their minds.

Two more jurors were of the view that

if the police arrested and charged someone, he must be guilty. Indeed, just as Whitaker was reviewing his position, one of these two was doing what the judge had warned the jury not to do – discussing the case outside. In his local public house, the juror expounded his view to a small group of close friends – all of whom bolstered his opinion by nodding in agreement.

A sixth juror, after suffering various physical assaults during her own difficult marriage, was adamant that this wife-murderer (as she thought of him) was not going to get away with his crime. She should, of course, not have been empanelled on the jury, and probably, had the United States system of jury selection with *'voir dire'* been used, would not have been.

Another juror practised as a spiritualist, and purported to see a coloured aura around the heads of certain people. She 'saw' a purple aura around Whitaker in the witness box, and immediately interpreted this supposed phenomenon in a very negative way. Worse, she had mentioned this to the juror seated beside her during the lunch break. He, somewhat attracted to this fey lady and thinking to get into her good books in order to meet up after the trial, not only didn't report her nonsense, but improved his prospects with her by suggesting he saw something similar himself.

No fewer than eight jurors were therefore prejudiced against the defendant.

A cynical lawyer, not exactly a *rara avis* in the criminal courts, might think this proportion was perhaps a little higher than normal at this stage in a trial, but certainly not unprecedented.

Whitaker, though, sitting in blissful ignorance of this deplorable situation, could not know that two thirds of his jury had already, at least provisionally, made up their minds.

He was therefore unaware that if he plumped for one of the males to try to get sympathy – a very long shot at the best of times, although he was too full of his own abilities to comprehend this – the odds of finding one of independent mind were already reduced to only three in seven.

In reality, the odds were even worse. There was only one male juror of the possible three with even the smallest degree of empathy for Whitaker. This had nothing to do with the 'little man fighting against the power of the state'. It was solely because this juror suffered at the hands of a genuinely abusive wife. However, although he might empathise with the defendant, he was not the sort of person who would stick his neck out and argue for acquittal if the facts suggested otherwise. In short, he took his oath seriously.

Whitaker was deluding himself – yet again.

CHAPTER 30

When the court convened the following morning, Whitaker was already seated in the dock as the jurors filed in. For the first time, he really looked at them. Attempting to catch a few eyes as they took their seats, he put on what he thought was a friendly smile.

As a ploy, this was disastrous. Two of those in direct receipt of a smile reacted almost in revulsion, as did several others who observed the defendant's attempts. Whitaker failed to notice any adverse reaction, and ranging over the jury made an instant decision – to target an inoffensive looking man near the centre of the front row. With no evidence whatsoever, Whitaker decided that this apparently insignificant little man (he was indeed small) was likely to be sympathetic. He gave the juror a particularly beatific smile.

Had Whitaker been a fly on the wall of the jury room during a break in proceedings later in the morning, he would have been utterly aghast at some of the comments openly bandied about:

"Never looked at us at all yesterday; today

he's grinning at us like a Cheshire Cat".

"What a sickening smile – I preferred it when he looked the other way."

"I do wish he wouldn't grin at me so inanely."

One, rather more perceptive juror, remarked, "he knows we have to decide whether he lives or dies, and he probably thinks if he befriends us it'll make us less likely to convict."

"More fool him!" was the vigorous response from the clairvoyant, accompanied by "hear, hear" from her admirer.

Clearly, the 'smiling' policy was not bearing much fruit. Whitaker's target didn't join in the conversation, but privately raged about the defendant's chutzpah. This juror was, in fact, one of the men who believed that simply being in the dock was sufficient to prove guilt.

Whitaker had got it wrong again.

****

Livesey stood to introduce his next witness. There was no need to call the hotel manager, as in interview the defendant hadn't disputed the location of his room. Instead, the barrister called the night porter.

O'Leary, who was clearly nervous, took the oath. Livesey asked him:

"Is the back door of your hotel regularly left unlocked at night, when the front door is locked?"

The hapless porter, now dreading dismissal, could only confirm that it was.

"Would that be so that guests who chose to do so, could entertain ladies – of one sort or another – in their rooms, and without anyone else being any the wiser?"

The judge considered asking counsel not to lead, but decided to let it go.

"I suppose so, yes."

"Was this arrangement common knowledge in the city?"

Here the judge did step in – as no doubt Reynolds would have done were he still involved:

"No, Mr Livesey, that isn't a question the witness can possibly answer. Rephrase it, if you please."

"Of course, my lord – apologies. Mr O'Leary, for how long had this arrangement been in place?"

"Upwards of ten years."

"Do guests occasionally come to ask you how a prostitute or other lady friend can be admitted?"

O'Leary winced. "From time to time, yes."

"Are such requests made as frequently now as they were in the early days of this, er, arrangement?"

"No, sir, I don't get so many now. The local girls can let their punters know about it," he added guilelessly.

"Thank you, Mr O'Leary. Wait there a

moment; there may be more questions for you."

Whitaker didn't move from his seat.

The judge, after a moment, asked the porter "Have you ever spoken to the defendant – the man in the dock over there?"

"Never even set eyes on him until now, your lordship."

"Thank you, Mr O'Leary, you may step down."

Inevitably, Whitaker wasn't best pleased with the judge's intervention. The given answer was to his advantage, certainly, but if the judge was going to 'help him out' it didn't exactly support his idea of showing how the whole establishment was biased against him. However, there was nothing he could do about it.

Livesey called Professor Hamilton, Mr Harris, Mr Armitage, and Mrs French in turn. All said much the same thing. Yes, they spent time with the defendant that evening. Yes, he had appeared to empty a number of glasses of whisky remarkably quickly. Yes, he seemed to be very much the worse for wear by bedtime. No, they couldn't recall seeing him actually drink anything.

Mrs French, who managed to keep the annoyance she felt for Whitaker out of her voice during her testimony, was asked by Livesey to explain where the defendant had been sitting. In doing so, she described the proximity of large pot plants on either side of his chair. For the jury's benefit, Livesey remarked that a later witness would refer to these pots again.

Whitaker declined to cross examine any of his symposium companions.

Urquhart decided to involve himself again. "The implication the Crown is drawing out here is clear enough, Mrs French. Did you see Dr Whitaker dispose of any drinks into one of these pots?"

"No, my lord; I didn't actually *see* him doing that."

The judge, instead of hearing the simple 'no' he had expected, realised he'd left himself open to Anita French's meaningful supplement and decided it was best not to press further.

After Mrs French, the bartender, Cole, was called. He added little, except to confirm the seating layout, and the brand of whisky – Morven Glen – taken by Whitaker.

At this point, the judge decided to break for lunch. Livesey and Frith, aware that in the absence of a defence representative they could not receive an invitation to the judges' lodgings, again resigned themselves to an inferior meal.

****

Livesey called the analyst, Burton, as first witness in the afternoon. As in the case of Bailey, the witness detailed his qualifications and experience. Whitaker again declined to raise any objection.

"Dr Burton, the jury has heard about a box of soil collected by Detective Sergeant Haig, and labelled exhibit ABH1. Did you receive that box, and if so did you analyse the contents?"

Burton confirmed he had received the exhibit, and that his analysis of the soil sample revealed traces of a number of chemicals which would not be expected in soil, peat or in any other medium in which plants were grown.

The combination of the chemicals found in one of the plant tubs, he stated, could only be explained by the presence of one of a very limited number of Scotch whiskies. He had tested some sixty-three varieties of Scotch whisky, both single malts and blends, and found that in only two did their chemical residue in soil correspond to that found in the hotel sample.

Livesey asked him if Morven Glen was one of the two. Dr Burton confirmed that it was.

Livesey thanked the witness, looked meaningfully at the jury, and sat down.

As Whitaker again declined to cross-examine, the judge felt obliged, in the interests of justice, to make a point in favour of the defence. "Dr Burton, can you say with any certainty for how long these traces might have been present in the soil sample?"

"No, my lord, I cannot. Alcohol, as your lordship will be aware, evaporates very quickly. Possibly over a long period of time these trace chemicals would also fade, but I have no data on the point."

"So you can't say that these traces didn't appear in the soil some significant time before, or even possibly *after,* the defendant's visit to the hotel?"

"That is correct, my lord."

"I'm obliged to you, Dr Burton; thank you."

Livesey contemplated re-examining, but decided against. After all, having given his original statement, Burton had 'come up to proof'. And he really couldn't complain that the judge was asking questions to assist the defence. If Reynolds were still present, he would have made exactly the same points as the judge, and probably a lot more forcefully.

Giving Burton time to leave the stand and return to his seat, Frith rose.

"I call Desmond Aloysius Hargreaves."

The solicitor took the oath, and Frith began. "Mr Hargreaves, please tell the court, as far as this matter is concerned, what your function is."

"I am the late Dulcie Whitaker's executor."

The judge interrupted again. "What is the thrust of this evidence to be, Mr Frith?"

"It goes toward motive, my lord, supporting my leader's remarks in his opening." Frith inclined his head deferentially towards Livesey.

The judge nodded. "Very well."

"I believe you've been valuing Mrs

Whitaker's estate for probate, Mr Hargreaves. Can you give the court the result of your calculations?"

"The work is not yet complete. However, I can say that for probate purposes the value will not be less than three hundred and eighty thousand pounds."

Apart from the press and public shuffling in and out of their seats each day, the courtroom had been a still and quiet place throughout the trial so far. Hearing that figure, a collective intake of breath, followed by animated and astonished comment, rippled around the room, as members of the public turned to the strangers sitting around them and shared their surprise.

Urquhart banged his gavel down hard. Once was sufficient.

"And who benefits under the will, Mr Hargreaves?" continued Frith.

"The sole beneficiary is the widower, Dr Robin Whitaker."

This time the courtroom received the information in total silence.

Frith looked to the dock and to the bench, but no questions were forthcoming from either quarter. Hargreaves stepped down.

Livesey rose. "That, my lord, concludes the case for the Crown."

"Thank you, Mr Livesey."

Urquhart looked towards the dock. "Stand up, please, Dr Whitaker. This is where you take the leading part. First, you need to decide whether you intend to call any witnesses other than yourself. If you do, then you have the right to make an opening speech – as Mr Livesey did for the Crown yesterday. If you have no witnesses to call, then you can only make a closing speech – summing up your case for the jury.

"It is entirely your decision whether you take the witness stand yourself. But remember, after giving your own evidence, one of the prosecuting barristers will cross-examine you on it.

"We will break for fifteen minutes; that will give you some time to think about how you want to proceed."

When the court reconvened, Whitaker remained standing, and addressed Urquhart. "I do not intend to call other witnesses, my lord, but I do wish to give evidence myself."

The judge motioned the dock officers to bring the defendant across the room to the witness box, where he took the oath.

"Thank you, Dr Whitaker. Give your evidence in a clear voice. The stenographer can take down what you say, however fast you speak, but counsel and I also take notes, and we need a bit more time. Carry on."

Unsurprisingly, Whitaker was a good speaker, well-used to addressing packed lecture halls during his academic life. He said his piece without using notes, and stuck rigidly to his original story. He was in Bristol at the time his wife was shot; and far too drunk to have found where he parked his car again, never mind driven it anywhere. The unlocked back door was irrelevant because he hadn't known about it.

He emphasised that producing witnesses who hadn't noticed him drinking was not evidence that he hadn't imbibed, and went on to embellish the point. He asked the jury why anyone should be surprised that, as an alcoholic, he would drink extremely quickly. That, he said, was what alcoholics did – they lacked the restraint to sip and savour. He suggested the jurors should be far more surprised by the ridiculous suggestion that he would throw away good Scotch.

He was scathing about Bailey's evidence, saying he himself remained strongly of the opinion that Kent forged the cheque, and that Kent had the ideal motive for killing Dulcie. As for the 'so-called' expert's opinion that he himself was the forger, Whitaker suggested it proved the incompetence of the witness and the hocus-pocus nature of his sham activity.

Bailey, still in the courtroom, smiled grimly.

Whitaker went on to complain that the police had made no real attempt to check Kent's alibi, nor those of McNamara and Forrest. There were good reasons, he insisted, for either of these men to kill Dulcie. He also made great play of the fact that the prosecution hadn't called either of the two 'adulterers', as he called them.

Livesey and Frith, listening to all this, wondered for how long the judge would allow it to continue.

Almost immediately, Urquhart intervened. "Dr Whitaker, the courts traditionally allow considerable leeway to defendants without legal representation. However, there are limits. You started off in good order, giving your evidence. But the latter part of what you have been saying is a speech – including a lot of unsubstantiated opinion. You will have your chance to make a closing speech later.

"I understand, my lord, and I apologise. It's very hard for me to appreciate the correct procedures of a criminal court – this is the first time I've ever been in one. I hope the members of the jury will understand that I'm simply overwhelmed by the complexity of the process, as well as by the unfairness of the allegations against me, and how I have been treated by the police." He looked piteously towards the jury box as he spoke these last words.

"Damned improper remark," muttered Livesey to his junior. The judge was thinking exactly the same, but decided to let it go.

"In fact, my lord, I think I have finished now." Whitaker turned sad eyes towards the judge. "I apologise again to you, and to the jury, that I am unable to conduct my defence in any way other than as a rank amateur." It was a nice act of contrition by 'the little man', humbly delivered and calculated to win sympathy and approval.

Livesey and Frith whispered together for a moment, before Livesey rose to cross-examine. He looked hard at the defendant without speaking for what seemed like an age, but was in fact only a few seconds.

"Before going to Bristol on the Monday afternoon, you had already planned to kill your wife, isn't that right?"

"No! Nothing of the kind ever entered my mind."

"Really. Well, let's take a look at what we know."

Livesey went through Whitaker's military training and the issue of the Webley. Whitaker easily deflected any suggestion that the gun used to kill Dulcie was his.

In the absence of having the weapon as evidence, there was little more Livesey could say on the subject. Whitaker sensed this, and was heartened. He felt sure that if he could dispose of all other questions in the same way, he must surely be acquitted.

Livesey moved on. "You accused Mr Kent, a friend of yours, of stealing one of your wife's cheques, making it out to himself in the sum of two hundred and fifty pounds, and forging your wife's signature, yes?"

"Yes."

"An expert witness has told the court that you were the likely forger. Why didn't you challenge him on the point?"

"I was flustered, being without counsel by then."

Livesey abruptly changed focus. "You've also complained that the Crown chose not to call two of the three men you accused. But there was nothing to prevent your counsel calling them in your defence – and before you dispensed with your legal representation it seems they didn't call either of them. Earlier this afternoon his lordship asked if you wished to call witnesses. Why didn't you call both of them yourself, even at that late stage?"

Whitaker hesitated. "I didn't think," he replied.

"Let's briefly turn to the matter of paying the cheque into the Flixton Road post office. You were offered the chance to stand in an identification parade. Why did you turn the suggestion down?"

"I should have thought it was obvious. As I didn't pay the cheque in, the woman could not have identified me. But she might have made a mistake. I still say it was Geoffrey Kent who paid it into his own account, and he's not unlike me to look at – as anyone can still see." He pointed across to where Kent was sitting. "So if I had agreed to take part, she might have inadvertently picked me out."

"I see," replied Livesey. "A cynic might suggest that in fact you selected the unfortunate Mr Kent as your dupe, precisely because the two of you might be confused. What do you say to that?"

Whitaker was genuinely annoyed about the suggestion. He hadn't even thought about his resemblance to Kent until after he'd purloined the post office book. He was therefore able to answer with a degree of truthful assertiveness. "It's a figment of your imagination!"

"So you say. Let's turn to the hotel in Bristol. You had, on your own admission in interview, stayed there before. Is that when you learned about the lax security on the back door?"

"I knew nothing about that. I didn't even know there was a back door, although, if I'd thought about it, I suppose I could have surmised there must be one."

Livesey took Whitaker through the early part of the evening and dinner. Again, Whitaker found no difficulty in responding – here, the truth would do.

"After dinner you returned to the lounge with four others – the witnesses we saw earlier. According to your account, this is when you started to drink heavily?"

"Yes. I don't care what anyone said – I drank three or four double Scotches."

"Why were you abstemious before and during the meal, and only started to drink afterwards?"

Whitaker forgot about his original lie about not wishing to muddle the flavours of food and alcohol, but gave a plausible alternative explanation. "I weakened later as I saw others drinking."

He answered the rest of Livesey's questions about his time at the Arden hotel without difficulty, and was almost feeling comfortable in the witness box. The more questions he answered, the more he felt the prosecution would never make a successful case against him.

Livesey again changed focus. What about the two men you described to the police as the 'adulterers' – for how long had you known about Mr Forrest's extra-marital affair?"

"I knew about it four or five weeks before my wife was killed. I discovered it quite by accident."

"And you informed your wife?"

"I did, yes. I told her as soon as I got home – she knew Forrest as well as I did, and was friendly with his wife."

"What was her reaction?"

"Horrified, naturally. She said she would confront him. She said it was unfair on his wife."

"Really?" intoned Livesey, in a voice which conveyed to the rest of the court *'no one should believe this twaddle'.*

"Do you seriously suggest it would be natural for her to be horrified, Dr Whitaker? After all, she was engaged in similar activities herself.

"I suggest it would be far more likely that she would simply shrug her shoulders. You didn't actually tell her anyway, did you? I put it to you that you simply filed this information away in your mind, to be used to offer the police yet another false suspect for use after you carried out your plan to kill your wife."

"That's ridiculous!"

"No, I don't think it is, Dr Whitaker. By your own evidence there was a delay of four or five weeks between your telling your wife, and her being shot. I suggest it's unlikely in the extreme that your wife would wait such a length of time before confronting Mr Forrest. Or, if she *had* confronted him sooner, that *he* would wait several weeks before deciding to eliminate this alleged threat."

Whitaker, fully grasping the logic of Livesey's thrust and also how damaging it was to him, was saved by a sudden burst of inventiveness. "He'd hardly come knocking on the door in the middle of the night while I was at home though, would he? He'd obviously wait until I was out of the way." He turned in semi-triumph towards the jury, feeling sure his rebuttal was unanswerable. Let the prosecution try and poke holes in that!

Livesey pounced. "For once, Dr Whitaker, I find myself in agreement with you. We've heard from two witnesses that the back door of your house was unlocked and standing ajar when they arrived on Tuesday morning. That is how they entered and found your wife dead.

"I put it to you: had your wife threatened Mr Forrest as you allege, she would *never*, I repeat, *never*, have admitted him into the house in the middle of the night – via the back door particularly – whilst she was alone and defenceless!"

Whitaker stood, dumbfounded. This was unassailable. He could think of nothing to say. Since, arguably, he hadn't really been asked a question he decided to remain silent, dreading what might come next.

Livesey, satisfied he'd made his point, moved on. "Let's leave Mr Forrest for a moment. You'd been aware of your wife's infidelity with Brian McNamara for some months, hadn't you?"

"Yes."

"I put it to you that Mr McNamara was another very convenient alternative candidate for the murderer. An alternative to you, in other words. Yes?"

"No! When I received the terrible news about Dulcie's death, the police asked me to name anyone who might have murdered her. I did my duty and informed them of her lover."

"We've heard evidence of your wife's infidelity and your alleged acceptance of it. You claim you had no intention of confronting her with your knowledge, is that correct?"

"Yes. Our marriage was not an exclusive one from the start, and we were very happy with the arrangement. Dulcie remained loyal and supportive to me in every other way. I explained all this to the police. This affair of hers was one of many."

"Really?"

To be consistent with the lies he'd already told, there was no choice but to answer "Yes."

"I see. Tell the court about some of your wife's other lovers, please."

Whitaker was stunned. "I beg your pardon?" was as much as he could manage in response. He sensed a massive and all-enveloping chasm was opening to swallow him up, simultaneously realising he couldn't allow any great silence to develop, as this would surely be read as a sign of guilt by the jury.

"I'm asking you to name a few of your wife's many lovers," said Livesey, with mock patience. "Hardly a difficult job, if everything was as open as you claim. We've heard from the police how you told them that you gave your wife the freedom to pursue her passions from the outset of your marriage. You've just reconfirmed this.

"Or do you expect the court to believe,

having made such an agreement with your wife prior to your marriage – and at her alleged instigation, no less – *she waited ten years to act upon the arrangement?*"

The disbelief in Livesey's voice pervaded the entire court. He pressed on. "You've told us about Mr McNamara and how you were curious to establish his identity. If we're to believe you were still curious after ten years about who your wife was seeing in your free and open marriage, then tell us: who were the others?"

Whitaker knew he'd been hoisted with his own petard. If he gave no names it would be clear he'd lied to the police about Dulcie's Bloomsbury leanings and their open marriage – and also her loyal support. Once that fell away, his motive to murder her for her money increased immensely.

On the other hand, if he made up some names, he would inevitably have to give additional details as to who the fictitious men were. The police would check, and again he'd be exposed as a liar.

The same applied if he gave the names of real men of Dulcie's acquaintance; the police would check and the men would deny any association.

He would be exposed, whatever he did.

Ignoring Livesey, who was waiting expectantly, he looked instead at Urquhart, and made the only excuse he could think of. "My lord, I wasn't expecting my late wife's private and intimate conduct to be lasciviously examined in this way. I cannot see how it is appropriate for me to give out her lovers' names in open court!"

The judge was having none of it. Reynolds, had he still been involved, would have leapt up and objected to Livesey's tack (and tactics), but in fact Urquhart had already resolved in his own mind that he would have overruled such an objection. The defendant had deliberately offered up McNamara as a murderer along with Kent and Forrest. If it was the case that the deceased had taken many lovers and never made threats against any of them, it greatly undermined the defendant's claim that she would have taken such steps against the solicitor or the dentist.

"I understand your reluctance Dr Whitaker," said the judge.

Whitaker happily took this as an endorsement of his unwillingness to produce names. He was quickly returned to reality.

Addressing the court usher, Urquhart instructed: "Provide the defendant with pen and paper, if you please."

Whitaker forestalled the action. There was nothing he could conceivably write. Better by far to make a show of being 'the bigger man' for the benefit of the jury. Looking squarely at Urquhart again, he spoke in what he hoped was a dignified and honourable-sounding voice. "I refuse to impugn innocent men and drag them into this nightmare, my lord!"

Livesey remained silent for a moment, before asking, very quietly:

"Why, when you have publicly impugned three other innocent men, including one of your wife's lovers, do you cavil at privately submitting the names of others to his lordship?"

Whitaker remained silent, not meeting his questioner's eyes. First allowing a heavily pregnant pause to open up, Livesey continued:

"I see. Well, I suppose my question is unanswerable. Let's talk about the car mileage log book instead. You heard the police evidence, to the effect that at interview the existence of it came as a complete surprise to you. Correct?"

Whitaker hesitated, before admitting, "I didn't know about it."

"It must have come as quite a shock, then, to be told of its existence. Particularly since, on separate occasions, you'd told three different police officers how you'd driven directly to the hotel and directly back home the next evening, never venturing out of the house again before your arrest.

"You repeated that statement again in front of your solicitor, Mr Egerton. It must have come as an even greater shock when you were informed that this log book showed your car having gone a hundred and twenty miles further than you told the police you'd travelled. How do you explain that?"

Whitaker didn't reply immediately, fresh inklings of doubt about his defence now entering his mind. Quickly assessing whether it was wise to even suggest a second forgery, he felt there was no alternative. "Dulcie made an error in writing the last number," he said presently, before adding, "or someone else altered it to trap me."

"Let's deal with your second suggestion first. If you yourself weren't aware of the existence of the book, how on earth would some stranger know about it?"

It was a very good question, but Whitaker thought of a very good answer. "Easily. Dulcie's lover wasn't a stranger. Nor was Geoffrey Kent."

"But there's no evidence that Mr McNamara ever entered your house. And whilst it's true that Mr Kent was a regular visitor, do you expect the jury to believe your wife would tell him about the book when she hadn't even mentioned it to you?"

"I can't say. Perhaps she mentioned it in casual conversation."

"Really," said Livesey, again imbuing the word with heavy meaning. "Let's look at your first suggestion; the possibility of your wife making an error in her last entry. I've calculated she would need to make not one, but two errors – in two separate digits.

"The first two digits have to be correct. For your theory to work, she would have incorrectly recorded two digits out of the remaining three. Very unlikely, wouldn't you say?"

"Strange and unlikely things happen all the time. It's not for me to understand them all."

"Allow me to help you understand, Dr Whitaker, why nothing strange or unlikely has happened to your wife's log book! We don't actually need to consider the digits. It's far simpler.

"Your wife's reading, when she returned home at two-fifteen on the Monday, corresponds perfectly with the reading immediately above. She recorded the exact few miles of her trip into the centre of Draycaster and back home.

"Unless you're suggesting she drove a hundred and twenty miles in the time she was shopping in the city, her recording of the mileage when she arrived home at two fifteen *must* be correct. What do you say to that?"

Whitaker realised, far too late, that the prosecution barrister had deliberately 'walked' him through the weakest evidence against him first, in order to ambush him with the strongest now.

He felt himself getting hot. "I can't say anything," he muttered, "you're deliberately muddling me."

"No, Dr Whitaker, you are in a muddle of your own making. The plain fact is that either, in that short period of shopping and lunching, your car travelled one hundred and twenty miles further than your wife recorded – totally impossible in the time available.

"Or, that *you* drove the car the additional one hundred and twenty miles to Draycaster and then back to Bristol in the early hours of the Tuesday morning!"

"I didn't."

"I put it to you that you did – and that the purpose of the additional journey was to kill your wife."

"I didn't do it!" Whitaker was almost shouting now.

Livesey, still on his feet at this point, shrugged his gown higher up onto his shoulders. With heavy disbelief in his voice, replied, "So you say." and again looked towards the jury before sitting down.

Mr Justice Urquhart was left to ponder. Had Whitaker been represented, his counsel would now almost certainly re-examine him on the points raised by the Crown. This, he thought, would be almost impossible for an unrepresented defendant to tackle on his own. Always bearing in mind the Court of Appeal, however, he decided Whitaker must be offered the chance. He explained the procedure to him.

"Thank you my lord. I wouldn't know how to ask myself questions – I can't compete with a King's Counsel and his skilled junior in these proceedings. I'll leave it until my closing address."

"As you wish, Dr Whitaker.

"I think it's best we adjourn until tomorrow. It would be better to fit both closing addresses into the same day – and my summary too, if possible. Ten o'clock, ladies and gentlemen, please."

CHAPTER 31

The following morning, Livesey rose to his feet as soon as the jury settled in their box.

"It is my job at this stage to summarise the case for the Crown, members of the jury. I shall not keep you long."

When drafting his address the previous evening. Livesey considered whether to mention the various occasions when the defendant suggested that his puny efforts were ranged against the power of the Crown's barristers, solicitor, and policemen. Livesey and Frith had not been pleased that Whitaker had almost been given licence to persuade the jury that he was being unfairly attacked, by several people to his one.

However, after talking over the point with his colleague, he decided not to mention it in closing.

The KC was true to his word, speaking for almost exactly twelve minutes. But he still managed to hammer home every key point brought out in evidence.

He ended by saying:

"You have heard evidence of the clearly planned and ultimately fruitless attempt to provide an alibi. You have heard how the defendant arranged for innocent people to be accused in his stead. And you have heard how the evidence provided by the victim herself, in the form of a car log book, finally shows that all his stories were false.

"You will no doubt be aware that in criminal matters the burden of proof lies on the Crown – we must prove guilt 'beyond a reasonable doubt'. His lordship will very probably address you on what that means in everyday language.

"But, on the evidence you have heard, and with respect to the learned judge, I submit that in this case such explanation is hardly necessary. Here, there can be no doubt whatsoever – Dr Whitaker callously shot his wife. I ask you to return a verdict of guilty."

Livesey gathered up his gown and sat down.

"Perfect," whispered Frith to his leader. "Pound to a penny Whitaker bleats to the jury about being outgunned and browbeaten by the beastly forces of the Crown."

"I can't take that bet," replied Livesey; "it's a certainty."

The judge was turning to Whitaker.

"Dr Whitaker; it's your turn now. You may summarise your case for the benefit of the jury."

"I feel at a considerable disadvantage, my lord. The prosecution addresses the jury from the well of the court. I shall be speaking from the dock, flanked by two prison officers. Even a witness appears to carry more weight than I. It must appear to the jury that I am an inferior citizen – and it hardly seems fair."

The judge recognised there was some force to the argument. However, it could equally be said that perhaps, pre-conviction, a defendant shouldn't be put in the dock at all, for fear of biasing the jury against him. And that, he told himself, would be a nonsense. (The judge was of course unaware that certain members of this jury had already proved the defendant's point.)

However, this being a capital case, Urquhart was determined to make every reasonable allowance for the defendant, but without prejudicing the prosecution case. He asked counsel if they wished to comment.

Frith rose. "The Crown has no strong view on the matter, my lord. As far as I am aware, the arrangement has always been for an unrepresented defendant in custody to make his case from the dock. However, if your lordship allows Dr Whitaker to make his address from this level, or perhaps even from the witness box, the Crown will make no objection."

"Thank you, Mr Frith, I am much obliged. On reflection, I think the witness box should be reserved for people under oath. Dr Whitaker, you may come into the well of the court to address the jury. Officers, please escort the defendant down. There is room for him towards the end of a bench, and you can sit behind."

"Thank you, my lord," said Whitaker when he was in his temporary position. This time holding some notes, he began his final address.

"Members of the jury, the police investigation into my wife's death was not carried out expeditiously. I concede that the senior officer in charge is an experienced, and in his field even an eminent, man; but he and his colleagues decided early on, quite wrongly, that my version of events was untrue.

"I was wrongly arrested and most unfairly charged. Eventually, I was brought before you, ladies and gentlemen. Outnumbered by a team of police officers, and prosecuted by another team of heavyweights, led by a King's Counsel. They have sought to paint me as a murderer. They are wrong – you are looking at an innocent man. My wife was shot dead by someone while I was sixty miles away. I was not the killer.

"You have heard it alleged that I planned the murder, and means and motives have been ascribed to me. I refute them all. I accept my wife has left me a great deal of money, but there is no doubt that I am far worse off without her. I am very lonely, and without her steadying hand I shall very probably spiral downhill into alcoholism again.

"One suggested motive was that I killed my wife because of her affair. It may sound plausible, but it simply is not true. Dulcie's continuing presence was essential for me.

"That Dulcie effectively took charge of me is certainly correct. However, it was exactly what I wanted her to do. I was not – and perhaps may never be – able to control my drinking and gambling habits. She was my support; my prop if you like. I am ashamed, but I have to admit it. I did not have any notion of eliminating her so I could be 'master in my own house'. That is fanciful in the extreme.

"I went, in all good faith, to a symposium in Bristol, as a delegate from the museum for which I work. You have heard how I met a number of other delegates in the hotel. When the police told me about my wife's death, I naturally offered them the names of some of those with whom I spent much of that evening. Whatever those witnesses say, the fact is that I drank far too much after dinner, and was probably nearly comatose by the time I reached my room.

"Some of the evidence you have heard is irrelevant. It is implied that I poured several glasses of whisky away into a potted shrub. I did not, and there is no evidence I did.

"It is said I was aware of some arrangement regarding the back door. I was not aware, and there is no evidence I was. Nor is there any evidence of my ever using that door.

"I knew of three people, each of whom, I thought, would have a reason to get rid of my wife. One of these was Dulcie's lover, and I still think he had a good motive. Another was a man my wife and I both knew. I accidentally became aware of his own extra-marital affair, and told my wife. She was going to tackle him, to give him a chance to reform before she informed his wife. I remain of the view that he too had a good reason for murder.

"Unfortunately, the police decided not to look too deeply into either of these two men – both, I should say, with prominent positions to maintain in our town, and with a great deal to lose if their infidelities were exposed.

"I should have liked to cross-examine these two men, but it was not to be."

The prosecuting team and the police officers all sat unhappily at this travesty of the facts. Whitaker continued unabashed:

"You heard how I then discovered a cheque, apparently written by my wife, which was in fact a forgery. That it was a forgery was not disputed by the police. But the man I believed to be responsible was able to wriggle out of this – you saw him give evidence." Whitaker waved towards Kent, seated only a few feet away.

"A so-called handwriting expert tells you that in his opinion Geoffrey Kent didn't write the cheque. That is an opinion, not fact – and it is wrong. I should call it quackery."

Bailey, still sitting not far away, smiled grimly once again. Similar comments about his discipline were not unknown – some from defence counsel whose clients went on to be convicted.

"That cheque was paid into Kent's account, and in due course his wife, knowing the account should be empty, drew some of the money out and spent it. What more proof do you need?

"I am having to speak for myself, ladies and gentlemen. I'm not a professional orator like the learned counsel here. I'm an ordinary man who has found himself in the middle of a nightmare. I ask you to reject the prosecution's case, which is based on faulty investigation, and the flimsiest of circumstantial evidence at best."

There was a silence for a few seconds, and then as the judge motioned the guards to take Whitaker back to the dock, a burst of whispering broke out in the court. On the press bench, a reporter from the local evening newspaper drew a crude little sketch of a gibbet and a noose with a question mark beside, and passed it to his neighbour. A solemn nod was the response.

With Whitaker back in the dock and the courtroom quiet again, the judge addressed the jury.

"It is my task to summarise the case for you. Fortunately, there are no legal complexities involved. It is simply a matter of deciding on the facts. And facts are entirely a matter for you. So I collate and pass on to you what seem to me to be the key points from both sides. But if I should put weight on one particular fact, it is open to you to disagree with me – and perhaps to prefer some other fact as being more important.

"Before I begin, I must make a point. The defendant has, several times, emphasised that he is unrepresented by a barrister. In so saying, he has implied – and indeed stated – that he is a little man being browbeaten by the weight of two powerful barristers employed by the Crown.

"I really cannot allow this to pass without reminding you it was the defendant who chose to dismiss his very experienced barrister, and also his instructing solicitor. The decision to be unrepresented was Dr Whitaker's alone, and he is not now entitled to ask for your sympathy on the grounds that he has no legal advisor. As I told you previously, the fact that he is unrepresented has no bearing on your considering the evidence and coming to a verdict.

The judge required only a little longer than Livesey to conclude his summary. He ran through the crucial points and very fairly emphasised the purely circumstantial nature of some of the evidence – especially much of that from the hotel.

On the other hand, he suggested the jury might think the mileage readings were crucial. The defence had not, in his opinion, succeeded in providing anything approaching a viable alternative explanation for the surplus one hundred and twenty miles.

Indeed, he drew the jury's attention to the fact that the defendant in closing had not even mentioned this key piece of evidence.

He went on to point out that the defendant, in maintaining his allegation about one of three other men being the guilty party, had produced no evidence to support these assertions, nor had either he or his previous representative called as witnesses either of the two men not called by the Crown.

The judge mentioned the question of motive, confirming that the prosecution was not obliged to provide such a thing, if the facts of the case spoke without the need for it. But he suggested that the jury might think it was worth bearing in mind one or more of the three possible motives put forward by the Crown.

As Livesey had anticipated, Urquhart addressed the burden of proof. The jury were told the meaning of 'beyond a reasonable doubt' is not always easy to construe.

"It is not enough for you to think the accused is probably guilty or even very probably guilty. However, you do not have to be absolutely certain – in real life there are very few cases where that would be possible. But if you have *a genuine doubt*, not just a doubt based on some extremely remote possibility, you should acquit.

"I have said all I need to say. It is time for

MACHINATIONS OF A MURDERER

lunch. You will have some food delivered to your room. Retire, refresh yourselves, remember the oath you have taken, and consider your verdict."

Livesey and Frith came over to Bryce for a chat.

"What do you think?" asked Livesey.

"I watched the jury for the last couple of days," replied the DCI. "Most of them aren't enamoured of the defendant. Urquhart summed up for a conviction, of course – but he could hardly do anything else."

"Yes," added Frith, "I bet the whole business of sacking Reynolds was a deliberate ploy, resorted to after realising he had no defence."

****

In the jury room, the twelve men and women were helping themselves to the sandwiches and beverages provided. They had elected a foreman during an earlier break, and it was this gentleman who called them to order.

"None of us has experience of this, and no doubt we could spend a long time reviewing every scrap of evidence. But it might be an idea to have a sort of straw poll first, to see what the feeling is."

This proposal immediately found favour.

"I think we normally vote openly, but perhaps for this purpose we should simply write down something on a piece of paper – that way nobody will feel he or she has to do the same as others.

"I suggest each of us writes 'guilty'; 'not guilty'; or 'unsure' on a piece of paper. No names or signatures needed. Write so your neighbours can't see, and then fold the paper over and put it in my hat as I pass around the table."

This was also welcomed as a sensible suggestion. The chairman quickly folded three sheets of foolscap in half and then half again, tearing them to produce twelve nearly identical slips of paper. He passed these around the table. Each juror took one, and wrote on it.

Folding his own slip and dropping it into his hat, the foreman collected the rest of the votes, and returned to his seat.

He drew out the slips one at a time, and read what each said, repeating the word 'guilty' twelve times. He sat back and looked around the table. The faces looking back at him were sober but relieved.

"That seems to be pretty clear. Does anyone want to raise any doubt at all?"

"I certainly don't," retorted one of the women. "Frankly, I think we heard an awful lot of poppycock in what was actually an open-and-shut case."

"Agreed," said the spiritualist's admirer. "After hearing everything, nobody could possibly have any serious doubts."

"Despicable man," said another.

There were nods all around the table.

"That wasn't too difficult," said the chairman, "but we're not quite done yet. Does anyone want to raise their hand and propose we add a rider, recommending mercy?"

No hand was raised.

"That's it then, for us. The judge and the others probably won't be back for another hour anyway, so I suggest we polish off the last of the sandwiches and have a bit of conversation."

A little before two o'clock, the usher informed the judges' clerk and counsel that a verdict had been reached. When the judge was ready, the usher went back to the jury room to collect his charges.

"Would the foreman please rise," instructed the clerk of the court.

Are you agreed upon a verdict?" he asked.

"We are," said the foreman.

"Do you find the defendant guilty or not guilty?"

"We find him guilty, my lord."

"And that is the verdict of you all?"

"It is, my lord."

There was a brief murmur around the courtroom. Two reporters jumped up and left the room before the foreman resumed his seat.

The judge ordered Whitaker to stand.

"Do you have anything to say why sentence should not be passed on you?"

Whitaker shook his head, unable to speak.

"The jury has convicted you of the murder of your wife. I may say that the verdict was inevitable, and based on the clearest evidence. It would be a waste of time to deliver some homily to you – your careful machinations were so evil that I doubt if any words would get through to your conscience. It only remains for me to pass the sentence prescribed by law."

The clerk placed a square of black silk on Mr Justice Urquhart's wig.

"Robin Christopher Whitaker, you will be taken from here to a lawful prison, and there, on a day to be appointed, you will suffer death by hanging; and thereafter your body will be buried in the prison in which you were last confined. And may the Lord have mercy on your soul."

"Amen," said the court chaplain.

"Take him down."

****

BOOKS BY THIS AUTHOR

The Bedroom Window Murder

It is 1949. Sir Francis Sherwood – WW1 hero, landowner, magistrate – is shot dead while standing at an open bedroom window in his country house. A rifle is found in the grounds.

The county police seek help from Scotland Yard.

Detective Chief Inspector Bryce and Detective Sergeant Haig are assigned to the case. The first difficulty for the Yard men is that nobody with even a mild dislike of Sherwood can be found.

But before that problem can be resolved, others arise...

The Courthouse Murder

In July 1949, an unpopular and deeply unpleasant man is stabbed in the courthouse of an English city. As the murder has been committed in a room to which the general public doesn't have access, it seems probable that the culprit is someone involved with the business of the courts.

Suspects include a number of lawyers, police officers, and magistrates.

For various reasons, the local Chief Constable decides to ask Scotland Yard to investigate the murder.

Chief Inspector Philip Bryce and Sergeant Alex Haig are assigned to the case.

Theirs is a recent partnership, but the two men worked well together in another murder case a few weeks before. (See 'The Bedroom Window Murder'.)

The Felixstowe Murder

In August 1949, Detective Chief Inspector Bryce and his new bride are holidaying in the East Anglian seaside resort of Felixstowe.

During afternoon tea in the Palm Court of their

hotel, a man dies at a nearby table.

Reluctant to get directly involved, Bryce nevertheless agrees to help the inexperienced local police inspector get to grips with his first murder case, turning his honeymoon into a 'busman's holiday'.

Multiples Of Murder

Three more cases for Philip Bryce. The first two are set in 1949, and follow on from The Bedroom Window Murder, The Courthouse Murder, and The Felixstowe Murder.
The third goes back to 1946, when Bryce – not long back in the police after his army service – was a mere Detective Inspector, based in Whitechapel rather than Scotland Yard.

1. In the office kitchen of a small advertising agency in London, a man falls to the floor, dead. Initially, it is believed that he had some sort of heart attack, but it soon becomes clear that he had received a fatal electric shock. A faulty kettle is then blamed. But evidence emerges showing that this was not an accident. Chief Inspector Bryce is assigned to the case.

2. Just before opening time, a body is found in the larger pool at the huge public baths in St

Marylebone. The man has been shot, presumably the previous evening. It is DCI Bryce's task, aided by Detective Sergeant Haig and others, to discover the identity of the victim, why he was killed, and who shot him.

3. For a few months in 1946, a traditional London bus was modified in an experiment to allow passengers to 'Pay-As-You-Board'. Doors were fitted, instead of having the usual open platform. The stairs rose from inside the saloon rather than directly from the platform. On the upper deck, a man is found stabbed to death. None of the passengers can shed any light on the murder, yet the design of this bus meant that no-one could have jumped off the bus unnoticed – one of them must be the murderer. Inspector Bryce, together with colleagues from Leman Street police station, solves one of his earlier cases.

Death At Mistram Manor

In September 1949, a wake is being held at a manor house in Oxfordshire, following the burial of the chatelaine. Over a hundred mourners are present.

Within an hour, the clergyman who conducted the funeral service is taken ill himself. The local doctor, present at the wake, provisionally diagnoses appendicitis, and calls for an ambulance. However, the priest dies soon after being admitted to hospital.

An autopsy reveals that the cause of death was strychnine poisoning.

The circumstances are such that accidental ingestion and suicide are both ruled out. The rector was murdered, and the timing means that the poison must have been taken during the wake.

The local police, faced with a lengthy list of potential suspects, ask Scotland Yard to take on the investigation, and the case is assigned to Detective Chief Inspector Bryce and two colleagues.

Although most of the mourners can easily be eliminated from the enquiry, around eight of them cannot. The experienced London officers have to sift through a number of initially-promising indications, before finally being able to identify the killer.

Printed in Great Britain
by Amazon